Emerald Green

Emerald Green

by

Charles Shelton

ISBN: 978-1-7336235-2-0

DEDICATION

I would like to dedicate this book to any and all who have had to put up with or struggle with any form of adversity, prejudice, or injustice in their lives; those, who, despite the difficult challenges or difficulties they currently may be facing, or that they have undergone in the past, have not allowed their struggles and sufferings to change or destroy the beauty of the true character and real person that they are inside.

CONTENTS

ACKNOWLEDGMENTS

I would like to give special thanks to my beautiful wife for her love and support.

Besides my wife, I would like to thank our children and grandchildren for their patience and understanding concerning the time and labors needed to bring forth this completed work; but, especially, for the joy and happiness that they bring to us.

In addition, I would also like to thank my brothers and sisters for the encouragement and support that they've provided throughout my life in general.

Lastly, and most of all, thanks be to God for all of the wonders of his creation and the marvelous demonstrations of his love.

1

A STRANGE MEETING

Two pair's of beaming human eyes lie intently fixed on one another; staring at each other through a tall, chain-link, metal fence that surrounds the playground at St. Agnes, Catholic Orphanage for girls. The chain-link fence is there for two purposes: 1) For keeping those who are on the outside from getting in, and 2) For keeping those on the inside from getting out.

The owners of these curious, but yet, innocent eyes, belong to two young children, who happen to be from two distinctly different and completely separate worlds.

As they stand there gazing upon one another, both of the children are thoroughly mesmerized, completely captivated by the appearance of one another. Why? Because neither one of them has ever seen anyone who looks like this before, someone so peculiarly unique and outwardly different from themselves.

The child on the inside of the fence is an orphan; a little

Caucasian girl; a dishwater blonde, with long spaghetti-like hair. She has an oval shaped face, and bright blue eyes, rosy shaded thin lips, and slightly oversized ears. The color of her skin is snow white in appearance, and she has a light sprinkling of a few tiny freckles splattered across the bridge of her narrow shaped nose and on the cheekbones of her face.

The child on the outside of the fence is a little colored girl. She has a round shaped face; and large, almond shaped charcoaled colored eyes, that sparkle like diamonds in the sunlight; a pug shaped nose; and full lips. Her hair is shiny black and it is tied up in two braided pigtails that droop downwards over her tiny ears. The complexion of her skin is medium dark brown, like the hue of a cup of coffee, with a touch of added cream.

Totally overcome with their fascination of each other, not a single word is being spoken by either girl during this unfamiliarly strange and unarranged meeting. Both of them just simply stand there in absolute silence, staring at each other through the restrictive and surrounding fence.

Suddenly, out of curiosity, the little Caucasian girl reaches her hand out, and she tries to squeeze it through one of the diamond shaped openings in the chain-link fence, in order to touch and feel the colored girl's hair. But, before she is able to reach her hand completely through to the other side, she is grabbed from behind by a Nun, who quickly pulls her back and away from the fence. Next, without missing a beat, the Nun takes hold of the girl by her ear, and she begins twisting and turning it. Immediately, in response, the girl yells: "Ouch, ouch, ouch, that hurts!"

"Elisabeth... Margaret... Baxter! Stay away from those little picaninnys!"[1] the Nun says, with a loud, commanding, and angry voice.

The Nun now proceeds to lead the orphan girl by her ear, all the way across the enclosed grassy field, and then pass a large group of

_____

[1] A picaninny is an offensive and demeaning term that is used for a black child.

other orphan girls, who happen to be playing various games on a paved playground. She marches her straight up to a door on the east wing of the orphanage. And after the two of them enter the building, the Nun slams the door shut behind them!

~

St. Agnes Orphanage is a home for girls only. It is housed within the structure of an old, large, and dingy gray colored brick building that was built back in the late 1800s. It is situated in the heart of St. Paul, which is the capital city of the State of Minnesota. A northern state that is located in the central part of the United States of America.

As regards the area surrounding St. Agnes is concerned, it is a highly developed and populated community that is solely occupied by middle class Caucasian families, who live in pretty nice homes.

~

It is a sunny and warm summer day here in St. Paul, with the heat index measuring 92 degrees Fahrenheit (33.3 degrees Celsius). Nevertheless, the playground at St. Agnes Orphanage is packed with children of different ages, shapes, and sizes. Some are big, a few are small, some are short, and others are extremely tall. However, the thing that is most interestingly is that all of the orphans here have two things in common with one another, which is, not only are they all of the same gender, but also they are of the same race or nationality — they are all Caucasian girls.

Suddenly, a loud voice, steep in volume and resonance, coming from a distant area outside of the enclosed orphanage, calls out: "Nellie!" In response, the little colored girl, who is still standing at the chain-link fence surrounding the orphanage, turns around, and she looks northward in the direction of the summonsing voice.

Glancing down the street, the colored girl, whose name is Nellie, realizes that she is being called by her Uncle Walter, who has finally changed the flat tire on his old, rickety, broken down vehicle. Nellie also sees that her Mother Eva, and her two older siblings, Charles, and Randall, are getting back into the car; for they had momentarily gotten out to stretch their legs, while Uncle Water was changing the flat tire.

Uncle Walter, now, with a sense of urgency in his voice, once again yells out, saying: "Come on Nellie! Let's go! We're already late enough as it is!"

"Ok! I'm coming Uncle Walter!" Nellie yells back. Then, she takes off running, as fast as she can, all the way to the car, and she gets in. And, after she is safety situated inside, her Uncle Walter drives away.

~

The year is 1939. Franklin D. Roosevelt is the current and acting President of the United States of America. It has been about 10 years since the Great Depression hit, but the American economy is resiliently bouncing back and showing signs of sustained improvement. It is a time of such things as: Betty Boop, Zoot suits, the Jitter bug, Hudson Motor Vehicles, Stamp Collecting, Stoop ball, Stick ball, Radio Shows, and Board Games, such as the ever popular game called "Monopoly." However, on the flipside of things, the social climate is struggling, especially in regards to racial equality. It is a time of deep racial prejudice and segregation, when socializing and integrating of the white race with the black race is neither encouraged nor tolerated, which makes this a considerably dark period in the history of the United States.

~

The next day, following her experience with the little colored girl, orphan Elisabeth Margaret Baxter is assigned the chore of dusting and polishing the wooden railings and balusters on a long and winding spiral staircase leading from the St. Agnes Orphanage downstairs lobby to the second floor upstairs.

As far as Elisabeth is concerned, polishing the wooden banister is neither a preferred or pleasant job. It is both tedious and boring. She wishes that there was a quicker and easier way to get the job done. Suddenly, an ingenious thought hatches in her highly imaginative little mind. One that she feels will make the job a whole lot easier, get it done quicker, and at the same time be a lot of fun.

Assuming that no one is watching her, Elisabeth spreads out her dust rag on top of the staircase handrail. Then, she climbs aboard and sits on top of it. Now, straddling the handrail with both legs, and holding on with her hands, she begins sliding down the long and winding handrail; all the way from the second floor upstairs to the first floor below. What a rush of excitement this brings! It's like being on a rollercoaster! As Elisabeth flies down the banister she giggles, and yells out: "Wee! Woo-hoo!" But, unfortunately, her joy is only short lived, for she is unexpectedly met by a Nun, who is waiting at the bottom of the staircase.

Coincidentally, this Nun happens to be the same Nun who disciplined Elisabeth yesterday for socializing with the little colored girl. Her name is Sister Mary Allen Francis. She is the head Nun in charge at St. Agnes. Her formal or official titles are Mother Superior, and Reverend Mother.

Sister Mary Allen is about five feet nine inches tall. She is clothed in a habit, with a long black gown, like all of the other Nuns at St. Agnes. In regards to the rest of her appearance, Sister Mary Allen has a narrow face, with itty, bitty, squinty eyes; and a long, downward hooking nose, that's shaped like a hawk's beak. Her lips are thin, and they curve slightly downwards in an arch-like shape that sort of resembles an upside down smile. When she walks, it sounds like loud claps of thunder! And when she speaks, a pair of clashing cymbals!

~

Upon catching Elisabeth in the act of sliding down the wooden railing, Sister Mary Allen, with a stern look on her face, and a scolding tone in her voice, says to her: "Good Lord, Almighty! Elisabeth… Margaret… Baxter! What in the world do you think you're doing?" And then, quickly reaching out her hand, she grabs hold of Elisabeth by her ear, and she proceeds to march her all the way down a long corridor to a door marked supply closet. And, after opening the door, she shoves her inside, and she says to her with a stern voice: "Now, you stay there young lady, until you learn your lesson!" Afterwards, she slams the door shut, locks it, and leaves.

~

Elisabeth Margaret Baxter is ten years old. She is stubborn by nature, extremely curious, highly mischievous, and full of life. She was born on January 24, 1926 to her parents named Ronald, and Ester Baxter. She is an only child. On May 12, 1929 she was awarded to the State of Minnesota, and placed here at St. Agnes Orphanage to live, after her mother died from a massive brain hemorrhage, and her father later mysteriously disappeared and was never found. Elisabeth was only three years old at the time.

~

Later that day, after an hour or so has passed by, Sister Mary Allen, now returns to the supply closet, where she had placed Elisabeth earlier. And she unlocks and opens the door, and proceeds to let her out. And she says to her, with a doubtful tone in her voice: "Did you learn a valuable lesson from all of this young lady? Only time will tell!"

2

A BEAUTY MAKEOVER

Three years have passed. Elisabeth is now thirteen years old. The first snowfall of a new winter season has just begun. Today, she is working inside the orphanage laundry, which is located in an adjacent building that was erected several years ago, next to the west wing of St. Agnes' main building.

Upon catching sight of the large and fluffy, gentle falling snowflakes; Elisabeth immediately runs over to a nearby window, so that she can get a closer look. "Wow, look at the sparkling snow! Isn't it beautiful!" she excitedly exclaims.

Unfortunately, Elisabeth's excitement is only short-lived. For Sister Michaels, the head Nun in charge of the laundry, catches site of her standing at the window, and she yells out to her with a loud and commanding voice, saying: "Elisabeth... Margaret... Baxter! Get back to work!"

"But, Sister, it's so beautiful!" Elisabeth replies.

"We don't have time for that... now get back to work!" Sister Michaels shouts.

"Yes, Sister Michaels," Elisabeth quietly grumbles under her breath, as she promptly goes back to work.

~

The sole purpose of the orphanage laundry is for helping to generate income for St. Agnes. Some of their biggest clients are the local passenger railway companies and hotels, such as: The Great Frontier and Northern Pacific Railway Companies, and the downtown Luxemburg, Wellington Stratford, and Grand hotels.

Laundry list items consist of: bed sheets, pillowcases, towels, washcloths, blankets, employee work uniforms, etc.

About sixty orphan girls work in the Laundry. Elisabeth's job is to sort through the incoming dirty laundry, separating whites from colors. Also, she has to make sure that there aren't any forgotten items that were left in the pockets of clothing. All found items, except for money and jewelry are to be discarded in a nearby waste can. Money and jewelry however, are to be immediately turned over to the laundry's 'Lost & Found Department.'

~

As soon as Elisabeth returns to her job (after gazing out the window at the falling snow) she begins sorting through the avalanche of incoming laundry. Suddenly, to her surprise, she discovers a woman's pocketsize makeup case, and also a tube of lipstick that were left in the pocket of a hotel employee's work apron. But, instead of throwing the items away, like she and her fellow co-workers have been instructed to do, she keeps and hides them in the bottom of the laundry cart, underneath the stack of laundry. And then, later, when no one is watching her, she retrieves them, and she secretly slips them into the pocket of her work uniform. Afterwards, she resumes work at her assigned station.

Later, at the end of the workday, as Elisabeth is walking from the Laundry to the main building of the Orphanage, she happens to run into her best friend, Betty Lu Macalester, and she secretively shows her the items that she found while she was working.

Shocked and surprised, Betty Lu says: "Where did you get those Elisabeth?"

"I found them when I was working in the Laundry today. They were left in the pocket of a hotel employee's work apron," Elisabeth replies.

"But, aren't you supposed to throw items like that away when you find them?" Betty Lu asks.

"Yes, I know the rules. But I've never found anything like these before. So I just had to keep them," Elisabeth says.

"What are you going to do with them?" Betty Lu asks.

Elisabeth thinks about it for a moment, and then she enthusiastically says: "I know! Let's have a beauty makeover day! You and I can put the makeup and lipstick on and pretend that we're grownups!"

"I don't know? Isn't that a little risky? If we get caught, we could get in a lot of trouble!" Betty Lu says.

"Come on! What's the harm? No one will ever know!" Elisabeth vows.

"When do you plan on doing this?" Betty Lu asks.

"How about tonight when everybody goes to bed?" Elisabeth suggests.

"I don't know Elisabeth? What if we get caught?" Betty Lu replies again.

"Don't worry, we won't get caught, everyone will be sleeping!" Elisabeth assures.

"Alright then, let's do it!" Betty Lu says.

~

Betty Lu Macalester is thirteen years of age — about six months older than Elisabeth. She stands about 4 feet 10 inches tall, with a noticeable gap between her two upper front teeth. By nature, she is a wide-eyed, happy-go-lucky kid, but also a bit naïve and flighty too. Apparently, she is somewhat new to St. Agnes. She was brought here to live about a year ago, when she was twelve years old.

~

Later that night, while the Nuns and all the orphan girls are sleeping soundly in their beds, Elisabeth and Betty Lu, whose beds happen to be located right next to each other, quietly sneak into the girl's dormitory bathroom. There they begin to work on giving each other the long anticipated beauty makeovers.

First, the two girls proceed to sit down in the middle of the bathroom floor. Next, Elisabeth reaches into the pocket of her pajamas, and she pulls out the makeup case and lipstick. Then, she says: "Betty Lu, I'll work on you first, and then when I'm done with you, you can work on me."

"Ok Elisabeth, that sounds good," Betty Lu says.

Elisabeth begins the makeover process by first applying makeup to Betty Lu's face. However, due to inexperience, and not knowing exactly what she is doing, she cakes it on pretty thick.

Next, after Betty Lu's face is completely covered in makeup, Elisabeth begins to apply the lipstick (a vivid, bright red color) to her lips. This too, she also puts on pretty thick.

Finally, upon completion of Betty Lu's facial makeover, Elisabeth says to her: "There, I'm done!"

Betty Lu is so excited that she immediately wants to jump up off the floor, and run over to a mirror, so that she can see what she looks like. She says: "I've gotta see what I look like!"

"Wait, not yet... hold your horses little lady!" Elisabeth says, as she quickly reaches out and grabs hold of Betty Lu, before she can get up. She continues: "Why don't you wait until after both of us are done? Then we can both look in the mirror together!"

"Ok, I'll wait. But it's not going to be easy. I'm just so excited!" Betty Lu says. She continues: "Let me work on you now Elisabeth!"

"Alright," Elisabeth says.

With good intentions, but also not knowing what she's doing either, Betty Lu proceeds to duplicate exactly what Elisabeth did to her — applying both the makeup and the lipstick on thick.

Later, after a little time has gone by; Betty Lu finally completes the finishing touches on Elisabeth's face.

"There, I'm all finished! Now we can look into the mirror and see what we look like!" Betty Lu eagerly says.

Filled with oodles of excitement and anticipated suspense, the girls quickly rise up from off the floor, and they hold hands. Afterwards, they walk over to a large wall mirror that is hanging on the wall, directly above the bathroom sinks, and they simultaneously look into it.

The moment that the girls catch site of themselves, they are so surprised that they can hardly believe their eyes! Now, reeling from gratifying satisfaction, and overcome with sheer joy, they begin sporting ear-to-ear grins, and in one accord they spontaneously erupt into elated comments about their fantastic new look!

Betty Lu says: "Wow! Is that really me? I can hardly believe it! I look so different!"

"Me too, I look so much older and sophisticated now!" Elisabeth proudly says.

"You look absolutely gorgeous Elisabeth!" Betty Lu exclaims.

"Thank you, Betty Lu, so do you! You're stunningly beautiful!" Elisabeth replies.

After admiring themselves and each other for a while, Elisabeth says: "My hair is so straight. I wish I had curls."

"Me too," Betty Lu says.

Pausing in silence for a moment, Elisabeth once again gets that harebrained look on her face, when she's hatching one of her brilliant ideas.

"What are you thinking about Elisabeth?" Betty Lu curiously inquires.

"I think I know how we can get curls," Elisabeth says.

"How do we do that?" Betty Lu asks.

"All we need to do is get our hair wet, and then roll it up. Then, after our hair dries, we will have beautiful, gorgeous curls," Elisabeth explains.

"But we don't have any hair rollers!" Betty Lu says.

"We don't need rollers," Elisabeth replies.

"What do you mean?" Betty Lu asks.

"Do you see those hand towels over there on the self," Elisabeth asks, as she points to them.

"Yep, I see them," Betty Lu says.

"Well, we can use those as a substitute for hair rollers to tie up our hair," Elisabeth confidently says.

"I don't think that will work Elisabeth," Betty Lu replies in a doubting tone.

"Sure it will! Let me show you," Elisabeth says.

Elisabeth now walks over to and takes a towel off of the bathroom shelf. Then, she opens the top drawer of a dresser that is stationed beneath the shelf, and she takes out a pair of large scissors. Next, she proceeds to cut the towel up into a bunch of separate ribbon-like strips. Afterwards, she takes one of the strips and she demonstrates the hair rolling and tying procedure by using a small section of Betty Lu's hair.

Immediately, upon seeing the results in the mirror, Betty Lu says: "Elisabeth, you're a genius! It does work! Let's do it!" Afterwards, both of them get busy working on each other's head. Elisabeth works on Betty Lu's hair first, and then, afterwards, Betty Lu works on her.

Later that night, after a couple of hours have passed by, Elisabeth and Betty Lu finally finish working on one another hair. However, because it's late into the night, both of them are beginning to feel pretty sleepy from staying up so late. After exchanging big yawns, Betty Lu says: "Boy, I sure am tired!"

"Me too," Elisabeth says.

"How long do you think it'll take for our hair to dry Elisabeth," Betty Lu asks.

"I don't know? But I'm sure it won't be too long!" Elisabeth replies.

While the girls wait patiently for their hair to dry, they take a seat beside one another on the bathroom floor. But, unexpectedly, within a short period of time, their minds drift off, and they fall fast asleep.

About an hour later, Elisabeth wakes up. However, she is still feeling pretty groggy. Dazed, weakened, and confused from lack of sleep, she leans over and she gives Betty Lu, who has fallen asleep beside her, a couple of gentle nudges, and she says to her in a long, drawn-out, sleepy tone: "Betty Lu. Let's go to bed."

At first, Betty Lu is slow to respond. She's just as tired as Elisabeth, if not more. But then she finally says: "Okay Elisabeth." Then, the two of them stand up, and in a sleepy, slumber, drunken-like state, they return to their beds and fall fast asleep!

Now, as it so happens, the next morning comes around early. And because Elisabeth and Betty Lu stayed up most of the night, they happen to oversleep, and they are not present in the Dining Hall for the morning breakfast.

Sister Mary Allen Francis enters the Dining Hall, and she takes her usual seat at the head of the Nuns table. And, before she begins to say the morning grace for the entire group of nuns and orphans as she ritualistically does every morning for breakfast, she first surveys the entire group of orphans, and she takes a headcount of all who are present.

As Sister Mary Allen is taking headcount; she notices that at one of the cafeteria tables, two chairs are empty. She also recognizes that the vacant seats are the assigned seats belonging to Elisabeth Baxter, and Betty Lu Macalester.

Concerned as to the whereabouts of the two missing girls, Sister Mary Allen immediately inquires of those who are present, saying: "Can anyone please tell me where Miss. Elisabeth Baxter, and Betty Lu Macalester are?"

In unison the entire group of girls at the breakfast table, where Elisabeth and Betty Lu routinely sit, speak up and they say: "They're still up in their beds sleeping!"

When Sister Mary Allen hears that the girls are still in bed, she instantly gets up out of her seat, and she leaves the table. And she quickly walks upstairs to the girl's dormitory.

As soon as Sister Mary Allen arrives at and enters the girl's dormitory; she observes that Elisabeth and Betty Lu are in fact still lying in their beds sleeping, just as the girls at the breakfast table had said.

Quickly, walking over to Elisabeth and Betty Lu's beds, which happen to be located right next to each other, Sister Mary Allen stops, and she stands between them. Then, in a fit of anger she reaches out and she simultaneously grabs hold of both of the girl's blankets, which happen to be pulled up over their heads, and she forcefully snatches them completely off of them!

The moment the blankets are removed, the girls immediately pop their heads up!

Both shocked and appalled at seeing Elisabeth and Betty Lu's new appearance, Sister Mary Allen says to them in a loud and disturbed voice: "Look at you! What have the two of you done to yourselves? You look like a couple of cheep whores!" Then, she reaches out and she quickly grabs hold of both of them by their ears, and she proceeds to lead them out of the room, and across the hallway, and then down a long flight of stairs that leads to the basement boiler room below.

What a rude and painful awakening this proves to be for both Elisabeth and Betty Lu. For all the while, as they are being lead by their ears, from the dormitory to the boiler room, they are yelling: "Ouch! Ouch! Ouch! My ear! My ear! That hurts!" However, little do they realize that this is not even half of what is to come!

Finally, upon reaching the boiler room, Sister Mary Allen leads the girls over to a wash basin, and she let's go of their ears. Next, reaching out her hand, she turns the water faucet on and she proceeds to fill up the wash basin with water. Afterwards, she grabs a rag and a bar of soap off of a wooden shelf that's situated above the wash basin, and she gets them both wet.

After the rag is thoroughly wet and lathered up with soap, Sister Mary Allen takes hold of Elisabeth, and she begins scrubbing her lips with the soapy rag. She continues to scrub and scrub until all traces of the lipstick are gone. Then, afterwards, she repeats the same process on Betty Lu's lips.

Now, because the bar of soap that Sister Mary Allen is using, happens to be lye soap, which is an extremely harsh product that carries the warning label: "AVOID CONTACT WITH SKIN. MAY CAUSE BURNS," the girl's lips immediately begin to sting, burn, swell up, and blister.

Finally, after Sister Mary Allen is finished scrubbing Elisabeth and Betty Lu's lips, she says to them: "Now, I want both of you to remove those stupid rags that you have tied up in your hair! And after you're done with that, I want you to go back upstairs and wash that horrible makeup off your faces! And, after you have completed those two tasks, I want you to stay in the dormitory. Don't you even think about coming out, until I say that you can!" Afterwards, Sister Mary Ellen turns and she storms out of the room, and she slams the door shut behind her!

As soon as Sister Mary Ellen disappears from their sight, Elisabeth and Betty Lu begin to cry big crocodile tears. They both feel so hurt and sad! Turning towards each another, they begin to hug, and comfort one another, all the while wondering within themselves: *"How could Sister Mary Ellen do such a terrible thing to them? After all, they didn't mean any harm. They were just trying to make themselves look pretty."*

From this moment onward, both girls vow to always remain close and loyal friends.

3

AN UNEXPECTED VISIT

Seasons and years have quickly rolled by. The year is now 1943. It is the end of another spring, and the beginning of a new summer. Elisabeth is now seventeen and a half years old. She has grown to become a very beautiful girl in appearance.

Today, Sister Mary Ellen Francis is thrilled and excited, because His Excellency, the Most Holy Archbishop, St. Oliver Earl Glance has just announced that he will soon be coming to pay an honorary visit to St. Agnes, during its upcoming fifty year anniversary, which will take place on August 15, about two months from now.

Because the 50th anniversary is such an important and momentous occasion, and also because it's been such a long time since an Archbishop has visited St. Agnes, Sister Mary Ellen wants everything to go especially well. So she initiates a comprehensive plan to ensure that everything will be absolutely perfect when the Archbishop arrives.

Without delay, Sister Mary Ellen has her fellow Nuns (who are under her charge) congregate all the orphan girls together into the dining hall for a short meeting. There she announces to everyone present the news of the upcoming Archbishop's visit, and she explains to them her plan for preparation. She also highlights the roles and responsibilities that the orphan girls will have in the implementation of it, and reminds them that they must all put forth their very best behavior, so that they can make a positive and lasting impression on the Archbishop when he arrives.

During the next two months St. Agnes undergoes a complete overhaul from top to bottom. All needed painting, touchups, and repairs are done. And everything is scrubbed, cleaned, polished and shined from top to bottom, until you can literally see your facial reflection in them. And, because of having so many things to do, and being so busy, time seems to quickly fly by for everyone.

Finally, the day of the Archbishop's visit has arrived. Luckily, just in the nick of time, everything has just been completed. St. Agnes looks magnificent, both inside and out!

Suddenly, a long and shiny black car pulls up and it stops in front of the Orphanage. Afterwards, the driver gets out and he walks to the back door of the vehicle, and he opens it up.

Noticeably, to the impression of all onlookers and passersby's, out steps the illustrious Archbishop, St. Oliver Earl Glance, dressed in his colorful and fanciful pontifical vestment.

The Archbishop is a ruddy looking Caucasian man, with a stout, corpulent build. He has a rectangular shaped face, with a long nose, and large bushy eyebrows. When he walks he keeps his body upright and erect, like a scarecrow in a cucumber field. It appears as though someone shoved a stiff board up his back. As he advances forward, he keeps his head cocked slightly backwards, with his chin arrogantly pointing upwards towards the sky. And, when he looks at you, his beaming eyes gaze down the bridge of his long and narrow nose, like a marksman staring through his sights, down the long barrel of his riffle.

As the Archbishop arrives, Sister Mary Ellen is on hand to greet and welcome him, along with two accompanying Nuns. As they approach the Archbishop, Sister Mary Ellen says to him: "Welcome to St. Agnes, Your Excellency, our Most Holy Reverend! It's a real pleasure to have you here with us! How was your trip?"

"Very nice, very nice indeed. And might I add, it's good to finally be here!" the Archbishop replies.

Shorty, after getting their greetings out of the way, Sister Mary Ellen and the Nuns proceed to escort the Archbishop into the building.

Upon entering the building, Sister Mary Ellen asks the Archbishop: "Would you like to rest up a bit, Your Excellency? I'm sure you must be tired after your long trip."

"No, that's alright, I'm perfectly fine. As a matter of fact, it feels good to finally stretch the old legs," the Archbishop says with a slight chuckle.

"Then, perhaps, you might want to go on a guided tour of the Orphanage," Sister Mary Ellen suggests.

"Sure, I'd like to do that," the Archbishop smiles and says. And without delay, off they go.

~

Sometime later in the day, after the Archbishop's completes his physical tour of St. Agnes, Sister Mary Ellen commands the Nuns to gather all the orphan girls together into the Chapel.

When all of the girls arrive at the Chapel (one hundred and twenty of them), they are quickly seated. Afterwards, the Archbishop enters the room through a door that is located at the front of the room. And, after walking over to a Bema or raised platform that is approached by steps. He climbs the stairs, and then he sits down upon a throne-like, red, crushed velvet, padded chair, that is situated at the top and center of the floor, just in front of the altar.

Upon seeing that the Archbishop is seated, Sister Mary Ellen walks over to a speaker's podium and proceeds to give a brief and rousing introduction. She says to the audience: "I would like to take this moment to welcome our most distinguished guest, His Excellency, the Most Illustrious, and Most Reverend, Archbishop, St. Oliver Earl Glance to our beloved St. Agnes. As you all know, the Archbishop comes to us on this most momentous occasion in celebration of St. Agnes' 50th anniversary. Yes, it was 50 years ago from today that St. Agnes' was first founded, and her doors were graciously opened to house girls that were in need of a home. And, as you, our beloved guests can see, we have come a long ways since then. Because of this, we would like to take this wonderful opportunity to thank the Archbishop from the bottom of our hearts for all the hard work that he and his fellow constituents have exhibited in contributing to St. Agnes' success."

The audience erupts in applause, giving the Archbishop a long and cheerful ovation. That is everyone, except, Elisabeth Baxter. She just sits there motionless and in silent observance.

Fearful of what Sister Mary Allen might think, concerning Elisabeth's lackluster response and non-participation, Betty Lu Macalester, who is sitting next to Elisabeth, leans over and she gives her a gentle nudge with her elbow. And she whispers softly in her ear, saying: "Ooh girl, you better clap!" However, Elisabeth just continues to sit there motionless and in silence.

After the applause dies down, Sister Mary Ellen steps away from the podium, and then she turns and she walks over to the Archbishop, who remains seated upon the throne-like chair.

As Sister Mary Ellen approaches the Archbishop, he stretches his right arm out towards her, with the palm of his hand faced downwards. In response, she bends over and she kisses his Episcopal ring. Afterwards, she prostrates herself at his feet, and then she rises and returns to her seat, which is located in a section that is exclusively assigned to the Nuns.

Next, following Sister Mary Ellen's solemn act of reverence to the Archbishop, all of the other Nuns come forth, one at a time, and they do the same, exact thing. They approach the Archbishop, kiss his ring, bow before him, and then they rise and return to their seats.

Finally, after all of the Nuns have completed their individual acts of homage to the Archbishop, a Nun who is standing in front of the seated orphans, motions for the girls in the first row of the middle section of seating to stand and form a line.

After the girls are in line formation, the Nun motions for the first girl to come forth. And with strict obedience, the girl does exactly what she was prepped to do. She approaches the Archbishop. And, after pausing for a moment to glance over at Sister Mary Ellen, who gives her an encouraging nod, the girl proceeds to bend over and kiss the Archbishop's Episcopal ring. Then she genuflects before him, rises, and afterwards she is immediately directed out of the Chapel by an assisting Nun.

As soon as the 1st girl exits the Chapel, the next girl in line is summons to come forth. And without hesitation, she walks over to the Archbishop, kisses his ring, genuflects, and then she too is directed out of the room.

Next, the third girl in line is called forward, and then the next girl, and the next, etc., until the entire first row is done.

Following the completion of the first roll of girls, the summonsing Nun now motions for the second row of girls to stand and form a line. As it so happens, Elisabeth Baxter is at the head of the line. It is now her turn to approach the Archbishop.

The Nun motions for Elisabeth to come forth. But, with a look of apprehension on her face, Elisabeth hesitates to do what she is told. She just stands there motionless and in silence.

Again, the Nun motions to Elisabeth a second time to come forward. However, she still remains unresponsive!

Upon observing that Elisabeth is still not responding to her signals, the Nun, in disbelief, begins to panic! She simply cannot believe that Elisabeth is not reacting to her commands! Now, feeling embarrassed and frustrated, and not knowing what to do, the Nun turns and she looks over at Sister Mary Ellen for help. However, she finds that she too is a bit puzzled and confused.

When a third Nun in the room, named Sister Beatrice, who is seated next to Sister Mary Ellen, observes that the Reverend Mother is not happy with Elisabeth's nonresponsive actions, and that she is starting to grow impatient and disturbed with her, she proceeds to get up from her seat, and she quickly walks over to Elisabeth. Approaching her, she looks her straight in the eyes, and with a cold-blooded stare, and a stern and threatening low key voice, she says to her: "Young lady, I'm giving you till the count of three to get moving!" Then, she proceeds to count (loud enough for Elisabeth to hear), saying: "One... two... three..." But, to her surprise, when she's finished counting, Elisabeth is unfazed and un-budged, still standing there in the same, exact spot!

When Sister Mary Ellen observes that Elisabeth is still refusing to budge an inch, she now personally gets up, and she walks over to her, and she says to her with raised eyebrows, and a muffled, but yet hearable and forceful tone: "Elisabeth... Margaret... Baxter! You better move young lady, and I mean right now!"

Upon hearing Sister Mary Ellen words, Elisabeth looks her straight in the eyes, and she says to her with an emphatic, loud voice (a volume loud enough for the entire room to hear): "No, I'm not going to do it! I refuse to kiss his ring and bow before him! He's not God, he's just a man!"

After Elisabeth is done speaking her mind, she quickly turns and she runs out of the Chapel, and down a long corridor that leads towards the front entryway door of the building.

Sister Mary Ellen, now, feeling highly embarrassed by Elisabeth's shocking outburst, and disobedient, renegade-like spirit and actions, turns and she says to Sister Beatrice: "Sister Beatrice, take over till I get back." Afterwards, she politely excuses herself to the Archbishop, and then she turns and she quickly leaves the room in pursuit of Elisabeth, along with two accompanying Nuns.

A short time later, when Sister Mary Ellen and the Nuns finally catch up to Elisabeth, they find her sitting near the main lobby, on the bottom steps of the long spiral staircase that leads to the second floor.

Sister Mary Ellen, slightly out of breath and seething with anger, says to Elisabeth: "I am totally fed up with your rebellious shenanigans young lady!" Next, pointing her finger at Elisabeth, she commands the two accompanying Nuns, saying: "Lock her in the supply closet, and don't let her out until after she agrees to come out and give due respect and homage to the Archbishop!" And then, afterwards, she turns and she proceeds to walk back to the Chapel, where she retakes her seat amongst the rest of the Nuns.

In the meantime, the two Nuns, now, with Elisabeth left in their custody; proceed to do just as they were instructed. They escort her to the supply closet, lock her in, and then leave.

~

Back at the Chapel, the next orphan girl standing in line is called forth. Without hesitation, she walks up to the Archbishop, kisses his Signet ring, genuflects before him, and then she is directed out of the room by an assisting Nun. Afterwards, all of the remaining girls, in turn, one at a time, follow suit, until the last one is finished.

~

Later in the evening, when the day is over; after the Archbishop has concluded his visit and he has departed from St. Agnes; the door to the supply closet, behind which Elisabeth was placed earlier, is now unlocked and opened. Slowly, but surely, out walks a mad and still thoroughly determined and stubborn girl.

Sister Mary Ellen, who happens to be standing at the supply closet alongside two accompanying Nuns, says to Elisabeth with a highly disappointed tone: "Never before, in the entire 50 year history of St. Agnes has this orphanage ever been subjected to such outright humiliation! Your insolent behavior has brought undeserved shame upon this great institution! I should have known better! You have been nothing but trouble from the moment you were first brought here 14 years ago!"

"I didn't ask to come here!" Elisabeth sharply replies. She continues: "I had no choice! I was forced to come! I hate this place! And I can't wait to leave! When I turn eighteen, I'm out of here for good!"

"Well, you have only six months to go before that happens, but in the meantime, you're mine! Now go on upstairs, and go to bed without supper!" Sister Mary Ellen commands.

Elisabeth, now fuming with anger, turns, and she proceeds to run all the way to the girl's dormitory. And after she enters the room she slams the door shut behind her. Next, running over to her bed, she throws herself upon it, buries her face in her pillow, and she begins to cry.

~

Elisabeth Margaret Baxter first came to St. Agnes Orphanage when she was three years old, following the tragedy of her Mother's death, and the mysterious disappearance of her father. At which time she was then awarded to the State of Minnesota, and placed at St. Agnes. She is now 17 ½ years old. She has spent pretty much her whole life here, a total of over 14 years. And she is assigned to stay here until she turn's eighteen, at which time she is then free to leave.

~

It is now late in the evening. Elisabeth is still lying in bed, after she was ordered earlier by Sister Mary Ellen to go to the dormitory. She is awake, but lying on her back with her blanket pulled up over her head. Suddenly! Out of nowhere a hand reaches out, and it grabs hold of the blanket, and it quickly yanks it off of her head. Elisabeth is startled! But wait! As she looks up, she sees that it's just her friend Betty Lu Macalester playing games! This makes Elisabeth so mad! With a highly irritated tone, she says: "Girl, you scared me half to death! What were you thinking?"

"I came to bring you some food, silly!" Betty Lu laughs and says.

Then, she hands Elisabeth a dinner plate with meatloaf, mashed potatoes and gravy, mixed vegetables, and a buttered biscuit on it.

"Thanks, Betty Lu! That was very nice of you!" Elisabeth appreciatively says. She then inquires, asking: "Does Sister Mary Ellen know about this?"

"Are you kidding? Of course not! But I figured that you were hungry, so I smuggled it out of the kitchen, and snuck it up here," Betty Lu says.

"Ooh, girl… if Sister Mary Ellen finds out, you're going to be in big trouble!" Elisabeth exclaims.

"Look who's talking, you're the one that's always in trouble. Besides, who cares? I'm out of here in two weeks anyways," Betty Lu replies.

"You lucky dog. I'm happy for you, but too bad it's you that's turning eighteen before me. I want to get out of here so bad!" Elisabeth reveals.

"Don't worry, your time will come. You'll get out soon. You only have six months left," Betty Lu says.

"I know, but to me that seems like an eternity!" Elisabeth laments.

"I'm sure it does, but, please promise me one thing," Betty Lu says.

"What's that?" Elisabeth asks.

"Promise me, that when you do get out, that you'll be sure to look me up. That way we can hang out together. And, if you like, perhaps we can even room together," Betty Lu encouragingly says.

"I will, you can count on it!" Elisabeth vows.

The girls now hug, and they reconfirm their loyalty and eternal bond of friendship towards one another.

~

Two weeks quickly fly by. Betty Lu Macalester has just turned eighteen years old, and today she is being released from the orphanage. For Elisabeth this is a bittersweet occasion. Sure, she is happy for her friend, but also, at the same time she is sad, because Betty Lu is leaving without her. Standing at a window on the second floor, Elisabeth can only wave goodbye to her dear friend as she gets in a taxicab and leaves.

Upon her release from St. Agnes, Betty Lu is awarded money by the State of Minnesota. Money that she is entitled to after she turned 18 years of age. The money was initially set aside in a trust fund for her by her parents, when they were still alive. The dollar amount that she receives is more than enough for her to get started in her new life. With it, she is able to lease a one bedroom apartment, buy furniture, clothing, food, and other items of necessity. And, whatever money is leftover, she keeps in a savings account that she opened up at the Bank & Trust City Bank, which is located close to where she moved.

4

FLYING THE COOP

During the next six months time drags by for Elisabeth at St. Agnes. To her it feels more like six years! However, the day for her release has finally come. She has just recently turned 18 years old, and today she is leaving St. Agnes for good.

Elisabeth is so excited that she can barely sit still. After all, this is the first time in fifteen years that she is about to step outside of the enclosed, chain-link fence that surrounds the Orphanage. To her, she feels somewhat like a caged bird that is about to be released into the wild for the first time, being freed from the confinements of its restrictive cage. Nevertheless, her release does not come without some mixed feelings. She can hardly wait to start her new life. But yet, at the same time, she is also a bit nervous too. This is because she has heard that the world outside of the Orphanage is so big in comparison to tiny St. Agnes. And, because she has been so sheltered and completely isolated from the rest of the world for practically all of her life, she doesn't know quite exactly what to expect.

As Elisabeth steps outside the front door of St. Agnes, with luggage in hand, it feels all so good to be finally released. Excitement floods her mind, and joy fills her heart, as she thinks about her dear friend, Betty Lu Macalester. She just can't wait to see and be reunited with her again! Suddenly, a yellow taxicab pulls up and it stops in front of the Orphanage. The driver then gets out, and he walks around to the back of the cab, and opens up the trunk. Next, he walks over to where Elisabeth is standing, which is next to an escorting Nun, who happens to be Sister Michaels (the head Nun in charge of the Orphanage Laundry), and he picks up Elisabeth's suitcase from off the ground. Then, he turns and walks back over to the cab, places the suitcase in the trunk and closes it shut. Afterwards, he walks around to the passenger side door of the vehicle and he opens it up for Elisabeth, and waits for her to get in.

"Goodbye, Sister Michaels," Elisabeth says.

"So long, Elisabeth, I wish you good luck in your new life," Sister Michaels replies with a smile.

"Thanks, Sister," Elisabeth says. Then she walks over to and gets into the cab.

After Elisabeth is seated, the cabdriver closes her door. Then he turns and reenters the vehicle.

Peering at Elisabeth through his rearview mirror, the Cabdriver asks: "Where to, young lady?"

"Take me to 1500 East Elm Street," Elisabeth says.

"Yes, Ma'am," the Driver says. Then, he drives off, and he proceeds to head in the direction of the vicinity of Frogtown.

~

Frogtown is a hustling and bustling, bright lights, big city sort of town. It is located within the district of Wright County in the state of Minnesota. It is called Frogtown because long before the land was excavated and the city was built upon it, the region was mostly a swampy area that was literally teeming with frogs. Today, it is a thriving metropolis and community, which is solely populated by upper and middle class white citizens, with good jobs, nice homes, and sleek automobiles.

~

Finally, after driving for some time, the taxi driver enters Frogtown, and then, shortly thereafter, he pulls over and stops in front of a large apartment building.

Elisabeth reaches into an envelope that she is holding in her hands, which contains a letter and some money that she received from her dear friend, Betty Lu, and she pays the driver according to the dollar amount that's registered on the cab's trip meter. And, she also gives him a tip. In response, the Taxi Driver says: "Thank you, Ma'am!" Afterwards, he gets out of the cab, and he retrieves Elisabeth's luggage from the trunk. Then he walks over to and opens up her car door, and customarily gives her an official and cordial greeting, saying: "Welcome to Frogtown, Ma'am!"

Elisabeth excitedly steps out of the cab with a big ear-to-ear grin on her face. Then, she takes a deep breath of fresh air into her lungs, retrieves her luggage from the driver's hand, and says: "Thank you, Sir!"

As the cabdriver gets back into the taxi and slowly drives away, Elisabeth walks up to the apartment building addressed 1500, and she begins climbing a cement staircase that leads to the front door.

After reaching the top stair, Elisabeth sets her luggage down beside her, and then she begins searching through a list of names on the apartment's posted registry. And, upon finding Betty Lu Macalester's name, she then proceeds to ring her doorbell.

Within less than a moment, a female voice answers on the apartment intercom, saying: "Who is it?"

"It's me, Elisabeth!" Elisabeth says. Suddenly, a dead silence occurs. Then, Elisabeth starts to hear loud banging noises coming from inside the apartment building. Curious as to what's causing all of the commotion, she glances through a narrow window pane that's located on the right side of the entryway door. And to her absolute delight, she catches sight of Betty Lu running down a long flight of wooden stairs towards her.

The moment Betty Lu reaches the bottom of the staircase, she quickly flings open the front door, and then, like a spry cat, she springs outside onto the platform where Elisabeth is waiting.

Immediately, the girls warmly embrace and hug each other. Afterwards, Betty Lu says with an excited voice: "Elisabeth, I'm so happy to see you!"

"I'm happy to see you too, Betty Lu!" Elisabeth replies.

"How was your trip?" Betty Lu asks.

"It was a little long, but nice," Elisabeth answers.

"Well, come on in girl! And take a look-see at your new home!" Betty Lu says, as she swoops up Elisabeth's suitcase from off the step. Then, they both enter the building, and climb the long staircase that leads to Betty Lu's apartment.

After the girls approach and enter the apartment, Betty Lu proudly proceeds to take Elisabeth on a full tour of her new home. She shows her the living room, kitchen "slash" dining area, bathroom, and also the shared bedroom, where Elisabeth will sleep.

"Wow, everything looks wonderful! It's perfect!" Elisabeth exclaims.

"Thanks, I knew you would like it!" Betty Lu replies. She continues: "Now, are you ready for the big news?"

"What's that?" Elisabeth asks.

"I got you a job too!" Betty Lu says.

"You're kidding me!" Elisabeth says, with a shocked and excited look on her face.

"I kid you not! You see, I work downtown at this restaurant called Little Ricky's Diner, and I told my boss about you. I said that you're my cousin from out of town, although you and I both know that you're not. I explained that you will soon be moving in with me, and that you will be needing a job," Betty Lu says. She continues: "My boss said, sure, bring her down anytime. We could use more help."

"Wow, that's amazing! Thank you so much Betty Lu for putting in a good word to your boss for me!" Elisabeth appreciatively says.

"No problem kid! After all, that's what friends are for!" Betty Lu, with a big smile replies.

5

LITTLE RICKY'S DINER

Following Elisabeth's arrival to Frogtown, the very next day, Betty Lu takes her down to Little Ricky's Diner, so that she can meet her boss. Interestingly, Little Ricky's is actually an old trolley car that was refurbished and made into a restaurant. Since its establishment, it has become a fun and popular place for the public to dine.

When Betty Lu and Elisabeth finally arrive at Little Ricky's Diner, Elisabeth is both interviewed and hired right on the spot. She can hardly believe it! She is so happy to have a job, and also surprised that she is being put to work so soon. For she is to start immediately as a waitress that very day. And, Betty Lu is assigned the privilege of training her in.

To get started, Betty Lu walks over to a tall, medal cabinet that is located outside of her boss's office, and she opens it up. Next, she grabs two new aprons off of the shelf, and she hands one of them to Elisabeth.

After the girls put their aprons on, Betty Lu gives Elisabeth a notepad and pencil.

"What are these for?" Elisabeth asks.

"To take food and beverage orders, silly," Betty Lu smiles and says. She continues: "Come on, let's go to work."

While Elisabeth and Betty Lu are talking amongst themselves, two young men happen to walk in the front door of the Diner, and they seat themselves in a vacant booth next to a window. Quickly spotting them, Betty Lu discreetly points her finger in their direction, and she says to Elisabeth: "Well, Elisabeth, it looks like your first customers are here. Let's go over and greet them and take their food orders."

As the girl's approach the boys table, Betty Lu smiles at them, and says: "Hello, welcome to Little Ricky's. My name is Betty Lu, and this is Elisabeth. We will be taking your orders today."

Immediately, one of the young men points his finger at Elisabeth, and he says to her: "Excuse me, but I don't believe I've ever seen you here before. Are you new?"

"Yes, this is actually my first day on the job," Elisabeth replies.

"I thought so," the Young Man says. He then begins to formally introduce himself and his friend to the girls, saying: "Hi, my name is Michael Harington. But my friends call me Mike. And this is my friend, Peter Dusek or Pete."

"It's nice to meet you Mike and Pete," Betty Lu smiles and says.

"Hi," Elisabeth says to the boys.

~

Michael Harrington is a Caucasian male. He is twenty years old, and about 6 feet tall, with a medium build. His skin completion is ivory white, and he has an oval shaped face with a narrow nose and thin lips. His hair is black, and his eyes are blue. Outwardly, he is very handsome in appearance.

Peter Dusek is also Caucasian. He too is twenty years old. He is about 5 feet 10 inches tall, with a stocky build. He has red hair, bluish gray colored eyes, and fair skin completion with freckles etched upon his square shaped face.

~

Noticeably, during the entire time that Elisabeth is at the boys table, Michael Harrington keeps staring at her. He cannot seem to take his eyes off of her.

"Well boys, what can we get for you?" Betty Lu asks.

"I'll have a ham and cheese omelet, and a tall glass of milk," Michael says.

"I'll have your 'pigs in a blanket,'[2] and also a tall glass of milk," Peter says.

"Ok gentlemen, we'll have those up for you shortly," Betty Lu says. And then she and Elisabeth turn and leave the boys table.

After the girls leave the boys table, Betty Lu leads Elisabeth over to the 'Food Order Pickup Station,' and she says to her: "Elisabeth, this is where you drop off the customer's food tickets that you write up, so that Freddy the cook can prepare their orders. And then, when their orders are ready for pickup, he'll let you know, both verbally and by ringing this bell that hangs over the pickup window.

As Elisabeth is being trained, she happens to glance back in the direction of Michael and Peter's booth, and to her surprise she notices that Michael keeps staring at her. Quickly, quietly, and yet inconspicuously bringing this to Betty Lu's attention, she asks: "Betty Lu, why does that boy named Michael, keep staring at me?"

"I think he likes you Elisabeth," Betty Lu smiles and says. Then,

---

[2] Pigs in a blanket are three individual sausage links that are wrapped separately in flapjacks.

picking up and handing a serving tray to her, she continues, saying: "I tell you what. Why don't you bring these glasses of water over to the boys?"

"Who me," Elisabeth asks, with a bashful and shy look.

"Yes, of course you," Betty Lu giggles and says.

"Ok," Elisabeth replies.

When Elisabeth returns to the boys' table with the glasses of water, Michael, who is still staring at her, asks: "Elisabeth, do you live around here?"

"Yes, I room with my friend, Betty Lu. We stay, not too far from here, over on East Elm St," Elisabeth says.

"Oh yeah, I know where that is," Michael exclaims. He continues: "Do you think that you and your friend Betty Lu would like to go to a movie with me and Peter sometime?"

"Gee, I don't know, maybe?" Elisabeth answers, in an embarrassed, awkward, and shy way.

"Please, don't get me wrong. I'm not trying to be pushy or anything. I just wanted to know if you guys would like to do that," Michael says.

"I guess, I'll have to check with my friend first, if you don't mind," Elisabeth replies.

"No problem. Take your time," Michael says.

Elisabeth now turns, and she walks back over to the area where Betty Lu is working.

As Betty Lu sees Elisabeth approaching her, she asks: "How are things going Elisabeth?"

"Fine, I guess?" Elisabeth says. And then, continuing, she leans over and she whispers in Betty Lu's ear, and says: "Those boys want to take us out to the Movie Theater."

"What? Do you mean on a date? Are you kidding me?" Betty Lu says, both shocked and surprised.

"I kid you not. That's what they said," Elisabeth confirms.

"What did you say?" Betty Lu asks.

"I told them that I needed to ask you first. Well, what do you think, should we go out with them, Betty Lu?" Elisabeth asks.

After quickly pausing to think about it for a moment, Betty Lu says: "Sure, why not. What do we have to lose? I think it would be a lot of fun!"

"Okay, then let's do it," Elisabeth says.

Suddenly, a bell at the food pickup window chimes, and a deep, and gravelly sort of voice yells out: "Order number 23!"

"It looks like the boys food orders are up," Betty Lu says, alerting Elisabeth. She continues: "Why don't you take it over to them?"

"Ok," Elisabeth says.

After retrieving Michael and Peter's food from the pickup station, Elisabeth turns and she walks over to them.

Without hesitation, Michael asks: "Well, Elisabeth, what did you and Betty Lu decide?"

Elisabeth places the food orders down in front of the boys, and then she says: "We decided that we'll go with you to the theater."

Upon hearing the good news, Michael and Peter flash ear-to-ear grins at one another, and in unison they say to Elisabeth: "That's great!"

Michael excitedly says: "If it's alright with you, Elisabeth, we'll pick the two of you up tomorrow night at seven o'clock?"

"Okay. Seven o'clock will be fine," Elisabeth replies.

"What is your address?" Michael asks.

"It's 1500 East Elm Street, Apartment 201," Elisabeth answers.

"Ok, thanks," Michael says.

Elisabeth now turns and she walks back over towards Betty Lu, who has just finished ringing up a customer's tab at the cash register.

Approaching Betty Lu, Elisabeth says to her: "Michael and Peter said that they'll pick us up at our apartment tomorrow night at seven o'clock."

"Super," Betty Lu exclaims.

"I'm so nervous! I've never been on a date before!" Elisabeth says.

"Oh, you'll be fine!" Betty Lu replies.

"But, I don't have anything to wear!" Elisabeth reveals.

"Don't worry; I have something that you can wear. And you're going to love it!" Betty Lu says.

"You do? Thank you, Betty Lu! You're a real life saver!" Elisabeth says.

"No problem. After all, that's what friends are for!" Betty Lu replies with a big smile.

6

THE BIG DATE

Today is Saturday. The time is 6:45 in the evening, and Michael Harrington and Peter Dusek will soon be arriving to pick up Elisabeth and Betty Lu to take them to the Movie Theater.

The girls are so excited! But at the same time they're also a bit nervous too, because this is the first time that either of them has ever been on a real date before.

Eventually, the hands on the clock on the living room wall roll around to seven o'clock, and the apartment doorbell rings. Elisabeth and Betty Lu gasp in excitement, and then they quickly gather themselves together. Afterwards, Betty Lu runs over to the intercom, which is located next to their apartment entryway/exit door, and after pushing the receiving button, she asks: "Who is it?"

"It's us, Mike, and Pete! We're here to pick you up for the movie," a voice on the other end says.

Betty Lu pushes the transmitting button on the intercom, and says: "Ok. We'll be right down!" Then, the girls quickly grab their sweaters; leave their apartment; and they walk downstairs and begin exiting the building.

As soon as Elisabeth and Betty Lu step outside the door, they find that both Mike and Pete are there, waiting at the top of the cement staircase to greet and complement them.

"Wow, you guys look really nice!" the Boys say to the girls.

"Thank you!" the girls reply with a big smile. Afterwards, the two couples walk down and over to a parked, shiny convertible automobile, with the top down. The vehicle is a 1944 Cadillac Convertible, with a V8 engine. It has a glossy, dark blue exterior; a tan, vinyl, convertible top; shiny chrome bumpers, moldings, front grill, and wheel covers; large whitewall tires; a sleek wooden dashboard; and tan colored soft leather seats, along with interior door trim.

Michael is the driver. So he arranges for Elisabeth to sit up front with him, and for Betty Lu to sit in the backseat with Peter.

After everyone is situated in the car, Betty Lu says to Michael: "Wow, this is a really nice car, Michael! It must have cost a fortune!"

"Thank you! I just got it! It's brand new!" Michael replies, with an ever so proud look on his face.[3]

"I like how the top goes down," Elisabeth says.

"Yes, that's my favorite feature too! I figured that we might as well take advantage of the beautiful night!" Michael says. He then starts up the car engine, and they head off to the Movie Theater.

While traveling to the theater, conversation between the boys and girls is a little awkward at first, but eventually everyone begins to relax and loosen up a bit. Breaking the ice, Betty Lu says to Peter: "So,

---

[3] The fact is Michael Harrington happens to be a spoiled, rich kid, who comes from money. His daddy, Richard Dupont Harrington is a big business executive.

Peter, what's the name of the show that we're going to see?"

"It's a movie that was just released. It's called 'Arsenic and Old Lace.' It stars actors: Cary Grant, Peter Lorre, and Pricilla Lane," Peter replies.

"I heard that it's supposed to be a pretty good flick!" Michael adds.

"That's great! I'm sure it will be a lot of fun!" Elisabeth smiles and says.

Not long afterwards, the two couples arrive at the 'Grand Starlight Movie Theatre,' which is located on downtown Main Street. The movie marquee is all lit up in bright lights, with the name of the film and main actors posted in big bold letters.

Michael quickly pulls his car over to the curb and parks and everyone gets out. Afterwards, the boys then proceed to escort the girls up to the front door of the theatre. However, before entering the main door, Michael politely excuses himself, saying: "Excuse me, I'll be right back." Then, he walks up to the ticket booth, which is located outside, and after purchasing tickets for everyone in his group, he rejoins them, and they enter the theatre door and lobby together.

As Michael, Peter, Elisabeth, and Betty Lu walk through the theater's lobby and approach the auditorium, they are warmly greeted by an usher dressed in full usher attire — hat, white gloves, flashlight, and all. And, after cordially welcoming them to the theater, he takes their tickets, and then he promptly escorts them to their seats.

A moment or so later, after the two couples are seated, and not long before the show begins, Michael and Peter arrange to get Elisabeth and Betty Lu some popcorn and refreshments. After ascertaining what each girl personally wants, the boys leave their seats, and they head off to the refreshment stand.

The theatre is quickly starting to fill up with people.

Elisabeth says to Betty Lu: "Wow, there sure are a lot of people here!"

"I'll say!" Betty Lu replies. And then she and Elisabeth spend the rest of the waiting time engaged in small talk, as they wait for the boys to return.

Sometime later, after a short period of time has elapsed, Michael and Peter return to their seats with popcorn and refreshments in hand. And just as quick as they are seated, the theatre's projection screen's vivid, red velvet curtains slowly open, and a large movie screen appears. The show now begins!

Elisabeth is so excited! She's as happy as a kid in a candy store. This experience is all so new to her. Never before, in all her life, has she ever attended anything like this before.

~

Later, as time progresses and they get further into the show, Peter, who happens to be sitting next to Betty Lu, raises his left arm up high above his head, as through he's trying to stretch-out, and then he slyly places it around her shoulders. Next, he slowly leans over and he gives her a kiss on her cheek. In response, Betty Lu smiles and then she turns and she kisses him on his cheek. Afterwards, they start to kiss one another on the lips.

When Michael, who is sitting next to Elisabeth, observes what Peter and Betty Lu are doing, he decides to follow suit. First, he slowly places his right arm around her shoulders. Next, he gently leans over and he kisses her on her cheek; and immediately afterwards, he kisses her on the lips. In response, Elisabeth kisses him back. But then, Michael proceeds to do something that Elisabeth didn't expect, and that highly offends her, and that is, he reaches out and he inappropriately touches her on the leg and he starts caressing her inner, upper thigh.

Elisabeth is completely shocked and appalled! She didn't expect Michael to behave like this at all, nor does she approve of it! And, in rapid response, she quickly pushes his hand away from her leg. Then, she looks him straight in the eyes. And with a sharp, angry, and forceful tone she says: "Stop it!"

Michael, quickly realizing that Elisabeth is angry with him and that she means business, immediately stops and he respectfully backs away from her. And he no longer tries to kiss or touch her during the remainder of the night.

~

Later that night, after the movie is over, while Michael and Peter are driving the girl's home from the theater; Peter and Betty Lu continue making out in the backseat of the car. Elisabeth, however, still shocked and disturbed by Michael's inappropriate actions back at the theater, isn't saying a word. She just keeps her face looking straight ahead during the entire ride home. Michael, knowing that she is angry with him, doesn't attempt to say a single thing.

When Michael, Peter, Elisabeth, and Betty Lu finally arrive back at the girl's apartment building, Michael promptly pulls the car over to the curb and stops. And then the girls get out.

Betty Lu says to the Boys: "Thanks for the movie. I had a great time. Good night." Elisabeth, on the other hand, doesn't say word. She just keeps silent. Then, she and Betty Lu quickly walk up to the front door of the apartment building and enter in. Afterwards, Michael drives off.

The remainder of the weekend quickly flies by.

It is now Monday, and Elisabeth is back to at work at Little Ricky's Diner. While she is busy waiting on several customers, who are seated on tall stools up at a long dining counter, which is located near the front door, just in front of the kitchen; Michael Harington enters the restaurant, and he promptly seats himself at an open stool at the end of the counter. Elisabeth happens to see him come in, but she deliberately ignores him.

Quickly observing that Elisabeth is giving him the cold shoulder, Michael eventually gets up out of his seat, and he moves to another open stool that's closer to her, so that he can get her attention. Elisabeth, now forced to acknowledge Michael, says to him with a disturbed, but quite whisper tone: "How dare you come here, after what happened last night! What kind of girl do you think I am anyways?"

"I'm sorry!" Michael replies. He continues: "But, I just couldn't help myself! I promise that it will never happen again! Please forgive me? Please!"

At first, Elisabeth doesn't respond to Michael's apology and plea for forgiveness. She just ignores him, and continues serving the other customers. But then, after giving the matter some thought (as to whether she should forgive him or not) she finally approaches him, and she says: "Alright, Michael, I'll forgive you this time. But don't ever let it happen again!"

Michael, now breathing a big sigh of relief, says: "Good! Thank you, Elisabeth! I appreciate that so much! As a matter of fact, to show you how sorry I am, please let me make it up to you, by allowing me take you out to a really fancy dinner!"

Elisabeth, feeling a little apprehensive about Michael's offer to take her out again so soon, shakes her head back and forth, and she says to him: "I don't know if that's a good idea Michael?"

"Come on Elisabeth, please! I know a great dining place, you'll love it!" Michael says.

Now, gesturing as though he's swearing on a Bible, Michael raises his right hand, and with a sad, puppy dog look on his face he says: "And I solemnly promise to be on my best behavior this time." He continues: "So what do you say? Will you let me take you out to dinner?"

"I don't know?" Elisabeth says, once again shaking her head back and forth in uncertainty.

"All come on sweetie. Give the poor guy another chance!" one of the customers at dining counter says, after having overheard and picked up on Elisabeth's and Michael's conversation.

"Yeah, give the guy a chance," other customers chime in and say, as they also begin pleading to Elisabeth in Michael's behalf.

Elisabeth, now recognizing that she's totally outnumbered, and that perhaps she should give Michael another chance; thinks about it for a moment, and then she turns to him, and says: "Alright Michael, I'll let you take me out."

Immediately, all of the customers erupt in loud applauds and cheers!

Michael, now, sporting a big smile; happily and enthusiastically says to Elisabeth: "Great! I'll pick you up Saturday night at seven o'clock."

"Okay. I'll see you then," Elisabeth says. Afterwards, Michael gets up out of his seat, says goodbye. And he quickly exits the restaurant.

7

AN UNFORGETTABLE NIGHT

It is Saturday night. And Elisabeth and Michael are on their second date. Both of them are dressed in formal attire, and they are seated at a table for two at Marbella's Restaurante, which is a very exclusive and expensive, fine dining establishment, that's located within a very prestigious downtown strip in the heart of Frogtown.

Marbella's is elegantly superb, with a romantic ambience. The entire restaurant is tastefully arranged and beautifully decorated. The large bay windows that surround the dining area are fitted with classy, custom designed, plush velvet fabric valances and formal draperies. And the floor is covered with complementary, strikingly beautiful, patterned carpet fit for royalty. Dazzling crystal chandeliers hang from the ceiling. And each of the tabletops are covered with lovely, ivory white, clean, fine linen, and centered with a scintillating crystal vase that's filled with a beautiful bouquet of fresh cut flowers. Also, beside each flower vase is a set of matching crystal candle holders, furnished with white lighted candles. And, lastly, to top it all off, in the background you can hear the mellow, sweet sound of smooth jazz music being played by a live orchestrated band. Truly, the entire setting is utterly delightful!

Michael Harrington now looks directly into Elisabeth eyes, and he says to her: "Elisabeth, I want to thank you for allowing me to take you out for dinner tonight. After all, it's the least that I could do, after having offended you."

"Thank you, Michael, I really appreciate that. It's very nice of you," Elisabeth replies.

"No problem. And, oh by the way, may I add, you look very lovely tonight!" Michael says.

"Why, thank you!" Elisabeth smiles and says.

Suddenly, a waiter of Italian decent, with a thick accent approaches Elisabeth and Michael's table. He is carrying a crystal glass picture of ice-cold water.

As the waiter begins to pour water into their drinking glasses, he smiles and says: "Welcome to Marbella's, Signore and Madame! I'm sure that the two of you will find this to be a most pleasurable dining experience!" Next, he hands them separate dinner menus, and he says: "Our Chef's special for tonight is a slow roasted honey glazed duck, served with minty carrots and herby roast potatoes." And then, continuing, he asks: "May I start the two of you off with a beverage?"

"I'll just have water," Elisabeth replies.

"The same here," Michael says.

"May I interest you in one of our appetizers?" the Waiter asks.

"Sure," Michael says, as he quickly glances at the menu. He continues, saying: "Why don't you bring us your *Medley of Appetizers for Two.*"

"Excellent choice, Signore!" the Waiter says. Then, he turns, and he leaves the table.

As Elisabeth browses through her dinner menu, she says to Michael: "Wow, there sure are a lot of items to choose from." She continues: "I'm stumped. I don't know what to pick?"

"What are you hungry for?" Michael inquires.

"I'm really not sure," Elisabeth says.

"I tell you what, why don't you let me choose for you?" Michael courteously suggests.

"Ok," Elisabeth replies with a smile.

Within a short time, the waiter returns to Elisabeth and Michael's table with the medley of appetizers, and he asks: "Have the two of you decided on a main course?"

Michael addresses the waiter and, he proceeds to place both Elisabeth's and his food order in Italian. He exquisitely says: *"Puoi portare la giovane donna, i tuoi gamberetti primavera, con salsa extra. E per il deserto, avrà la tua cassata silciliana! E per me, puoi portarmi esattamente la stessa cosa."*[4]

"Sono scelte eccellenti, signore! Grazie,"[5] the Waiter replies, with a big grin, after he hears Michael give both Elisabeth's and his food order in the Italian tongue. Then, he takes their menus and he leaves the table.

As soon as the waiter leaves, Elisabeth says to Michael, concerning his placement of their food orders: "That was very impressive Michael!"

Michael, now showboating a comical display of mocked arrogance, with an exceedingly proud look on his face, along with swagger mannerisms, and a stuffy, pompous tone of voice, kiddingly

---

[4] Which means, when translated: You may bring the young lady, your shrimp primavera, with extra sauce. And for desert, she will have your cassata siciliana! And for me, you can bring me the exact same thing.

[5] Which means, when translated: Those are excellent choices, Sir! Thank you.

says: "Well Madame, what can I say? I try." When Elisabeth observes Michael's silliness, it immediately triggers a spontaneously giggle from her, and then they both begin to chuckle and laugh!

Well, so far the night is going well. The Restaurant is lovely. The food is delicious. And Michael is being the perfect gentleman. As Elisabeth contemplates these things, she thinks, what more could a girl ask for?

~

Later that night, after dinner is over and Elisabeth and Michael have left the restaurant; he begins to drive her home. However, Elisabeth quickly observes that he seems to be going the wrong way, heading in the opposite direction to where her home is located. So she inquires of him, saying: "Michael, where are we going? Aren't you going the wrong way?"

"It's a surprise, you'll see," Michael says. Subsequently, he proceeds to drive his car to an area that is situated high above Frogtown, to a place on a hill that overlooks the city, a place called "Lookout Point." The advantage of Lookout Point is that it offers a spectacular view. For one can look out over the valley and see the entire city below. And, from up here, the view of the captivating city lights, along with the enchanting stars in the moonlit sky above; on a clear night like tonight, is absolutely breathtaking!

As soon as Elisabeth and Michael arrive at Lookout Point, Michael quickly pulls his car over and parks. And with the front of his car facing the edge of the cliff, and the convertible top conveniently down, he turns off the engine.

Immediately, upon observing the amazing panoramic view of the glimmering city lights below, along with the sparkling diamond-like starry sky above, that is situated within a complementary backdrop of black velvety expanse, Elisabeth exclaims: "Wow, the sight from up here is absolutely gorgeous!"

"Yes it is," Michael agreeably replies, as both he and Elisabeth proceed to sit back, relax, and enjoy the view.

~

A short time later, after Elisabeth and Michael have been sitting and appreciating and enjoying the amazing view of both the glimmering city lights below and the twinkling starry night sky above, Michael, without a moment's notice, slowly leans over and he kisses Elisabeth gently on her cheek. In response, Elisabeth quickly pulls away from him. And in a nervous tone, she says: "I don't think this is a good idea."

"What's that?" Michael asks.

"I don't think we should be here," Elisabeth says.

"No, it's ok. Trust me," Michael says. Afterwards, he proceeds to lean over again, and he gives her a kiss on the lips.

Again, Elisabeth quickly pulls away from Michael, and she says: "We should go! This isn't right!"

Michael tries to put her at ease, saying in a soft and gentle tone: "Don't worry! It's ok!" Afterwards, he leans over and he attempts to give her another kiss on the lips. However, this time, instead of pulling away from him, Elisabeth begins to relax, and she kisses him back. She reasons that perhaps she should believe and trust Michael; after all, as she contemplates or thinks back on how the evening has gone thus far; he's been a perfect gentleman all night. But wait, could her judgment and assessment of him be slightly off?

Unfortunately, for Elisabeth, as time elapses, Michael proves to be in sync with his true character. As the two of them continue kissing, he slowly reaches his hand over and he touches her on her breasts. In quick response, Elisabeth forcefully pushes him away from her. Then she slaps him really hard in the face. And she says to him in a sharp, angry tone: "Stop it!" Michael, however, doesn't listen to her. He only becomes more aggressive. Now, forcing himself on Elisabeth, he pulls her into his arms and he passionately kisses her on the mouth; and at the same time, he reaches his hand down and he touches her near her private area.

Elisabeth is furious! Once again she pushes Michael away from her, and she says to him with a loud and commanding voice: "I said, stop it!" But Michael still doesn't listen. Becoming ever more aggressive, he starts to forcefully climb on top of her.

With Michael's body now lying on top of her, Elisabeth panics and becomes overwhelmed with fear! And, at the top of her voice she screams: "Get off of me!" However, her pleas are falling upon deaf ears. So she begins pushing and fighting him with all of her might! But to no avail. There's simply no stopping him! He's like a wild dog in heat!

As Elisabeth continues to struggle with Michael, she eventually manages to reach her right hand down to her right foot. And, quickly slipping her high-heel shoe off, she takes it and she strikes Michael in the head as hard as she can with the butt of the heel! As a result, the blow is so hard that he monetary releases his hold on her. The fact is, he simply has no choice! Now, reeling and clutching his head in pain, he submissively let's go.

Without hesitation, and taking full advantage of the opportunity to escape, Elisabeth quickly opens her car door, and she gets out and she starts running away, down the long and winding road and steep hill. Michael, however, still hurt, dazed, and confused from the blow, can only manage to sit up, lean forward, and slump his head against the steering wheel. All the while, Elisabeth keeps on running... getting further and further away from him and his car.

Poor Elisabeth! Running both rattled and scarred, with only one shoe on and clutching the other one in her hand, has no clue as to where she is going. Oh no! Suddenly, she trips on the shoulder of the road, and she falls down fast and hard to the ground! Now, wincing and grabbing her twisted ankle in pain, she proceeds to take her other shoe off. Then, she immediately gets back up upon her feet, and she starts running again; barefooted, down the middle of the long and winding hillside road.

In the meantime, back at the car, Michael is finally starting to recover from the blow to his head. Peering into the rearview mirror, he notices that there are drops of blood running down his face (the blood is flowing from an open gash that he sustained when Elisabeth hit him on top of his head with her high-heel shoe).

Michael, now fully realizing what Elisabeth has done, and noting that she is managing to get away (although not knowing where she is or in what direction she has fled) quickly starts up his car, and in seething anger he begins to chase after her in hot pursuit!

Interestingly, as Elisabeth is running, she eventually happens to come upon a long and cascading staircase that is situated down and alongside a grassy hillside on the left side of the roadway. Fortunately, the entire staircase from top to bottom is illuminated by a series of lighted street-like pole lamps. Stopping and gazing down the long staircase from above, she observes that it leads to the Frogtown city streets below. So without hesitation, she quickly enters the staircase and she begins rapidly descending down the stairs.

In the meantime, Michael is still driving his car, frantically and diligently searching for Elisabeth. But, she is nowhere to be found! He's not seeing her anywhere! Fuming within himself, he says: *"Where in the world can she be?"* And then, suddenly, it dawns on him. Knowing the area like the back of his hand, he has a hunch that she might have found and took the hillside staircase that leads to the Frogtown city streets below. Now, feeling confident that he knows where she is, and that he can catch up to her, he speeds onward!

While Michael is flying down the road in a desperate attempt to catch up to Elisabeth, she, on the other hand, is beginning to feel tired and exhausted from all the running. So she stops and she sits down on the staircase, in order to rest for a moment. However, little does she realize that Michael is close by. For he has just arrived at the staircase. And after immediately pulling his car over to the shoulder of the road, he gets out, and he proceeds to approach the stairs.

Elisabeth, not knowing that Michael is near, but realizing that she can't rest too long, and that she has to keep on moving, gets back up on her feet, and she continues descending down the long staircase.

As Michael approaches and peers down the long staircase from above, he quickly spots Elisabeth. Quietly whispering to himself, he says: *"Aha! There she is! I thought so!"* Yep, his hunch was right after all. Elisabeth is indeed on the staircase, and she is swiftly descending down it towards the city streets below. Now, angrier than ever, Michael quickly gets back into his car, and he speeds off down the road!

Eventually, after trekking down the long flight of stairs, Elisabeth finally reaches the bottom of the staircase, and she exits onto the city streets below. Coincidently, an old man and woman happen to be walking by. So Elisabeth, not knowing exactly where she is, or which way to go, approaches and stops the couple to ask them for directions. She says: "Excuse me, but I'm not from around here. Can you please tell me which way it is to 1500 East Elm Street?"

"Sure. I know where that is," the Man replies. Raising his hand, he points his finger towards the east, and he says: "It's about a mile and a half east of here, in that direction."

"Wow, that's a long ways to walk," Elisabeth exclaims.

"Well, there's a city bus that goes that way," the Man says.

"There is? Where do I board it?" Elisabeth asks.

"The Street that we're standing on is Grand Avenue. The Bus Stop is on the corner of Sunset Boulevard and Main Street," the Man explains. And then, pointing his finger again, he continues, saying: "If you walk two blocks in that direction, you will come to Main Street. And when you get to Main Street, turn right; which is east, and go one block. There you will find the Bus Stop. If you wait there, a bus should be coming through shortly."

"Thank you so much for your help, Sir!" Elisabeth says.

"No problem," the Man replies. He continues: "And, oh, by the way, after you board the Bus, be sure to tell the driver where you're going, so that he can inform you when he's approaching your bus stop. That way you'll be prepared to get off."

"Thank you, Sir! I really appreciate your help!" Elisabeth says.

"I'm glad that I could be of some assistance to you young lady. Goodbye and good luck," the Man smiles and says.

After giving directions and instructions to Elisabeth, the old man and his wife resume walking south in the opposite direction that Elisabeth is now traveling. They proceed to walk down to the end of the block. And then, they turn left at the corner, and disappear from site.

~

After having walked for a short period of time, Elisabeth finally arrives at the Bus Stop. And she sits down on the bench and waits for the bus to arrive. But then, suddenly, out of nowhere, a car pulls up and it stops in front of the Bus Stop where she is waiting. To her surprise, she sees that it's Michael Harrington. Oh no! He has found her!

Elisabeth, now in a state of complete panic, immediately gets up, and she begins to flee! But, within a flash, Michael hops out of his car. And before she can get too far, he quickly chases her down; grabs hold of her by her arm; and he begins dragging her back to his car. Elisabeth, however, is not giving up easy! She is resisting and fighting him every step of the way! But, unfortunately, because Michael is bigger and stronger than she is, his strength proves to be too much for her, and eventually he manages to drag her back to his car. And, after opening the driver's side door, he begins shoving her; head first, inside. Elisabeth, however, who is still continuing to put up a hard fight, somehow manages to twist her body around, so that she's now facing Michael, and with her back now lying firmly against the car seat, she delivers a swift and hard kick to his groin area! Instantly, upon feeling the blow, Michael grabs his crotch, doubles over in pain, and he drops to the ground upon his knees!

Now, with Michael momentarily down and incapacitated, Elisabeth immediately takes full advantage of the opportunity to escape. First, she quickly takes the car keys out of the ignition, and she throws them as far as she can across the street. And then, without hesitation, she takes off running as fast as she can, at breakneck speed, heading westward, down Sunset Boulevard.

~

After a moment or so elapses, and the initial shock and blow to his groin begins to wear off, Michael finally gets up off of the ground and he stands upon his feet. And, although, still in a lot of pain, he cries out with a loud voice, saying: "Elisabeth Baxter, come back here!" But Elisabeth doesn't listen to him. She doesn't even stop to look back. She just keeps running, and getting further and further away.

Now, Michael is really mad! Not wanting Elisabeth to get away, he begins running after her in hot pursuit.

Poor Elisabeth is so frightened! Not knowing where she is headed, she just continues running straight down Sunset Boulevard. And after running several blocks, she eventually comes to a bend in the road. As she rounds the bend, looking ahead, she observes that there is a long and tall, brick wall across the street, on the opposite side of the Boulevard. Unbeknown to her, it is the Bayridge Dividing Wall, which merges into Sunset Boulevard at the West Bend end of the road.

~

The Bayridge Dividing Wall is a long and tall, brick barricade-like structure that separates Frogtown from Shytown. It is about ten feet high and about four feet thick. Also, it runs diagonally up to and then adjacent with West Sunset Boulevard as it stretches endlessly onward.

~

Quickly crossing the street, Elisabeth runs up to and alongside the massive wall for a short distance. Now, breathing heavily and tired from running, she has no choice but to stop and catch her breath.

As Elisabeth stops and stands there leaning against the wall and resting, she happens to discover, just above her head, that there seems to be some bricks missing in one section of the wall. Upon further examination she notes that there appears to be just enough bricks missing to perhaps provide an opening large enough for a human body to possibly squeeze through.

Elisabeth, uncertain as to what lies on the other side of the wall, pauses for a moment. Then, she turns, and she glances back in the direction from where she came. And, immediately, she spots Michael Harrington. Unfortunately, he stubbornly refuses to give up on her. And he's running towards her, and getting ever so closer.

Elisabeth, now fearful that Michael is going to catch up to her, proceeds to climb up to the hole in the Bayridge wall, and then she begins to squeeze her body through it, until she passes completely through and into Shytown on the other side.

~

Shytown is a community that is solely populated by people of the black race. Years ago it was labeled Shytown by the white community of Frogtown, because as legend has it, that due to heavy jurisdictional restrictions that were placed upon the inhabitants of that community by the legal system, that, as a result, they, "The Negro People" are too afraid or intimidated to leave their assigned area to venture into Frogtown, where the prominent and dominant people of the white race live (a story of course, which in time has become grossly exaggerated and highly embellished upon).

~

Michael Harrington is tired of running, but he still refuses to give up on pursuing Elisabeth. He's absolutely intent on catching her. He lost sight of her for a moment, when she first rounded the bend on West Sunset Boulevard, but now that he is catching up, he once again has his sights completely fixed on her. But wait! When he sees that she has climbed through the Bayridge Dividing Wall into Shytown, he stops running. And he begins shaking his head back and forth in extreme disappointment and disbelief.

Elisabeth, now on the other side of the Bayridge wall and feeling that she has gotten away safe, walks over to and she sits down beside a nearby tree, so that she can catch her breath, and rest up a bit. But, just as soon as she is starting to feel at ease and safe from harm, suddenly, out of nowhere jumps Michael Harrington.

Quickly, grabbing hold of Elisabeth from behind, Michael begins dragging her back to the opening in the wall. Elisabeth tries hard to break free from his strong grip. But, to no avail. Now, feeling completely overpowered, she starts to scream: "Help! Help! Somebody, help me!"

Suddenly, out of the darkness and into the light steps a male figure. It is a young black man. He is about nineteen years old, and six feet tall.

Addressing Michael, in regards to his rough treatment of the young lady, the young black man yells out to him, saying: "Hey you! Leave her alone!"

Michael quickly turns around and he looks in the direction of the voice, and after seeing who it is, he says: "Mind your own business, boy!" Afterwards, he turns and he continues to drag Elisabeth towards the opening in the wall.

Once again, the young black man yells out to Michael, saying: "I said! Leave her alone!" In response, Michael throws Elisabeth forcefully to the ground. And in a fit of rage he turns, and he quickly charges at the young black man, tackles him, and they begin grappling and wrestling around on the ground.

At first, the young black man initially is putting up a pretty good fight, but then, Michael manages to rap his right arm around his neck, and he begins to squeeze and apply a lot of pressure. The pressure is so great that the young black man can barely breathe!

Michael, now realizing that he has the upper hand, and that he is inflicting a lot of pain on his opponent, begins to laugh.

When Elisabeth sees that the young black man is being hurt and that the very thought of it is somehow sadistically bringing Michael inner joy, she is appalled, and she yells out to him, saying: "Michael!

Stop it! Let him go!" But Michael doesn't listen to her plea. He just continues to crank up the pressure on the young man neck.

The young black man, gasping for air, finally manages to lift his right arm up high above his head, and then, with an ever forceful driving force, he drives his elbow downwards into the pit of Michael's stomach. As a result, the force from the blow is so hard, that it knocks the wind clear out of Michael, causing him to release his tenacious hold. Afterwards, the young black man slowly gets up from off of the ground and he rises to his feet.

Michael, with the wind completely knocked out of him, is curled up in pain on the ground, holding his stomach and gasping for air. However, within a short time he is able to regain his wind.

As soon as Michael gets his wind back, he gets up from off of the ground, and he throws a quick right punch at the young, black man's face. However, the young man swiftly wards off the blow with his left hand, and then in a flash he throws a quick counterpunch with his right hand and lands his fist squarely on Michael's chin. The blow is so powerful that it knocks Michael clean off his feet, and he falls down fast and hard, with his back landing flat against the ground. In response, Michael quickly grabs his chin, and grimaces in pain. And then, without delay he proceeds to pick himself up from off of the ground.

Now, up and on his feet once again, Michael looks the young black man straight in the eyes, and then, for some unexplained reason, Michael abruptly turns around, and like a bat out of hell, he begins to flee, running as fast as he can towards the opening in the Bayridge wall. And, immediately upon reaching it, he turns around and he looks back at the young black man. And with a whimper in his voice, he yells out with a loud and angry tone to him, saying: "I'll get even with you, Nigger! Just you wait!" Then, he quickly turns and he squeezes his body through the narrow opening in the wall, and disappears from sight.

The moment Michael is gone, the young black man turns towards Elisabeth, and with a concerned, sympathetic, and soft and gentle voice, he asks: "Miss, are you alright?"

"Yes, I am now. Thanks to you," Elisabeth replies in a grateful tone. She continues: "Let me formally introduce myself. My name is Elisabeth Baxter. What's your name?"

"My name is Randall; Randall Pascale," the young man says.

"Thanks again, Randall," Elisabeth appreciatively says, as she reaches out and cordially shakes his hand. Continuing, she says: "If it wasn't for your help, I can't imagine what might have happened to me?"

"You're welcome, Elisabeth, I'm glad I could be of help," Randall replies.

~

Randall Pascale was born in Clinton, Illinois on January 7, 1926 to an African American mother named, Kathryn, and a Native American father named, Cherokee Pascale. Randall is about 6 feet tall with an athletic build. He has dark brown skin complexion, and wavy, jet black hair, with large loose curls situated on the top, towards the front of his head. He has an oval shaped face, a long slender nose, thin and narrow lips, and slightly big ears. He and his family moved to Shytown after his father died. Randall was 10 years old at the time.

~

Elisabeth, feeling a little jittery and worried, as to whether Michael has truly left or not, says to Randall: "I wonder if Michael is gone, and if it's safe for me to leave now?"

"I don't know? But I think it would be best for you to wait awhile longer to make sure," Randall replies.

"That's probably not a bad idea," Elisabeth responds.

"So Elisabeth, who was that guy anyways? Is he your boyfriend or something?" Randall inquires.

"No, he's not my boyfriend. He's just some boy that I recently met. And we went out on a couple of dates together," Elisabeth reveals.

"Wow, some kind of date that turned out to be!" Randall says.

"You're telling me!" Elisabeth exclaims, in wholehearted agreement.

"How did you get here Elisabeth," Randall asks.

"I came on foot, but I was going to take the city bus home," Elisabeth answers.

"If you'd like, when it's time to leave, I'd be happy to walk you to the bus stop and see that you get on board safely," Randall says.

"Will you?" Elisabeth says, now feeling a big sigh of relief.

"Sure," Randall replies.

"I would appreciate that very much!" Elisabeth says.

While Elisabeth and Randall are waiting, they spend the rest of their time sitting on the ground engaged in small-talk.

"Where do you live Randall?" Elisabeth asks.

Randall raises his hand and he points his finger in the direction northward, and he says: "I live in a little house that is just a few blocks north of here, on Wilborn Street. You can't miss it. It has an open front porch and a huge maple tree in the front yard, with a tire swing hanging from one of its large limbs." Suddenly, the very thought of mentioning the tire swing, causes him to begin reminiscing about the past. Giggling a little, he says: "That old tire swing has been there for many years; ever since my brother and I were kids."

"Oh, so you have a brother," Elisabeth says.

"Yep, I have one brother. His name is Charles. I also had a sister. Her name was Nellie. But she died when I was twelve," Randall reveals.

"I'm sorry to hear that," Elisabeth replies.

"My Mother's name is Eva," Randall says. He continues: "Where do you live Elisabeth?"

"I stay with my best friend, Betty Lu Macalester. We rent an apartment together on East Elm Street, over in the Frogtown District," Elisabeth replies.

"Do you have any brothers or sisters?" Randall inquires.

"No. I'm an only child," Elisabeth says. And then, quickly changing the subject, she raises her hand, and she points her finger at the Bayridge Dividing Wall, and she asks: "Randall, why is this massive wall here?

"It's there to separate the white community from the black community," Randall says.

"Why are whites and blacks separated?" Elisabeth asks.

"I really don't know. I guess it's just a rule that somebody made up a long time ago," Randall answers.

"Well, I think it's a stupid rule!" Elisabeth exclaims.

"Me too, and someday I hope to do something to change it!" Randall says.

"I'm sure you will!" Elisabeth replies.

After a moment of silence, Randall says: "Well, Elisabeth, I think that the coast is clear now (meaning that Michael Harrington is gone). Why don't we get you to the Bus Stop?"

"Ok," Elisabeth replies. Afterwards, they both rise up from off of the ground, and they walk over to the Bayridge wall. And then, one at a time, they proceed to squeeze their bodies through the narrow opening.

After successfully passing through the Bayridge wall into Frogtown, Elisabeth and Randall proceed to walk together towards the bus stop.

Because it is late at night, the city streets are both quiet and empty. There's not a single person in site. The reason being is because, routinely, everything, except for the bus service, shuts down at ten o'clock at night. And, because there's nothing to do, people in general are normally at home during this time.

After walking for awhile, Elisabeth and Randall finally get near the bus stop. They are about 50 feet away. Looking up and over in the not so far distance, to the left of them, they spot the bus coming. It's about two blocks away.

Randall, fearful that he will be seen with a white girl, which is something that is strictly forbidden during this time period in US history, stops and he discontinues walking; deliberately dropping behind Elisabeth so that he doesn't get her in trouble.

When Elisabeth realizes that Randall has stopped walking alongside of her, she turns around, and she asks: "Aren't you coming Randall?"

"No, this is as far as I go. You'll be ok from here," Randall says.

"Ok. Thank you, Randall," Elisabeth replies, with a puzzled look on her face.

"You're welcome, Elisabeth," Randall replies. Afterwards, they both wave to each other and say goodbye.

As Elisabeth turns back around to leave, she observes that the bus is getting closer, so she picks up her pace and quickly hustles the remaining distance to the bus stop.

The instant Elisabeth reaches the bus stop, the bus arrives. So she boards it; pays the fare; tells the driver where she's going; and inquires from him when and where she needs to disembark. Afterwards, she takes a seat next to a window at the front of the bus. And, as soon as she is seated, the bus driver begins to drive away.

Quickly, turning and looking out her window, Elisabeth peers back at the spot where Randall is standing. But, she sees that he is gone. However, in reality, he really is not gone. He just happens to be hiding and watching in the not so far distance, from a secret and undisclosed location. And, after the bus is completely out of his sight, he leaves. And, like Elisabeth, he too heads for home.

8

A VISIT TO WHISPERING POND

Today is Sunday, and a good day for sleeping in. But instead of using the day to sleep a little longer, Elisabeth rises early, takes a shower, reenters the bedroom, and proceeds to get dressed.

As Elisabeth is getting dressed, her roommate, Betty Lu, who shares the bedroom with her, starts to wake up, and she says to her in a somewhat groggy tone: "Hi Elisabeth, you're home. I didn't hear you come in last night."

"Oh, hi Betty Lu. Yeah, I got in a little late. You were sleeping, so I snuck in quietly, so that I wouldn't disturb you," Elisabeth replies.

"Do you want to go shopping or something today?" Betty Lu asks.

"That sounds wonderful, but, I think I'll have to take a rain check on that, because I've got something important that I need to take care of today," Elisabeth answers.

"Sure, no problem kid, we can do something together another day," Betty Lu says.

"That sounds good," Elisabeth replies.

Elisabeth is now fully dressed. And after grabbing her purse, she says: "Goodbye, Betty Lu!"

"Goodbye, see you later!" Betty Lu says.

Quickly exiting the apartment, Elisabeth proceeds to walk to the local bus stop. And the moment she gets there the bus arrives. So she boards it, and the driver pulls off.

After traveling on the bus for awhile, Elisabeth disembarks at the corner of Main Street and Sunset Boulevard. Then she proceeds to walk west on Sunset Boulevard in the direction of the Bayridge Dividing Wall.

~

Eventually, after walking for a while, Elisabeth finally arrives at the Bayridge wall. And she immediately begins searching for the narrow opening that she climbed through the night before. Upon successfully finding it, she proceeds to climb up to it, and after squeezing her body through, she enters the other side into Shytown.

Shytown is a poor community that is located within the District of Wright County, in the State of Minnesota. It is a poverty-stricken area that is solely populated by black people, who are forced to live in impoverished, destitute conditions, consisting of rundown shanty houses, and old and rusty automobiles.

~

After entering Shytown, Elisabeth heads due north on Vinewood Avenue. And after walking several blocks, she finally comes to Wilborn Street. There she turns right, and then she keeps walking until she comes to a small house with an open front porch, and a huge maple tree in the front yard, with a tire swing hanging from one of its large limbs; just as Randall Pascale had so distinctly and thoroughly described to her last night. And then, without any hesitation at all, she walks straight up to the house and onto the front porch, and she knocks at the door.

Within a moment or so, a colored woman dressed in a long, purple colored robe, with matching house slippers on her feet, opens the door, and she asks: "Can I help you?"

"Yes, I'm looking for a young man named, Randall Pascale. Does he live here?" Elisabeth asks.

"Yes, Randall lives here. I'm his mother, Eva," the Woman replies.

"Is there something wrong?" Eva asks.

"No, nothing is wrong, I was just wondering if I can speak with him for a moment," Elisabeth says.

"Sure, hold on but a second child, and I'll fetch him for you," Eva says. Then, she turns, closes the door, and she calls out with a loud voice, saying: "Randall, somebody's at the door for you!"

~

Eva Marie Pascale is a colored woman, who is very comely in appearance. She is about 5 feet 7 inches tall. She has a round shaped face, and dark brown skin complexion. Her hair is black and is styled in sort of an afro look. She has large, almond shaped, charcoaled colored eyes, a pug shaped nose, and full lips. By nature, she is gentle and quiet spirited, strong willed, and as cautious as a serpent.

~

As soon as Randall hears his Mother calling for him, he yells out to her from a room on the second floor, saying: "What is it Mom?"

"Someone is here to see you, son!" Eva yells back to him. In response, Randall immediately comes running down the stairs, and he quickly enters the living room where Eva is standing.

As Randall enters the living room, he asks Eva: "Who is it Mom?"

"I don't know. It's some white girl," Eva says, as she walks over and takes a seat on the couch.

Acting a bit puzzled, curious, and little sassy, Eva puts her hand on her hip, and she says to Randall: "Randall, can you tell me why a white girl would be at my door?"

"I don't know Mom," Randall replies. And then, without delay, he walks over to and opens up the front door.

When Randall opens the door and sees that the person standing there is Elisabeth Baxter, he is shockingly surprised. And with a stunned look on his face, and an inquisitive tone in his voice, he says to her: "Elisabeth! What are you doing here?"

"I just wanted to stop by to thank..." Elisabeth begins to say, but, before she can finish talking, Randall immediately cuts her off, and he quickly steps outside onto the porch, and shuts the door behind him.

Elisabeth continues, saying: "I just wanted to stop by to thank you Randall once again for what you did for me last night."

"You didn't have to do that, besides, it's a little risky for you to have come into this area all alone," Randall says.

"I'm not afraid," Elisabeth says.

"Do you mind if we go somewhere else?" Randall asks.

"No, I don't mind," Elisabeth says.

Randall now opens the front door, and he yells to his mother Eva, saying: "I'll be right back Mom!" Afterwards, he closes the door, and then he and Elisabeth leave the house and they proceed to travel on foot together to a densely wooded area that surrounds a body of water, called "Whispering Pond."

Whispering Pond is a fairly large, fresh body of water that is fed from a nearby lake. It is situated in a secluded area that is surrounded by a thick forest of trees and wild bushes. It's located about a half a mile away from Randall's house.

A short time later, after walking for a bit, Elisabeth and Randall finally arrive at Whispering Pond.

"This is a nice and quite area!" Elisabeth says.

"Yes it is! It's called 'Whispering Pond,'" Randall replies.

"Why is it called that?" Elisabeth asks.

"Legend has it, that the Native Americans that once populated this land, named it 'Whispering Pond,' because it was believed that on a breezy day that they could hear the surrounding willow trees that line its banks, whispering to them," Randall says.

"Whispering what?" Elisabeth asks.

"Words of knowledge, truth, and wisdom," Randall says.

"Wow, do you ever hear them?" Elisabeth asks.

"Sometimes," Randall says.

Suddenly, the wind starts to blow a stiff, gentle breeze, which causes the willow trees to gently sway in the wind; the effect of which produces a soft, rustling sound, like the sound of people quietly speaking in the not too far distance. In response, Randall abruptly stops talking, and he pauses for a moment. And then, with eyes-wide-open, he continues, saying with a whispering tone: "Elisabeth, did you hear that?"

"What?" Elisabeth asks.

Randall turns and he looks Elisabeth square in the face, and he says to her: "The trees. They said that you're beautiful." In response, Elisabeth smiles. And then, she and Randall begin to giggle and laugh.

Randall, now, feeling ever more at ease, opens up to Elisabeth, and he says: "This has been my favorite place to visit since I was a little kid. I know every square inch of the area. I often come here to get away from it all, in order to relax or to go for a swim." He continues: "My favorite time to come here is at night, so that I can lie beneath the midnight sky, and look up at the myriads of stars, and let my mind wander and think."

"What do you think about?" Elisabeth asks.

"A lot of things," Randall, replies.

"Things like what?" Elisabeth asks.

"Oh, I guess, about life in general. You know, like the future, and what I want to be, and so forth," Randall says.

"What do you want to be?" Elisabeth asks.

"Well, with me being a colored boy, there aren't a whole lot of career choices to currently choose from. But, if I had my wish, I'd like to become a professional dancer," Randall says.

"Why a dancer," Elisabeth asks.

Randall, now exhibiting a spark of enthusiasm and excitement in his voice, along with a glimmering, sparkle in his eyes, says: "Because I feel it's what I was born to do. I can't remember a time in my life when I didn't' dance." He continues: "My Mother says that she believes that I was dancing before I was even born. She says that when she was pregnant with me, if she happened to be in a place where music was playing, that I would hear the music and begin moving and dancing inside her womb to the rhythm of the beat."

"Is that right? Wow, that's pretty impressive!" Elisabeth says.

Randall now begins to joke, and he says: "It's a good thing that I wasn't wearing any shoes!" The silly thought of this tickles Elisabeth, and they both begin to giggle and laugh. But then, suddenly, like the flip of a light switch, Randall's facial expression quickly changes—from that of being joyful, over to being very somber. And with a sad tone in his voice, he says: "Someday, I hope to use my God given gift to breakdown some of the ugly barriers that divide people."

"I'm sure that you will," Elisabeth says.

"That's enough about me. What about you Elisabeth? Have you given much thought about what you want out of life?" Randall asks.

"Well, unfortunately, I spent most of my life growing up in an all girls orphanage. Because of that I feel like I've missed out on so much!" Elisabeth says. She continues: "I want to first see and experience as much of the world as I can, and then, after I get my fill of everything, I would like to eventually settle down, get married, and have lots of kids."

"Well, as smart and pretty as you are, you won't have any problem finding the right guy," Randall replies.

"Why, thank you," Elisabeth smiles and says.

As Elisabeth and Randall are talking, suddenly, a loud snapping sound occurs. It sounds as though a large tree branch is breaking. Looking up and in the direction of the noise, Randall observes that it's just some neighborhood kids that have come to spy on them. Randall yells out to them, saying: "Hey! You kids! Get out of here!" In response, one of the boys boldly and tauntingly yells back at him, saying: "Why don't you make us, you big ugly gorilla!"

"Why, I'll get you... you little!" Randall yells. And he begins running after the kids.

When the kids see that Randall is chasing after them; which is really what they desire him to do. They become startled, and they scream, and they quickly begin to scatter and flee!

A short time later, after having chased the kids for a short distance, Randall returns to the pond smiling and shaking his head back and forth. And he says to Elisabeth, with a happy tone in his voice: "Those kids are little stinkers! They sure do like to mess with me!"

"Do you know them?" Elisabeth asks.

"Yeah, they're just some of the neighbor kids. Occasionally, they will randomly stop by when I'm in the area just to play jokes on me, and give me a hard time," Randall says.

Now, realizing that time has flown bye, Randall, says to Elisabeth: "It's getting a little late Elisabeth. I think we better start heading back."

"Sure," Elisabeth says, as they begin to leave.

After leaving Whispering Pond, Randall walks Elisabeth to the opening in the Bayridge Dividing Wall. There they say goodbye to each other, and then Elisabeth squeezes her body through the narrow passage in the wall.

Coincidently, as Elisabeth climbs through the wall into Frogtown, Michael Harrington happens to be driving by in his car. Upon catching sight of Elisabeth at the Bayridge wall, he quickly pulls his car over to the curb and parks, so that he can secretly spy on her from a distance.

Totally unaware of Michael's presence, Elisabeth begins to walk in the direction of the Bus Stop. But wait! Just as she's walking away from the opening in the Bayridge wall, Randall comes climbing through. And he urgently calls out to her, saying: "Elisabeth! Elisabeth! You dropped your bracelet!"

Immediately, upon hearing Randall's voice, Elisabeth quickly turns around, and she walks back towards him. And then, taking her bracelet from his hand, she says: "Thank you, so much! I didn't even realize it had fallen off! I don't know what I would have done if I had lost it! It was my mother's! It was the only item of hers that was passed on to me after she died!"

"I'm glad that I spotted it!" Randall says.

Elisabeth now opens up to Randall, and says: "I had a good time Randall!"

"I did too. Feel free to come back again, anytime," Randall replies.

"Thank you, Randall, I think I will," Elisabeth smiles and says. Afterwards, she turns and she proceeds to walk towards the Bus Stop. Randall, on the other hand, returns to the opening in the wall, squeezes his body through, and disappears from site.

When Michael Harrington, who is watching in secret, observes Randall climbing back through the Bayridge wall, he audibly says to himself, with a stone cold look on his face and with malice in his voice, in regards to Randall: "As sure as the sun rises, I'll get that Nigger, if it's the last thing I do!" Afterwards, he quickly starts up engine of his car, and he drives away.

~

For the next two months, Elisabeth and Randall spend a lot of time together at Whispering Pond — during which time they both become well acquainted with each other. One day, while they are there, Randall looks at Elisabeth (to whom he now affectionately calls by the nickname, 'Lizzie'), and says: "Hey Lizzie, let's go for a swim!"

"I can't," Elisabeth responds.

"Why not," Randall asks.

"I didn't bring my swimsuit," Elisabeth exclaims.

"That's alright, we don't need swimsuits," Randall says. He then strips down to his boxer shorts, and then he runs and dives into the pond, and quickly submerges beneath the surface of the water.

After being submersed under water for a moment or so, Randall finally pops his head up out of the water, and he yells to Elisabeth, saying: "Lizzie, come on in! The water feels great!"

"Ok, but turn around first, and then I'll come in," Elisabeth says.

Immediately, obeying Elisabeth's request, Randall turns and he faces the opposite direction.

The moment Randall turns his back to her, Elisabeth quickly undresses down to her undergarments, and then, afterwards, she runs and she jumps into the pond. But, instead of diving completely beneath the surface like Randall did, she intentionally keeps her head up out of the water, so that she doesn't get her hair wet.

The water is cold. Elisabeth is shocked! Quivering and shaking, she says: "Burr, its cold! Randall, you tricked me! This water is cold!"

"No it's not! It feels great!" Randall remarks. Then, he dives beneath the surface again, and he swims towards her feet.

After approaching Elisabeth, Randall slyly grabs her by her ankles. Then, he yanks her feet out from under her, and he pulls her beneath the surface of the water. Afterwards, he quickly swims away from her, as fast as he can.

After being pulled under water for a moment, Elisabeth's head quickly pops back up above the surface. Now, looking at Randall with revenge and a devilish look in her eyes, she says in a playful tone: "You got my hair wet! I'll get you, you dirty rat!" And then, swimming as fast as she can, she chases after him.

As Randall flees from Elisabeth, he swims towards the middle of the pond, and then back over towards the shallow end, but, because she's a good swimmer, she finally catches and grabs him by the arm. And, after pouncing upon him, she begins dunking his head under water, over and over again. All the while, he doesn't bother to put up any resistance.

After, Elisabeth gets her fill of repeatedly dunking Randall's head beneath the surface of the water, she stops. And then she and Randall begin to laugh. Afterwards, they embrace and kiss a long kiss.

When Elisabeth and Randall finish kissing, he picks her up, and he carries her out of the water and onto shore. And after gently laying her down upon a large, spread out blanket in the grass, he lies down beside her with his back against the ground. In response, Elisabeth lifts her head up and she lays it upon his chest. Then, Randall reaches over and he grabs a corner of the blanket and he pulls the blanket over them, so that they can cover up and keep warm. And as the two of them lie there cuddling, they fall fast asleep.

Sometime later, after a considerable time has passed by, Elisabeth and Randall wake up. It is now dark, and they find themselves lying beneath a majestic night sky. Immediately drawing her attention to the canopy of twinkling stars above, Randall says: "Lizzie, look up at the sky!"

"Wow, Randall, you were right! It's breathtakingly beautiful!" Elisabeth exclaims, as she stares in absolute wonderment.

A short time later, after stargazing for a while, Randall says: "Well, Lizzie. I think I better get you to the bus stop." So after getting dress, they walk to the Bayridge Dividing Wall.

~

When Randall and Elisabeth arrive at the Bayridge wall, they embrace and kiss. And then, Elisabeth says: "Goodbye, Randall."

"Wait a minute! Don't you want me to walk with you to the bus stop?" Randall asks.

"No, that's ok; I can make it by myself this time. You go home and get some rest," Elisabeth says.

"Are you sure?" Randall asks.

"Yep, I'll be perfectly ok," Elisabeth smiles and says. Next, she gives Randall a quick peck on the cheek, and then she turns, squeezes her body through the opening in the wall, enters Frogtown, and heads to the Bus Stop.

After Elisabeth leaves for home, Randall does the same.

9

FORGET-ME-NOTS

Today is Sunday. And after breakfast Elisabeth travels to Randall's house. Shortly after she arrives, she knocks at the front door. Within a moment, Randall's mother Eva answers the door, and she says: "Randall's not here."

"Do you know where he is?" Elisabeth inquires.

"No, he got up early this morning and left home. He didn't say where he was going," Eva explains.

"Ok, thanks," Elisabeth says. And then she turns and begins to leave.

Thinking and assuming that Randall must be at Whispering Pond, Elisabeth proceeds to head in that direction.

After walking for awhile, Elisabeth eventually approaches the wooded area surrounding Whispering Pond. And then, quickly entering the woods, she begins walking along a narrow and worn path that leads to the pond.

As Elisabeth steps deeper into the wooded area, suddenly, a strange and eerie noise occurs, and then it abruptly stops. Startled by the sound, she immediately stops in her tracks. And, looking around, she quickly scans the area with her eyes to see where the noise might have come from. However, upon investigation, she doesn't see anything. So she resumes walking.

Suddenly, the strange and eerie noise reoccurs again. Once again, frightened by what she hears, Elisabeth immediately stops and stands frozen in her tracks. Once more, scanning the area with her eyes, she looks to see where the noise came from. However, she still doesn't see anything. So she begins walking again, but this time at a much faster pace.

As Elisabeth gets a little further down the path, the strange and eerie noise occurs again. But this time she doesn't even bother to stop. Instead, she picks up her pace, and she hurries down the path. Suddenly! Out from behind a large tree, the large figure of a man jumps out in front of her, and he yells: "Boo!" Elisabeth stops and screams! But then, after quickly coming to her senses, she sees that it's just Randall playing a stupid game.

When Randall observes Elisabeth's dramatic theatrical reactions, in response to his practical joke, he begins to laugh. But as far as Elisabeth is concerned, she doesn't think that it was funny at all! As a matter of fact, she is so angry and upset with him, that she spontaneously begins hitting him repeatedly with her fists, over and over again, in his chest, like a drummer wailing on his drums. While at the same time, she begins chewing him out, saying with an angry and scolding voice: "Randall! Don't you ever do that again! That scared me half to death!"

Randall, now stops laughing. And then, grabbing hold of Elisabeth by her arms, he gently pulls her body close to his. Next, looking her straight in the eyes, he sincerely and tenderly says: "I'm sorry my darling!" Afterwards, he kisses her gently on the lips, and they embrace and kiss a long kiss.

After Elisabeth and Randall quickly make up, he takes her by the hand, and he says to her in a soft tone: "Come here, Lizzie. I want to show you something." He then proceeds to lead her off the narrow path, and he begins escorting her through a densely wooded area.

A short time later, after they have walked a little ways, Randall stops, and he says to Elisabeth: "Now, close your eyes Lizzie!" And then, still holding onto to her firmly, but yet gently by the hand, he continues to lead her up and out of the trees to the edge of a large, wide open field that's surrounded by tall trees.

It's a beautiful pristine-like day. The air is fresh. And the sun is shining brightly in a cloudless, cheery, blue sky.

"You can open your eyes now Lizzie," Randall says.

When Elisabeth opens her eyes, she sees the most loveliest sight! The entire field is covered with beautiful pink and purple flowers.

Highly impressed by what she sees, Elisabeth exclaims: "Wow! They're beautiful!"

Elisabeth and Randall now proceed to walk together deep into the flowery field. And then, Randall stops, and he bends over at the waist. Reaching down, he gently hand picks a small bouquet of flowers, and then he rises, and he hands them to Elisabeth.

Elisabeth immediately lifts the flowers to her nose. And after smelling them, she says: "Um, they're lovely! And they smell so sweet! What are they?"

"They're called 'Forget-Me-Nots,'" Randall says. Continuing, he says: "They're the symbol of true love!"

Next, secretly reaching into his pants pocket, Randall pulls something out, but, momentarily he keeps the item concealed.

A moment later, now feeling that the time is right, Randall drops down on one knee in front of Elisabeth. And he looks up and into her eyes, and he says to her: "I love you, Elisabeth, and I always will." And then, quickly raising his hand, he shows her a beautiful wedding ring, and he asks: "Will you marry me?"

In response to Randall's wedding proposal, Elisabeth is so overcome with happiness that she starts to shed tears of joy. And with joy in her heart and excitement in her voice, she says: "I love you too, Randall! Yes, I'll marry you!"

Randall is absolutely thrilled! Quickly rising to his feet, he carefully places the ring on Elisabeth's finger. Then they embrace, and kiss a very long kiss. Afterwards, they begin walking slowly, arm over arm together to Whispering Pond.

Unfortunately, as soon as Elisabeth and Randall begin to leave the flowery field, suddenly, her bracelet slips off her arm and it falls to the ground. However, neither she nor Randall is aware of it.

~

When Elisabeth and Randall arrive at Whispering Pond, they spread a blanket out upon the grass. And then they sit down to eat a picnic lunch that Randall had specially prepared and securely set aside for them. Afterwards, they remain at Whispering Pond for much of the day.

Sometime later in the evening, as Elisabeth and Randall are sitting by the pond talking and enjoying one another's company, dark clouds begin to quickly roll in. And shortly afterwards a few honking geese fly by, followed by a light rain shower. Luckily, Randall had thought in advance to bring an umbrella along.

Rising quickly to their feet, Elisabeth and Randall begin scrambling to gather up their belongings, so that they can leave the area before the downpour gets any worse. Then, suddenly, Elisabeth happens to notice that her bracelet is missing. In response, she says: "Oh, no!"

"What's the matter Lizzie?" Randall asks.

"I lost my bracelet! It must have slip off my arm!" Elisabeth says.

"All, that's too bad," Randall sympathetically says. He continues: "Don't worry sweetheart, I'm sure it will show up somewhere, but for now we better get you out of this rain!"

The sky now opens up, and a heavy downpour occurs. Randall quickly opens up the umbrella and he holds it up over Elisabeth and himself. Afterwards, the two of them promptly leave the area and they head for the Bayridge Dividing Wall.

As it so happens, by the time that Elisabeth and Randall arrive at the Bayridge Wall the rainfall has completely stopped. Nevertheless, Randall hands his umbrella to Elisabeth, and says: "Here Elisabeth, take my umbrella."

"Are you sure?" Elisabeth says.

"Yep, you better keep it with you, just in case the rain picks up again," Randall replies.

"Ok. But can you hold onto it until after I get through the wall," Elisabeth asks.

"Sure," Randall says.

After Elisabeth squeezes her body through the narrow opening in the massive wall, Randall successfully passes the umbrella through to her. And then they both leave, and they go to their separate homes.

10

THE BIG DANCE

Today is Friday. And after working the day at Little Ricky's Dinner, Elisabeth leaves her job, and she boards and travels on the city bus to visit Randall.

When the bus arrives at the corner of Main Street and Sunset Boulevard, Elisabeth disembarks, and then she proceeds to travel on foot to the Bayridge Dividing Wall.

After walking for a while, Elisabeth finally arrives at the Bayridge wall. Strangely, as it so happens, Michael Harrington is nearby. But, she doesn't realize it. He has been secretly tailing her from a safe distance, ever since she left work today, following and spying on her from his car.

Totally unaware that she is being watched, Elisabeth begins squeezing her body through the narrow opening in the Bayridge wall. And as soon as she steps foot into Shytown, she quickly shuffles off to Randall's house.

When Michael sees that Elisabeth has successfully passed through the Bayridge wall, he gets out of his car, and in a hurried pace, he speedily follows after her. Quickly approaching the wall, he begins squeezing his body through the opening. And after entering Shytown, he scans the horizon with his eyes, and immediately spots Elisabeth. She's about 100 yards away, traveling due North on Vinewood Avenue. So he continues to follow her, but all the while, he intentionally keeps a safe distance back, for fear that he may be spotted by her.

Eventually, Elisabeth arrives at Randall's house, and she walks up to and knocks at the front door. Michael, who continues to follow her discreetly (observing from a safe distance), now scrambles to seek cover, as he jumps and hides behind a large bush nearby.

A moment later, Randall comes out of his house with a neatly rolled up blanket under his arm, and then he and Elisabeth head off to Whispering Pond. Curious as to where the two of them are going, Michael secretly follows after them.

After walking for awhile, Elisabeth and Randall finally approach the wooded area surrounding Whispering Pond. And after quickly entering the woods, they begin walking along the narrow path that leads to the pond.

Today is a beautiful sunny day. And although the thick forests of trees provide a lot of shade, flashes of sunlight occasionally breakthrough the canopy of leaves and it sporadically illuminates and shines upon Elisabeth and Randall as they walk along the path.

Because of the distance between them, Michael cannot see Elisabeth and Randall as he secretly follows them along the path, but he can hear them talking and laughing in the not so far distance ahead of him.

Eventually, Randall and Elisabeth arrive at the Pond, and he immediately begins spreading his blanket out upon the ground for them to sit on.

When Michael (who is still following and watching secretly from a safe distance), observes that Elisabeth and Randall has stopped and camped out at the pond, he quietly sneaks over to an area on the opposite side of the pond, so that he can continue to spy on them, and at the same time conveniently keep himself concealed.

As Elisabeth and Randall are sitting and enjoying one another's company, Randall smiles at Elisabeth, and he says to her: "Hey Lizzie, would you like to go to a party with me tonight?"

"A party," Elisabeth replies, with a surprised voice and look.

"Yes, a party," Randall confirms. He continues: "You see, every now and then, some of the guys and girls in our neighborhood get together down at Mr. Jones Warehouse, to listen to music, to dance, eat food, and have a good time."

"I'd love to go! But, I'll need to go home first. So I can fix myself up," Elisabeth says.

"You already look beautiful!" Randall exclaims.

"Thank you. But I can't go there looking like this," Elisabeth replies.

"Okay. How about, after we leave here today, you go home, get ready, and then come back. I'll meet you by the opening in the Bayridge Dividing Wall at seven o'clock tonight," Randall conveniently suggests.

"Okay, that sounds great!" Elisabeth says. Afterwards, they hug and kiss.

When Michael, who is spying on them, sees that Elisabeth and Randall are both thoroughly enjoying one another's company, he becomes highly agitated. And then, with a look of anger and disgust on his face, he gets up and he quietly slips away from the area, totally undetected.

A short time later, after Michael has gone, Elisabeth and Randall also leave Whispering Pond. And they return to their homes, so that they can rest up a bit, and also get ready for tonight's big party.

~

Later, during the evening, when seven o'clock rolls around, Elisabeth and Randall meet by the opening at the Bayridge wall as planned.

When Randall sees Elisabeth all dolled up in her makeup and fancy clothes, he is absolutely stunned by her beautiful appearance, and he says to her: "Wow! Look at you! You're as pretty as a picture — absolutely gorgeous!"

"Thank you, Randall! You look wonderful too!" Elisabeth smiles and says. Then, the two of them leave, and they head off to the party at Mr. Jones Warehouse.

Eventually, after a relatively short period of time has elapsed, Elisabeth and Randall finally arrive at the warehouse. And as they are approach the building, they hear the sound of music playing. It's coming from inside.

Entering the building, Randall and Elisabeth proceed to walk down and along a narrow hallway, and then into a large, crowded room. As they work their way through the crowd, which happens to consist solely of colored people, Elisabeth can't help but to notice that she's getting some very strange looks. Now, beginning to feel a little uncomfortable, she turns to Randall and she inquiringly asks: "Randall, is it alright for me to be here?"

"Yes, Lizzie, it's perfectly okay for you to be here," Randall says.

As Randall escorts Elisabeth through the crowded room, they eventually come to a large table that is full of a variety of well prepared foods. Also, at the end of the table there's a large glass bowl that's filled with fruit punch, topped with a sprinkling of mixed fruit.

Quickly, eying up the assortment of foods, Randall flashes a big smile, and in a delighted and elated mood, he says: "It sure looks and smells good! Boy, I'm as hungry as a bear!" Then, promptly picking up two paper dinner plates, he hands one to Elisabeth. And they begin to fill their plates with personal selections of food.

As Randall and Elisabeth are busy dishing up their plates, a few people walk by, and they enthusiastically greet Randall, saying: "Hey, Randall!" In response, Randall smiles, and he returns friendly greetings to them, saying: "Hey! What's up guys? It's good to see you!" Afterwards, he and Elisabeth turn and they proceed to take their plates, along with two prefilled cups of fruit punch, and they walk over to and sit down at a vacant dining table that's located near the dance floor. All the while, loud music is continuously playing, as a group of people are dancing within a special, reserved area that is specifically assigned only for dancing, that's located in the center of the room.

A short time later, after Randall and Elisabeth have finished eating, several girls at the party walk up to Randall, and they say to him: "Dance for us, Randall!" In response, Randall politely says: "No, not now; perhaps later." However, the girls refuse to take no for an answer. But instead, they keep on insisting that he get up and dance for them.

Because of the failure of the girls to respect his wishes, Randall now becomes a little agitated in his spirit. And he repeats his words to them. But this time with a more forceful tone, saying: "I said, no; not now!"

When Elisabeth observes that Randall is getting upset with the girls, she turns and she looks at him. Then, she smiles, and she says to him with a gentle voice: "Go ahead Randall, dance for them!" In response, Randall respectfully listens, and he says to Elisabeth: "Okay Lizzie, if you say so." Then, quickly rising from the table, he walks over to the DJ (Disk Jockey) and he puts in his favorite song request. Afterwards, he slowly proceeds to enter the dance floor.

The moment Randall steps out onto the dance floor, the music stops playing. And the entire dance floor begins to clear, until Randall is the only person left remaining on the floor.

Suddenly, a new song begins to play. It is Randall's selected song. The song has a strong, pulsating and rhythmic beat. Now, with all eyes in the room intently fixed upon him, Randall begins to dance.

As Randall dances, he performs a medley of popular dance steps, and then he breaks out into some dance steps of his own originality, including jumping high into the air and then gently dropping down into the splits upon the floor.

Upon watching Randall dance, all of the people in the room become extremely excited! And they begin to cheer him on, saying: "Go Randall! Go Randall! Go Randall! Go!"

"Look at him go!" one enthusiastic onlooker says.

"Man, that cat can really dance! No one else even comes close!" someone else exclaims.

"He's the best!" another person relates.

"Now… that's what I call poetry in motion," another highly impressed bystander adds.

When Elisabeth observes Randall dancing, she is simply blown away! Completely amazed! Standing there with her face aglow with excitement, and her heart overfilled with joy. She can hardly believe what she is seeing. Fred Astaire has nothing on him. Randall's dancing skills are extraordinary. He is so electrifying and thrilling to watch! But, what's even more amazing is that he performs even the most difficult steps and dance moves so smoothly and effortlessly!

Elisabeth, however, is not the only one at the party that's fascinated and thrilled. The entire place is jumping with joy and excitement at seeing Randall dance.

Finally, after the song has finished playing, and Randall is done dancing, he receives a loud and standing ovation from everybody in the room.

Randall now exits the dance floor. And he makes a beeline over to Elisabeth. Then, taking her by the hand, he cordially asks: "Young Lady. May I have this dance?"

Initially, Elisabeth is a bit shy and she puts up a little resistance at first. But then she eventually gives in and willingly surrenders to Randall's request.

When a girl at the party, who is standing nearby with a group of her girlfriends, observes that Randall is about to dance with Elisabeth, she gets upset. And in a jealous tone and mad spirit, she outspokenly says to her friends, concerning Elisabeth: "Oh no she doesn't! Don't tell me, she's going to dance with him?"

As Randall leads Elisabeth by her hand onto the dance floor, a soft and slow, romantic dance song begins to play. As a matter of fact, the song happens to be a secret request of his.

Randall now places his free hand around Elisabeth's tiny waist, and he gently pulls her body close to his, and they begin slow dancing to the beautiful music. As they dance, there's a special spark in their step, and pure magic in the air. Elisabeth looks so ravishingly lovely, and Randall looks so handsome and debonair.

Randall now looks Elisabeth straight in the eyes, and he says to her: "You're so beautiful!" Then he leans in and he whispers softly in her ear, saying: "I love you, Lizzie!"

Elisabeth, beaming with a happy and radiant glow, smiles, and she gently whispers back in his ear: "I love you too, my darling Randall!"

While Randall and Elisabeth are dancing together, they're starting to get some strange and odd looks from some of people at the party. A few of them have even begun to talk amongst themselves, about how wrong they think it is for Elisabeth to be dancing with Randall.

Suddenly, Randall's brother Charles enters the room. And he immediately spots Randall on the dance floor with Elisabeth. The very sight of the two of them dancing together highly disturbs him. He watches them for a moment. And then, after spotting a group of his friends, who are standing in a corner of the room, he proceeds to walk over towards them.

~

Charles Pascale is twenty one years old, just two years older than Randall. He has dark brown skin complexion, and black hair. He is 5 feet 10 inches tall, with a stocky, muscular build. He has a round shaped face, a pug nose, slightly oversized ears, and full lips. By nature, he is known to be a pretty tuff and rough character, that no one would even dare mess with. Also, he's bullheaded; stubborn as a mule; hard as nails; and as strong as an ox.

~

As Charles approaches his friends, one of the young men in the group who has the street name "Snake," says to him: "Hey, Charles! What's shakin, Man? Long time no see!"

"Hey, Snake! What's up, man?" Charles replies.

"What I'd like to know, is what's up with your little brother, Randall, and that white girl?" Snake asks.

"Man, I don't even know. I'm just as surprised as you are! Who is that white chick anyways? And how did she get here?" Charles says.

Another one of Charles friends in the group, a young man named, Bootsie, who has picked up on the conversion between Charles and Snake, decides to put in his opinion or two cents, saying: "Hey Charlie, man! We don't know? We thought that you could shed some light on the subject for us. Man, you gotta say somethin to Randall, man. He can't be bringin no white chicks up in here like that!" In response, Charlie (as Charles is sometimes affectionately called by his family and friends) says to Bootsie: "I'll talk to him, man."

Now, as it stands, Charles Pascale is inebriated. In fact, he is higher than a kite! He had been boozing earlier, long before he even came to tonight's party. However, according to him, he hasn't had his full fill of liquor yet. Addressing his group of friends, he asks: "Does anybody have any fermented spirits up in here?"

Immediately, Bootsie, quickly pulls a pint of whiskey out of the inside pocket of his jacket, and he hands it to Charles. In response, Charles says: "Now Bootsie, that's what I'm talkin about man!" He then unscrews the bottle cap, takes a big swig, and then he hands the bottle back to him.

The music now ends. And Randall and Elisabeth proceed to exit the dance floor. As they head towards their seats, Charles spots them, and he begins walking towards them.

As Charles approaches his brother, he calls out to him to get his attention, saying: "Randall! Hey, Randall!" But, unfortunately, Randall happens to be facing the opposite direction, with his back to Charles. However, when he hears his name being called, he quickly turns and he looks in the direction of the summonsing voice.

Upon turning and seeing his brother Charles, Randall smiles. Then, he turns and he says to Elisabeth in an excited voice: "Hey, look, it's my big brother, Charlie!" And then, turning back towards Charles, who is now standing in front of him, Randall says to him: "Hey, Charlie! I thought that voice sounded familiar! It's good to see you, man! When did you get here?"

"Hey, Bro. I just got here, man," Charles says.

"Let me introduce you to someone," Randall says. Quickly turning his attention towards Elisabeth, he says to Charles: "Charlie, this is Elisabeth."

"Hey, Elisabeth," Charles says.

Next, formally introducing Charles to Elisabeth, Randall says to her: "Elisabeth, this is my big brother, Charles."

"Hi Charles, it's nice to finally meet you. Randall has told me so much about you," Elisabeth says.

"Oh yeah, well he never said anything about you!" Charles replies, in a cutting, rude tone.

Randall, quickly picking up on Charles's sarcasm, and also, now realizing that he's drunk, turns to him, and he says: "Man, have you been drinking again?"

"Don't worry about me! Worry about yourself! I'm a grown man! I'll do what I want!" Charles says in an irritated and angry tone. He continues: "The one that you need to pay attention to is yourself! Like, what's you doin brinin this white girl up in here! This is our place! She doesn't belong here! What you doing? Sleeping with the enemy?" In response, Randall says to Charles in a highly disturbed and threatening tone: "Watch your mouth, man!"

Elisabeth is shocked! Feeling highly offended by Charles' hurtful words, she turns and she proceeds to run out of the room.

Oh boy! Now Randall is really mad! Upon seeing his dear Elisabeth being hurt and leaving the party, he says to Charles: "Charlie, you shouldn't have said those mean and hurtful things to Elisabeth! That was very cruel! She didn't deserve that!" In response, Charles coldheartedly looks Randall in the eyes, and he shouts in his face, saying: "Who gives a damn, man!"

Charles's words and tone trigger an immediate, responsive chord in Randall. And in a fit of fury, he quickly swings his right fist at Charles and decks him clear on the chin with a powerful blow! The force of the blow is so strong that Charles staggers backwards and topples over and onto a nearby table. Instantly, the table breaks and collapses from the weight of his body, and he hits the floor really hard!

After hitting the floor, Charles struggles to get up, but he can't. His head is still reeling from the all so dynamic blow.

Randall now walks over to Charles, and he stands directly over him. And peering down at him, he says to him with an angry voice, in regards to Elisabeth's hurt feelings: "I care!" Then, he turns and he quickly exists the building, in order to join and be with Elisabeth.

Immediately, upon exiting the warehouse, Randall looks for Elisabeth, but he doesn't see her anywhere. So he begins calling out her name, saying: "Elisabeth! Elisabeth!" However, she doesn't answer. Now, assuming that she's a good distance away, and headed for home, he begins running as fast as he can in the direction of the Bayridge Dividing Wall, in hopes that he can catch up to her, and stop her before she passes through the opening in the wall.

∼

After running several blocks, Randall finally spots Elisabeth. She is walking in the distance, about a couple of blocks ahead of him. So he proceeds to call out to her in a loud voice — loud enough to be heard by her, yelling: "Elisabeth! Elisabeth!" But she doesn't respond. She just keeps walking forward in the direction of the Bayridge wall.

When Randall observes that Elisabeth's is not responding to his voice, he starts to feel a bit discouraged. Nevertheless, he is determined not to give up on her. So he just drops his head, picks up the pace, and continues to speedily run after her. Finally, after she gets to a distance of about 100 yards or so away from the Bayridge wall, he manages to catch up to her. And, immediately, reaching out his hand, he tries to take hold of her by her hand. But she quickly pulls it away from him. And she keeps walking.

Randall, now stops, and in an entreating tone, he calls out to Elisabeth with a pleading voice, saying: "Lizzie! Please stop!" However, to no avail. For she is still ignoring him.

Randall, still not giving up on her, in a last ditch effort, again runs to catch her, but this time when he approaches her, he tries something different. Instead of reaching for her hand, this time he runs right pass her, so that he can get in front of her, to block her path.

It works! Elisabeth stops walking. Now, standing in front of and facing her, Randall asks: "Lizzie! What's the matter?"

"Nothing," Elisabeth says.

"Come on now, I know there's something's wrong. What is it?" Randall asks.

Elisabeth begins to breakdown and cry, and she says: "Why didn't you tell your brother about me? Are you ashamed of me?"

"No. I would never be ashamed of you! I love you!" Randall says.

"Well then, why didn't you tell him about me?" Elisabeth asks.

"I would have, but he's never home," Randall says. He continues: "My brother, Charles, is a drunk. And often, when he goes on his drinking binges, he will disappear for several weeks on end. This last time he was gone for over two months!"

When Elisabeth hears Randall's explanation, she believes him. Now, changing the subject, she asks: "Why am I not wanted and accepted around here? You saw how the people at the party were looking at me. They treated me like I was some kind of freak or something!"

"People are ignorant!" Randall replies.

"But why, I haven't done anything to hurt any of them," Elisabeth says.

"It's not you babe, it's just the way that things happen to be," Randall says. Now, raising his hand and pointing a finger at the Bayridge Dividing Wall, he continues, saying: "This huge dividing wall here, that separates the white community from the black community, has, over the years, become a symbol of what people's lives have become! They're so use to it being here, that they can't see or accept anything different! The crazy thing is, they don't even realize how greatly it has adversely affected them! Sad to say, not one of them is even aware of the real treasures that lie on the opposite side. For example, if it wasn't for that most unforgettable night when I first met you, even I, myself, would have never known. But, because of that totally unexpected and very special night, I found the most amazing, and most beautiful woman in the whole world! The woman that I both love and cherish, and the person that I want to spend the rest of my life with! And that makes me feel extremely blessed and happy!"

As soon as Randall is finished speaking, Elisabeth is so deeply touched by his words that she throws her arms around him, and she begins kissing him repeatedly on his face and lips. And, she says: "I love you, Randall!"

"I love you too, Lizzie!" Randall says. Afterwards, he gently takes her by the hand, and he says to her: "Come on sugar, let's get you home." And then they leave.

11

AN UNEXPECTED SURPRISE

Today is Saturday. When the early morning sun arrives it finds Elisabeth sleeping in bed. As the sunlight penetrates through her bedroom window, its warm and gentle rays begin to reach out and touch her soft face, as if to say: "Arise you sleeping beauty!"

Feeling the warmth of the sunlight upon her face, Elisabeth begins to awake and wipe the sleep from her eyes. And then, she smiles and whispers to herself, saying: "What a beautiful day!"

Elisabeth is as happy as a lark! She can barely wait to see Randall again. So she quickly hops out of bed, showers, gets dress, and grabs a light bite to eat. Afterwards, she leaves home and takes the city bus downtown.

After arriving downtown, Elisabeth exits the bus, and then she walks to Sir Frederick's Diamonds & Jewelry Store.

As soon as Elisabeth enters the Jewelry Store, a salesman behind the display counter warmly and readily welcomes her, saying: "Good Morning, Ma'am! Can I help you?"

"Yes, I would like to purchase a man's wristwatch," Elisabeth says.

"Well, we certainly have plenty to choose from. Is there any particular brand or style that you're looking for?" the Salesman asks.

"No, not exactly. But I'd like something special," Elisabeth remarks.

"I think I have exactly what you're looking for," the Salesman says. Reaching into the glass display case, he pulls out a watch. And, showing it to Elisabeth, he says: "May I suggest this one? It's a 14 karat gold watch with 21 jewels, with a 14 karat gold basket weave wristband. It's a very unique watch, in that, not only is it reasonably priced for its high quality and extraordinary beauty, but also it's the only one of its kind."

"It's absolutely perfect! I'll take it!" Elisabeth says.

"Excellent! Would you like me to gift wrap it for you," the Salesman asks.

"Yes, please!" Elisabeth replies.

After purchasing the wristwatch, Elisabeth leaves the Jewelry Store, and she returns home. There she prepares and packs a picnic lunch for her and Randall to eat. And then, shortly thereafter, she leaves home, takes the bus, and she heads to Randall's house, so that the two of them can spend the day together at Whispering Pond.

～

The time is 10:00 AM. Randall is at home sitting at the kitchen table. Suddenly, in walks his brother, Charles. At first, the two of them make brief eye contact, but then they both quickly turn, and look away in different directions.

Charles proceeds to walk over to a cupboard nearby, and after opening the door; he grabs a drinking glass, and then he closes the door. Next, he walks over to and opens up the refrigerator, takes a carton of milk from off the top shelf, and then he shuts the door. Afterwards, he walks over to and he takes a seat at the kitchen table, directly across from where Randall is sitting.

After filling his drinking glass with milk, Charles looks across the table at Randall. Now, breaking the code of silence, he says to him: "I'm sorry about what happened last night at the party, Randall."

"Forget about it," Randall says.

Charles pauses for a moment. And then he says: "Man, I just don't want to see you get hurt."

"What do you mean?" Randall asks.

"You know what I mean, man," Charles replies.

"No. I don't," Randall answers.

Charles begins to explain to Randall what he means, saying: "We're the enemy! Whitey doesn't care about us! That heartless oppressor treats us like crap, calls us 'Niggers,' spits in our face, condemns us to a life of poverty, and uses our women and men as slaves to do his dirty work!"

"But, Elisabeth isn't like that! She's different!" Randall replies.

"They're all the same, man! And you're only going to get hurt by being with her! You know that whitey doesn't want us messing with his women!" Charles says.

"But, I love her!" Randall exclaims.

Charles, now, showing signs of disapproval on his face, shakes his head back and forth in disappointment, and he cautions his little brother, saying: "Man, you're gonna get hurt!"

Randall, quickly stands up, grabs his sweater from off the back of his chair, and says: "Why don't you just leave us alone!" Afterwards, he storms out of the room, heads towards the front door, and he begins to exit the house.

The moment Randall exits the front door, Elisabeth arrives. Happy and excited to see her, his face lights up with a big smile, and with a joyful tone in his voice, he says: "Hi Lizzie! I'm so glad you're here!" And then, immediately observing that she's carrying a picnic basket and blanket, he points to the basket, and he says: "Hey, what do we have here?"

"I brought us some lunch!" Elisabeth smiles and says.

"Wow, that was very nice of you! Here, let me carry it for you!" Randall says, as he takes the basket from her arms. Afterwards, they promptly leave and they begin strolling along together to Whispering Pond.

As Elisabeth and Randall travel to Whispering Pond, Randall never says a word to her about the argument that he just had with his brother, Charles, back at the house. Instead, he keeps the conversation on a positive note.

Eventually, when Randall and Elisabeth finally arrive at Whispering Pond, he first sets the picnic basket down. Next, he helps Elisabeth spreads the blanket out upon the ground. And then they sit down upon it.

While the two of them sit there enjoying each other's company, Elisabeth says: "Randall, can I ask you a question?"

"Sure, Lizzie," Randall answers.

"What's the story with your brother, Charles?" Elisabeth asks.

"What do you mean?" Randall inquires.

"Why does he do that to himself?" Elisabeth asks.

"Do what?" Randall says.

"Why does he drink so much?" Elisabeth asks.

"I don't know? I guess it's because he's mad at the world or something," Randall remarks.

"I'm worried for him. It's as though he's on a self destructive course," Elisabeth replies.

"Yep, that's Charlie alright! He's so stubborn! You can't tell him anything!" Randall says.

"That's too bad," Elisabeth exclaims.

Randall, now changing the subject, looks Elisabeth straight in the eyes, and with a proud tone in his voice, he says to her: "I composed a poem for you, Lizzie."

"You did?" Elisabeth says, with an appreciative look and surprised tone.

"Yep, it's entitled *'Tantalizing Beauty.'* Would you like to hear it?" Randall asks.

"Yes! Please! I'd love to!" Elisabeth says.

Randall is a little nervous at first. So he clears his throat, and then he begins to recite his poem, saying:

"She walks in beauty, a tantalizing sight,

A sheer beauty of exquisite delight

With velvety smooth skin, and long satin hair,

The likeness of her beauty is beyond compare

She has a smile so bright, it lights up a room,

A voice so mesmerizing, it makes you swoon

Captivating eyes that put you in a trance,

Movements of her walk, a graceful ballet dance

Her body's sweet fragrance sparks a fire,

Her soft, voluptuous lips stir desire

Everything in perfection so elegantly arrayed,

Her enticements my heart so easily persuades."

~

After Randall concludes his poem, Elisabeth says: "Wow, that's a beautiful poem Randall! I love it!" Then, she leans forward, and she gently kisses him on the lips. Afterwards, she sits back, and she says: "Now, I have something for you. So close your eyes, and stick out your hand."

As Randall closes his eyes and holds out his hand (palm up), Elisabeth quickly opens her purse. Then, she reaches in and pulls out Randall's gift. Afterwards, she places his gift, that is concealed within a beautifully gift-wrapped box, in his hand, and she says: "Ok. Now you can open your eyes!"

When Randall opens his eyes, he is so surprised that he becomes frozen for a moment.

Elisabeth smiles and says: "Well, aren't you going to open it?"

"Sure," Randall says, as he begins to carefully remove the gift-wrap paper. Then, he opens the box.

"Wow, it's absolutely stunning! Lizzie, you didn't have to do this!" Randall excitedly says, as he beholds his beautiful, new, shiny wristwatch.

"I know, but I wanted to! Here, let me help you put it on,"

Elisabeth says.

After Elisabeth helps Randall put his wristwatch on, he says: "Thank you so much Lizzie for this amazing gift! I will always cherish it!" Then they embrace and kiss. Afterwards, Elisabeth says: "Well, how about some lunch!"

"Sure," Randall replies. Afterwards, they open the picnic basket, serve themselves, and eat.

Sometime later, after spending the fun filled day together, Elisabeth and Randall eventually leave Whispering Pond, and they go to their separate homes.

~

The very next day, Sunday morning, Randall leaves home early, and he travels on foot to Whispering Pond, so that he can search the area for Elisabeth's lost bracelet. He's hoping that he will be able to find it and surprise her with it the next time they meet. Thinking back to the time period when she lost her bracelet, he begins to retrace their steps. However, it's not going to be an easy task. For attempting to find the bracelet in the wooded and grassy surroundings of Whispering Pond is like trying to find a needle in a haystack.

After combing through and thoroughly searching the area near and around Whispering Pond for a while, suddenly, Randall luckily happens to stumble upon Elisabeth's missing bracelet. He finds it lying on the ground, in the flowery field, where the beautiful Forget-Me-Not flowers grow. Overjoyed with his find, he bends over and he picks it up from off of the ground. But then, suddenly, he hears the sounds of rustling leaves, and snapping twigs.

When Randall looks up and in the not too far distance, he sees Michael Harrington, along with two other white men approaching him. One of them is Peter Dusek, and the other is a man named, Jake Peterson. They are entering the clearing through a wooded area bordering the field.

~

Jake Peterson is a twenty year old, extremely big, city-farm like type of boy, who wears a sort of a blissful, stupor look on his face. He stands about 6 feet 4 inches tall, with a large, square shaped head, and a crew cut hair style.

~

Randall, now sensing danger, and realizing that he's outnumbered, immediately begins to flee!

When Michael and his friends see that Randall is fleeing from them, they begin to chase after him in hot pursuit.

Randall, hoping that he can lose his pursuers, hightails it as fast as he can across the open field, towards a densely wooded area, on the opposite end of the clearing.

Randall is swift and fast as a deer, and he quickly manages to carve out a good distance between him and his pursuers.

After reaching the wooded area, Randall immediately enters it, and he begins working his way through. However, he soon runs into difficulty, because the area is heavily overrun by wild bushes and densely populated with a thick forest of trees. Experiencing extreme difficulty, he continues slowly navigating and pushing his way through.

Randall's pursuers, now having significantly closed the gap on him, are nipping at his heals! However, when they reach the wooded area, they too, find themselves struggling to work their way through.

Finally, after much struggling and effort, Randall manages to eventually work his way out of the dense, wooded area, and he exits onto a dirt road. Tired and worn out from physical exertion, he stops for a moment in order to catch his breath. Quickly, surveying the area, he spots a house. It's located down the road, about 100 yards away. Wasting no time, he runs towards it.

In the meantime, Michael Harrington and his friends are still struggling to work their way through the densely wooded area. Nevertheless, determined and stubborn, they are not giving up in their pursuit of Randall.

After running nonstop down the dirt road, Randall finally arrives at the house. Immediately approaching the front door, he begins knocking hard on it, and yelling: "Hello! Hello! Is anyone home?" But no one answers. So he turns and he proceeds to run around to the backdoor.

When Randall arrives at the backdoor, he repeats the same process, knocking hard, and yelling: "Hello! Hello! Is anyone home?" But, still no answer.

As Randall continues pounding on the backdoor, suddenly, Michael Harrington and his two accomplices appear.

Michael, with a cocky look on his face, and an overconfident tone in his voice, says to Randall: "What's the matter? Is no one home?"

"Let's get that Nigger!" Peter yells.

Randall, realizing that all hell is about to break out, quickly turns and he takes off running, towards a detached garage that's located a short distance behind the house.

When Randall pursuers see him running away, they immediately chase after him.

Because Randall is fast, he reaches the garage before his pursuers can catch him. And he tries to open the side entry door. But it's locked. Now, realizing that he's at a dead end, he picks up a long ax handle that happens to be lying against the door, and he turns and bravely faces his foes, all the while, discreetly keeping his back close against the door; which is a very clever, subterfuge type of maneuver, to prevent them from being able to surround him.

As Michael, Peter, and Jake approach Randall, Michael looks Randall straight in the eyes, and he says to him: "I told you that I was going to get you! Didn't I, boy?" He continues: "What were you doing with that white girl, Elisabeth, anyways? Don't you know that Niggers aren't supposed to mix with whites?"

"I can't help it if she chose me over you, 'boy!'" Randall sarcastically responds back.

Randall's sharp words and stinging tone makes Michael furious! And losing all control, he lunges towards him. But when he does, Randall quickly swings the ax handle, and he strikes him real hard across the left side of his face with it! Immediately, Michael falls down flat to the ground.

Now, lying on the ground, and grimacing in pain, Michael grabs his face. Then, turning to his friends, he commands them to attack Randall at once, saying with a loud and angry voice: "Get him!"

As Peter and Jake begin to attack Randall, he starts swinging the ax handle again. This time he manages to strike Peter real hard across his left arm with it; and in the process the ax handle breaks in half.

Peter, although hurt from the blow of the ax handle, manages to shake it off, and then he and Jake quickly converge on Randall, pounce on him, and wrestle him to the ground.

While Randall is being pinned to the ground by Peter and Jake, Michael shouts out to them, saying: "Hold him there!"

Michael now picks himself up from off the ground. And he walks over to and stands directly over Randall. And, peering down at him with anger and rage on his face, he begins kicking him in the stomach, over and over again! Each repeated kick that he administers is more forceful and harder than the previous. And they hurt and weaken Randall greatly!

After Michael delivers his last kick to Randall's stomach, he says to his two accomplices: "Ok, now pick him up, and let go of him!"

As Peter and Jake lift Randall to his feet, they release hold of him, just as they were instructed. Immediately, Michael quickly charges at Randall, and he throws a swift punch at his head. But, somehow, Randall manages to duct out of the way. And then, as quick as a flash of lightning, he throws a counterpunch with his right hand, and lands his fist directly on the bridge of Michael's nose. The force from the blow causes Michael's head to snap backwards, and his nose begins to bleed!

Immediately, Michael grabs his nose! And now, with blood on his hand, and a stunned look on his face, he says to Randall with a furious and loud voice: "You broke my nose! You damn Nigger!" And in a fit of rage he charges at him, wildly swinging both of his fists. Randall however remains perfectly calm and he manages to dodge every blow. And then, pulling a punch from far left field, he unleashes a hard left hook to Michael's jaw! The blow is so powerful that it knocks Michael down, and his body hits the ground hard!

As Michael lies there on the ground once again, he looks up at Randall. Then he points his finger at him, and he yells to Peter and Jake, saying: "Get him!"

Peter and Jake, doing exactly what they're told, instantly converge upon Randall. First, Peter attempts to land a punch, but Randall is able to slip his jab, and then he quickly counters with a hard left cross to Peter's chin, which knocks him backwards.

At the exact moment Randall's blow hits Peter, knocking him for a loop, Jake sneaks around and he grabs Randall from behind. And he puts him in a full nelson wrestling hold. Randall tries hard to break free, but he can't.

Peter, now observing that Randall's arms are being securely restrained, confidently walks up to him, and he proceeds to punch him several times in the face. And then, he finishes with a hard blow to his stomach. This final blow knocks the wind completely out of Randall, and his body proceeds to fall limply to the ground upon his knees.

With Randall helplessly down on his knees and doubled over in pain, Michael now approaches him from behind, holding a large stone in his hands. Next, lifting the stone high above his head, he then proceeds to forcefully thrust it downwards, striking Randall on the back of his head. Immediately, upon impact Randall's body falls down lifelessly with his face to the ground.

Peter, recognizing that Randall is no longer moving, quickly approaches him, in order to check to see how he's doing.

After examining Randall, Peter turns and with a shocked look on his face, and a frightful tone in his voice, he says to Michael: "He's dead!" And then, continuing, he says: "Man, why did you do that? You didn't say anything about killing him! We were just supposed to scare him and ruff him up real good!" He continues: "I'm not going to take the rap for murder!"

In response, Michael looks at both Peter and Jake with crazy eyes (as though he completely lost his sanity). And with an intimidating and threatening voice, he says to them: "We're all in this together! And if the two of you know what's good for you, you'll keep your mouths shut!"

As it stands, both Peter and Jake happen to have a morbid fear of Michael anyways. Like a tyrant, he has always bullied and exercised an unhealthy, dominating influence over them, ever since they were growing up together as young boys in Frogtown. And, because of their extreme fear of him, and what he might do to them, if they were ever to squeal to anyone, especially to the authorities, Peter and Jake quickly vow to keep the matter of Randall's death a secret between them and Michael alone. Afterwards, the two of them turn and they proceed to run away from the scene of the crime.

Michael, who happens to still be standing over Randall's body, looks down at him. Suddenly, he notices that he's wearing a shiny and fancy wristwatch. So he bends over, and he quickly removes it from his arm. Then he takes it, turns, and runs away.

~

The very next day, which is Monday morning, Elisabeth rises from her sleep, hops out of bed, showers, eats breakfast, and then she travels off to work — like any other normal workday routine. Then, later, upon completion of the workday, she prepares to visit Randall. Although she's feeling a little tied from a long and tough workday, she's extremely happy, because she gets to spend the rest of her day with Randall at Whispering Pond. Luckily, she brought a change of clothes with her to work.

After using the restaurant's restroom to change, Elisabeth leaves Little Ricky's Diner, and she catches a bus to Main Street and Sunset Boulevard.

When the bus arrives at her destination, Elisabeth disembarks, and then she heads off on foot to the Bayridge Dividing Wall.

Upon reaching the Bayridge wall, Elisabeth proceeds to squeeze her body through the small opening in the wall, and she enters Shytown. And then, she quickly scurries off to Randall's house.

A short time later, Elisabeth finally arrives at Randall's house. And she promptly knocks at the front door. However, no one answers. So after waiting a moment or so, she knocks again. But still, no answer! Now, thinking that no one is home, she turns and she begins to leave. Suddenly, the door slowly opens.

As Elisabeth turns and looks back at the door, she notices that it's Randall's Mother, Eva. She has finally come to the door.

Upon seeing Eva, Elisabeth smiles and enthusiastically says to her: "Good morning, Mrs. Pascale! Is Randall home?"

Eva hesitates for a moment. And then, she says to Elisabeth in a very sad and mournful voice: "I'm sorry honey, but, Randall is dead!"

As soon as Elisabeth hears the tragic news about Randall, she immediately goes into shock, and she faints and collapses on the porch.

Sometime later, as Elisabeth begins to regain consciousness, she imagines that she had a bad dream. But then, looking around, she thinks to herself: *This is not my bed that I'm lying upon! Nor is this my home! Wait a minute! It's a hospital room!* Now, quickly and solemnly beginning to recall the truth about what really happened, Elisabeth panics, and she cries out with a loud voice, saying: "No! No! No! Not my Randall! Not my Randall! Please, God! Not my Randall!" And she begins crying and sobbing uncontrollably.

Suddenly, a Nurse comes running into the room!

The Nurse, attempting to calm Elisabeth down, says to her with a gentle and soothing voice: "There, there, now, it's ok honey. It's alright. Everything's going to be alright."

But it doesn't work. Elisabeth just becomes even more hysterical; crying and screaming, and saying: "Randall! Randall! No! No! No! Not my darling Randall!"

The Nurse, now realizing that Elisabeth must be quickly sedated, turns and she calls out for help, and immediately two other nurses come running into the room.

The 1st Nurse shouts to her fellow Nurses, saying: "Quick, help me sedate her!

When Elisabeth hears the Nurse saying: "Sedate her!" She begins to resist and fight them. However, the two assisting Nurses manage to grab hold of her, and they pin her to the bed, holding her there, while the 1st Nurse successfully administers the sedative.

Finally, after being successfully sedated, Elisabeth quickly begins to calm down, and she falls fast asleep.

Unfortunately, as it so happens, Elisabeth Margaret Baxter happens to be in the Trauma Unit at the Good Samaritan Hospital, where she was taken and admitted after her collapse. She has suffered a mental breakdown. And she is to be kept here under close observation until she fully recovers.

~

The next day, following Elisabeth's admittance to the hospital; while she is being thoroughly examined by a Doctor, it is discovered that she is pregnant. So the examining Doctor stops and he asks her: "Did you know that you are pregnant young lady?"

Shocked and with a very surprised look on her face, Elisabeth says: "No. I didn't," And then, she begins to cry. However, these tears are not the tears of sadness; but rather, they are the tears of extreme joy!

Elisabeth is so happy! She can hardly believe it! She is absolutely thrilled to be pregnant with Randall's child. But yet, in her heart she also feels a sense of great pain and sorrow, because she knows that he will never get the chance to see and help raise their child.

As the days and months slowly pass by, the news of Elisabeth's pregnancy greatly aides in the process of her recovery. And she is eventually released from Good Samaritan.

Two days later, following her release from the hospital, Elisabeth visits Arlington Cemetery, the place where she has ascertained where Randall was buried.

It's a cool and crisp autumn day, with a grey, overcast sky, and a blanket of colorful, fallen leaves spread out upon the ground. Elisabeth is wearing a warm trench coat, as she stands alone, in front of and looking down at Randall's grave.

"My dear, Randall, I miss you so much! What am I going to do without you?" Elisabeth audibly says with a very sad voice. Suddenly, a pool of tears begins to well up and flow from her eyes, and she begins to sob and weep profusely. But then, quickly pulling herself together, and drying her tears with a handkerchief that she pulls out of the pocket of her coat; she says with a smile on her face and excitement in her voice: "Hey, Randall! Guess what? We're going to have a baby! Isn't that wonderful! I hope it looks like you!" And then, after pausing for a moment in silence, she continues, saying: "I sure do miss you, Randall! And I wish that you were still here with me! You were everything to me! I love you with all of my heart! And I always will! Goodbye Randall, my darling!" Afterwards, she bends over, and she places a beautiful bouquet of Forget-Me-Not flowers (that she has been holding in her hand), down upon the ground in front of Randall's tombstone. And then she walks over to a waiting taxi; gets in; and goes home.

12

NEW BEGINNINGS

Many months have passed since Elisabeth was released from the Good Samaritan Hospital, and she now gives birth to a brand-new baby boy. She names him Christopher Maurice Pascale. The child is beautiful! He has a full head of straight and silky, dark brown hair; a small pug nose; and thin lips, with a tiny teardrop shaped groove positioned just above his upper lip.

Initially, the pigmentation of Christopher's skin has sort of an off white hue to it. However, with the passage of time, over the coming months and early formative years, the coloration of it begins to gradually darken, till it becomes light brown, with sort of a yellowish, golden hue. Also, his silky straight hair progressively begins to slowly transform from being straight and silky, into being a little bit coarser, with large, loose curls situated toward the top and front of his head.

Unfortunately, sometime later, after giving birth to Christopher, Elisabeth begins to experience some health problems. Her heart was weakened considerably from the stressful lost of Randall, and also from undergoing some serious complications during Christopher's birth. As a result, she often becomes easily fatigued.

~

Two years quickly pass by. The year is 1947. Elisabeth and Christopher are returning home from grocery shopping. Upon entering their apartment, Elisabeth quickly notices that her roommate, Betty Lu Macalester, appears to be upset about something, so she says to her: "Betty Lu, is something wrong?"

Betty Lu points to Christopher, and she says to Elisabeth: "Is that a colored man's baby?" In response, Elisabeth keeps silent.

"You heard me! I said, is that a colored man's baby," Betty Lu asks.

"Why do you ask," Elisabeth replies.

"Because, I want to know," Betty Lu says.

"What difference does it make?" Elisabeth answers.

"It makes a big difference!" Betty Lu says. She continues: "Well, is it?"

"Yes, it is," Elisabeth reveals.

"I thought so! Are you crazy? What were you thinking? Don't you know better than to get mixed up with those people? Our whole neighborhood is talking!" Betty Lu exclaims.

"I really don't see what the big problem is," Elisabeth remarks.

"Well, then let me spell it out for you! Interracial mixing of whites and blacks is not right!" Betty Lu says.

"Why not," Elisabeth asks.

"Because, it just is," Betty Lu answers.

"Who made that rule?" Elisabeth asks.

"I don't know? But that's not the point!" Betty Lu says.

"Then, what is the point?" Elisabeth asks.

"The point is, is that you just don't do it! Everybody knows that!" Betty Lu responds.

"That rule was made up by a cold and cruel, inhuman society! It's not God's will! He made all men equal!" Elisabeth says.

"That may be true, but in reality honey, coloreds are not considered equals, and until something drastically changes that's the way it's gotta be!" Betty Lu replies. She continues: "I feel sorry for you, Elisabeth! You've really gotten yourself into a big mess this time! But not only that, I also feel sorry for Christopher. It's totally unfair to him to have been brought into this world under these circumstances. The fact is, in reality, the world only love's those of their own kind. Haven't you ever heard the expression 'Birds of a feather flock together,' because of this, Christopher will never fit in or be accepted, he'll always be viewed as different from the rest. He'll be labeled a misfit, an outcast!"

"That's not fair! He's only a child!" Elisabeth says, as she begins to cry.

"I know, but that's the way it is! Society sets the rules!" Betty Lu says. She continues: "This is hard on me too! Everywhere I go, people are pointing, and staring, and talking behind my back! Our landlord is even threatening to evict us! I need a place to live! And because of this, I have no choice but to ask you to leave!"

Elisabeth is totally stunned! And she says: "But, Christopher and I need a place to live too! Where are we going to go?"

"I don't know? But you can't live here anymore!" Betty Lu answers. She continues: "At most, the best I can do, is give you a few days to find another place. Today is Saturday. I want you out of here by Friday of next week!"

"But, Betty Lu, I thought that we were friends forever? Remember the promise that we made to each other back at the Orphanage?" Elisabeth recalls.

"Well, it can't be that way anymore!" Betty Lu replies in a coldhearted tone. Afterwards, she turns and she exits the apartment.

Elisabeth is totally devastated! She is feeling both crushed and betrayed. Bending over and reaching down, she picks up Christopher from off the floor, and she holds him close in her arms, and she says to him with tears streaming down her face: "Momma loves you baby! And I always will!"

Early the next morning, Elisabeth quickly rises. And after getting both her and Christopher dressed, they sit at the kitchen table eating breakfast, while she diligently searches through apartment vacancy ads in the local news paper and circles all available apartments with an ink pen.

A short time later, after finishing breakfast, Elisabeth takes Christopher, and they leave and head out to find a new place to live.

Unfortunately, at the end of the day, after they have checked out a dozen or so vacancies, poor Elisabeth is sorely disappointed, because things didn't go so well for them. They are turned down by every landlord. Now, feeling tired and dejected, Elisabeth takes Christopher and they head for home.

Over the next few days, Elisabeth repeats the same process. She rises early in the morning; searches through apartment vacancy ads; and then her and Christopher travel to check out places to live. However, at each day's end, there is still no success. They are turned down at every place they visit.

~

It is now Wednesday. And it is late in the evening. Today, like all previous days, Elisabeth and Christopher have spent the entire day looking for a place to live. But now, she is beginning to lose all hope, because at the end of the day, even though all of the places they look at are vacant, every landlord still refuses to rent to them.

Poor Elisabeth! What is she going to do? She is feeling so down and stressed. And the pressure is mounting, for she knows that tomorrow, which is Thursday, is the last day for her and Christopher to find a new home, because, officially, Friday morning is the deadline. Unfortunately, at that time, she and Christopher must vacate Betty Lu's apartment, as she had so firmly stipulated.

~

Today is now Thursday, the last day for Elisabeth to find a place to live. And time is quickly flying by. It's already getting near the end of the day. And so far she and Christopher have visited and checked out about 10 apartments in the surrounding area, but still without success. Nothing but rejections! Feeling extremely rundown, tired, and dejected, Elisabeth starts to cry. But then, for the sake of Christopher, she quickly pulls herself together, and they proceed to head for home.

On the way home Elisabeth stops at the 'Super Subs & Soups Diner,' on Main Street, in order to get her and Christopher a bite to eat.

As Elisabeth enters the front door of the restaurant, she spots a sign that says 'Please Seat Yourself.' So she walks over to and seats Christopher and herself at one of the vacant booths next to a window.

Within a short time, a waitress approaches Elisabeth's table and she says to her in a rude tone: "I'm sorry honey, but we can't serve you here!"

"Excuse me, what did you say?" Elisabeth asks, with a confused look on her face.

"We can't serve you here!" the Waitress says.

Apparently, Elisabeth is not getting the point. Still confused, she asks: "What do you mean, by saying, you can't serve us here?"

The waitress proceeds to point at Christopher, and then to a sign that is hanging on a wall by the cash register. The sign reads 'Coloreds not allowed.'

"But my child is hungry!" Elisabeth declares.

"I'm sorry, but rules are rules!" the Waitress says.

"You've gotta to be kidding me?" Elisabeth exclaims. Then, she gets up, takes Christopher, and they start to leave.

Interestingly, as Elisabeth and Christopher are about to exit the diner, she happens to spot an apartment for rent advertisement that is hanging on a patrons information board by the front door.

Elisabeth, not wanting anyone to see what she's about to do, turns quickly and inconspicuously looks around inside the diner, to make sure that no one is watching her. Then, she secretly takes the rental ad off the board, and slips it into the pocket of her sweater. Afterwards, she and Christopher exit out the door.

After Elisabeth leaves the diner, she walks a short distance away, and then she stops and pulls out the ad, and begins examining it. The ad reads: 'One bedroom apartment for rent. Available immediately! Location: 423 Summit Hill. See back for directions.'

When Elisabeth looks at the back of the ad, she sees that it contains a map with detailed directions and instructions on how to get to the rental property, which happens to be not that far away from where she is. So without delay, she takes Christopher and they proceed to walk there.

After walking several blocks (in various directions), Elisabeth and Christopher finally come to a closed, tall, rod Iron Gate blocking a driveway, with an address affixed to it. The address reads: '423 Summit Hill.' Also hanging from the gate is an apartment rental sign.

Quickly gazing through the gate to see where it leads, Elisabeth's eyes follow a long and curved paved driveway. And at the end of the driveway there is a big white house sitting on top of a hill.

"Wow, that's a big house!" Elisabeth says. Then, she turns and she closely examines the rental sign.

Oh no! At the bottom of the sign, it says in small print "One bedroom apartment for rent. *For Single Person Only!*"

Elisabeth is so upset! How could she have missed this important part of the ad? She knows that this stipulation automatically disqualifies her and Christopher from being able to rent the apartment. How discouraging! It seems that no matter how hard she tries, she just can't seem to win!

But wait! For some unexplained reason, Elisabeth feels compelled to approach the house anyways. Opening the unlocked, iron gate, and with Christopher now fast asleep in her arms, she proceeds to walk towards the front door of the house.

~

When Elisabeth arrives at the front door of the house, she rings the doorbell, and then she waits.

Finally, within a moment or so, the door opens. It is an old, blind man, accompanied by his Seeing Eye Dog, which is a Golden Labrador Retriever.

The Man says: "Hello. Can I help you?"

"Yes, I'm here to see about the apartment. That is, if it's still available?" Elisabeth says.

"Yes it is, please come in," the Man says. Then he turns and he proceeds to walk, with his dog leading the way, into the living room. Afterwards, he sits down in a large, wingback chair. And his dog obediently lies down on the floor beside him.

Next, the Man courteously says to Elisabeth: "Please, have a seat."

Elisabeth, with Christopher still sleeping in her arms, proceeds to take a seat on a small couch that's located directly across from the man and his dog.

The Old Man inquires, saying: "How did you find out about the vacancy?"

"I saw your ad posted at a restaurant nearby," Elisabeth says.

"Oh, you must be referring to the 'Super Subs & Soups Diner,'" the Man replies.

"Yep, that's it," Elisabeth says. She continues: "But when I got to your house and read the sign, I noticed it says that the apartment is for a '*Single* person only!'"

"Yes, that's right," the Old Man confirms.

"Well, I have to be honest with you, Sir. I'm not alone. I also have my two year old son with me," Elisabeth reveals.

"Oh, is that right?" the Man remarks. He then inquires, asking: "What is your son's name?"

"His name is Christopher," Elisabeth answers.

"If I might ask, where is his father?" the Man says.

"He's no longer with us, Sir. He died about 3 years ago, before our son was born," Elisabeth relates.

"I'm sorry to hear that!" the Man says.

As Elisabeth and the blind man are talking, his dog gets up. And it walks over to Christopher, and it begins licking his face. In response, Christopher immediately starts to wake up.

When Elisabeth sees the dog licking Christopher's face she chuckles and smiles. And then she reaches out her hand, and she gently pets the dog on top of its head, and she says to it: "Nice doggie."

"I'm really surprised!" the Man says.

"What's that?" Elisabeth asks.

"Old, Maggie (the dog's name) usually doesn't take that well to strangers!" the Man says. He continues: "By the way, my name is Archer Tucker. But you can call me Art."

"Hi Art, I'm Elisabeth Pascale,"[6] Elisabeth says.

~

Archer Tucker is a middle aged Caucasian man. He is about 5 feet 11 inches tall, with a medium build. He's sort of an easygoing type of fellow. He was married once. But he and his wife of many years never had any kids. Sadly, she left him shortly after he became blind from a tragic hunting accident that happened about 12 years ago.

~

Elisabeth, continuing the discussion, says to Archer: "I wouldn't have answered your ad, Sir, but I'm desperate to find a home for me and my son!"

"Can you clean and cook?" Archer asks.

"Yes, Sir, I can clean. And I'm a very good cook!" Elisabeth replies.

"I've been looking for someone like you," Archer says. He continues: "Come with me." He then rises from his chair, takes hold of Maggie by her harness, and they proceed to lead Elisabeth and Christopher to the backdoor of his house.

When they reach the backdoor, Archer points out the window,

---

[6] Elisabeth changed her surname from Baxter to Pascale after Randall died and Christopher was born.

and he directs Elisabeth's attention to a small cottage-like house that's located on his lot, directly behind his home.

"Elisabeth, do you see that yellow house out there, with the big bay window in the front?" Archer asks.

"Yes, I see it," Elisabeth replies.

"That property belongs to me," Archer says. He continues: "It's a furnished guesthouse. My maid used to live there, up until the time before she got married and moved away. The house has one bedroom, a kitchen, a dining area, a bathroom, and a laundry room, plus a large den that can be turned into another bedroom. If you'd like, both you and Christopher can live there rent free. And in addition to that, I will pay you 50 dollars a week. That is, if you accept the job of cooking, cleaning, doing laundry, and running small errands for me."

Elisabeth is so excited that she can hardly believe her ears! She says: "I take it! When would you like me to start?"

"Immediately," Archer replies.

"What would you like me to do first?" Elisabeth asks.

"Why don't you take Christopher into your new home and get settled and acquainted with it first. And then, later this evening, you can cook some dinner for all of us to eat," Archer says.

"That sounds great!" Elisabeth remarks. She continues: "Thank you so much for the home and job, Sir!"

"You're welcome! And remember, you don't have to call me, Sir. You can just call me Art," Archer says.

"Ok, Art," Elisabeth smiles and says.

~

When Elisabeth and Christopher arrive at the guesthouse, she opens the front door and they walk inside. Wow! She can hardly believe her eyes! It's perfect! Now, overcome with emotion, she begins to cry tears of joy. And reaching down, she picks up Christopher, holds him in her arms, hugs him, and she says to him: "I love you, very, very, much, my little Christopher. And I always will! Your Momma's going to take good care of you, my beautiful Son!"

Later that night, when it's time to finally tuck Christopher into bed, Elisabeth sings him a song, as she customarily does every night during bedtime. The song that she sings is her favorite song, the one that she and Randall slow danced to on the night of the big party at Mr. Jones' Warehouse years ago.

As Christopher listens to his mother singing to him, the soft, soothing sound of her sweet voice immediately causes him to fall fast asleep. Afterwards, Elisabeth gently kisses him on his forehead, and then she whispers softly in his ear, saying: "I love you, Christopher. Sweet dreams my little sweetheart." Next, she reaches over, turns off the nightstand lamp, and then she quietly exits the room.

As future years pass by, Elisabeth and Christopher develop an extremely close attachment—an unbreakable bond.

13

SCHOOL DAZE

The year is 1950. Christopher is now five years old. And Elisabeth is taking him to the local Fitzgerald Grade School, in order to register him for kindergarten for the upcoming school year.

Christopher looks pretty much the same as he did when he was two years old, but now he's just bigger. However, the feature that stands out the most about him is his skin color. He is a rare breed. Because his father Randall was both African American and Native Indian, and his Mother Elisabeth is white, the pigmentation of his skin is a very light brown color, with sort of a yellowish, golden glow. For this reason, and also the fact that he is living at a time period in history when the white and black races don't interracially mix, he doesn't fit in.

When Elisabeth and Christopher arrive at the School, Elisabeth has him empty his hands of items that he picked up along the way as they were walking, items such as: dandelions, weeds, and twigs, etc.

And then, afterwards they enter the building.

The moment they enter the front door, Elisabeth spots a posted sign on the wall that reads "Kindergarten Registration. Location: Room 110." So she and Christopher proceed to walk to there.

Upon finding and entering Room 110, Elisabeth and Christopher enter a small line of people, who are patiently waiting at the student's registration table.

Unbeknown to Elisabeth, Christopher quickly wanders off. Leaving her side, he strolls over to a nearby table, where a Caucasian boy of his own age is sitting. The boy happens to belong to a couple who are also waiting in the registration line.

As Christopher approaches the boy, he doesn't say a word to him. He just stops in front of the table, and then he stands there in complete silence.

Interestingly, the boy's table is overflowing with some type of wooden puzzle-like building blocks that are randomly spilled out upon it, and he is diligently working to assemble them.

Neither the boy nor Christopher are aware of it, but the custom made, wooden, puzzle-like building blocks, when fully assembled, form into a complicated, structured bridge. Also, the puzzle-like structure is really not a toy, but rather, it is an instrument or tool that is used for testing and measuring a child's Intelligence Quotient (IQ) level.

So far, the boy has about one fourth of the puzzle-like structure put together. However, he seems to be stumped with the remaining pieces. Initially, he was doing quite well assembling the puzzle, but, now, he is beginning to have a hard time matching and putting the rest of it together. And, because of this, he is starting to get frustrated. All the while, Christopher remains standing there in front of him in complete silence, with his eyes intently fixed upon the building blocks.

Finally, after some time has passed, and realizing that the boy is totally stumped, and is in need of help, Christopher reaches out his hands, and he proceeds to dig deep into the large pile of wooden blocks. And then, immediately, pulling out a puzzle piece, he takes it and he places it in its proper place within the building structure. Next, in progressive and rapid succession he continues to select puzzle pieces, one by one, and he takes and places them individually in their correct place within the building structure. He continues to do this with absolute ease to all of the remaining pieces, until the entire structure is completely assembled.

Interestingly, because Christopher assembles the bridge so easily and quickly, you would think that he has seen or put it together before in the past. But, in reality, the fact is, he has never seen nor constructed anything like this before.

At the exact moment that the wooden puzzle-like structure is completed, a woman, who happens to be the head person in charge of the 'Fitzgerald School Welcoming and Registering Committee,' approaches Elisabeth, and she gives her a hardly welcome, saying: "Welcome to Fitzgerald! My name is Patricia Rice. I am the School Principle. We are very pleased to have you here! What brings you to Fitzgerald today?"

"Hello, my name is Elisabeth Pascale. I'm here to register my son Christopher in the Kindergarten class," Elisabeth says.

"That's wonderful! You won't find a better school than Fitzgerald! We're number one in academic achievement in the country!" the Principle proudly says. Next, she turns and she draws attention to all of the children there, who have become scattered throughout the room at the many different child activity stations, and she says to Elisabeth: "Well Elisabeth, which one of these handsome and gifted boys is yours?"

Elisabeth, now realizing that Christopher has roamed off to play, quickly scans the room with her eyes, and she finds him standing at the table where the boy with the wooden puzzle-like building blocks is sitting.

Pointing her finger at Christopher, Elisabeth smiles, and she says to the Principle: "There he is! There's my son Christopher standing over there!"

When the Principle sees Christopher, she is shocked, and she says to Elisabeth: "Do you mean that little colored boy standing in front of the puzzle table?"

"Yes, that's my Christopher!" Elisabeth proudly says. In response, the Principle, now with a snooty look on her face and an extremely rude tone in her voice, says: "I'm sorry, but we don't allow any Negro children in our school! This school is for white children only!" She continues: "Besides, it's also a school for exceptionally gifted children with high IQs!" And then, pointing her finger at Christopher, she sarcastically says to Elisabeth concerning him: "You might want to take him to a school where he'll fit in better, to a place where it won't be so taxing upon his tiny, little, inferior mind!"

Elisabeth is shocked and appalled by the Principle's words! And she immediately proceeds to walk over to Christopher to retrieve him, so that the two of them can leave.

As Elisabeth walks over to get her son, the Principle follows closely behind.

Quickly approaching Christopher, Elisabeth reaches out her hand, and she says to him: "Come, Christopher! It's time to leave!"

Suddenly, the Principle notices that the complicated wooden bridge is completely assembled. Totally stunned and shocked! And not believing what her eyes are seeing! She quickly turns her attention to the Caucasian boy who is sitting at the table, and she says to him: "Wow! Did you put this puzzle together? How in the world did you do it?" But, before the boy can respond, she continues: "My goodness! Aren't you an extremely bright one! No one has ever even come close to assembling this complicated structure before!"

As it so happens, the Caucasian boy's mother, and his father, who is a world renowned physicist, are presently chatting and socializing nearby with some of the other parents. And when they overhear what the Principle is saying about their child, they hurry over to him. And, with lit up smiles on their faces, they proceed to give him big hugs. And they say to him with highly impressed and ecstatic tones: "Good job, William! You make your Mommy and Daddy so proud!"

Sadly, not one person there, except for Christopher and William, really knows the real truth of the matter. That it was Christopher, and not William that completed the wooden structure.

Elisabeth now takes Christopher by the hand, and she says to him: "Come, Christopher." And they turn and proceed to promptly exit the building.

As Elisabeth and Christopher exit the school and begin walking away from it, Christopher suddenly recalls the items that his mom had him place on the ground before they entered the School — the dandelions, weeds, and twigs, etc. So he says: "Mom, I forgot my stuff!"

"Ok, then go and get them," Elisabeth says, as she patiently waits for him to retrieve them.

Immediately, Christopher quickly turns, and he runs back and gathers up his things, and then he returns to his mother; takes hold of her by her hand; and they head for home.

~

Interestingly, unknown to Elisabeth or anyone else, Christopher's spatial intelligence is extremely high; as a matter of fact, it is way off the charts!

Spatial intelligence is a combination of multiple intelligences that deals with spatial judgment and the ability to see or visualize with the mind's eye. With Christopher, these areas of intelligence are highly overdeveloped. How this happened is a mystery. But, apparently, it's a special, innate, God given gift that he was born with.

It's not easily understood or explained, but the way that Christopher's mind works is through a series of sophisticated and elaborate pictures or moving scenes, which enables him to envision and create complex things within his mind's eye. In other words, his extraordinary ability enables him to see, turn, rotate, maneuver, and completely build and construct, entire, complicated structures and objects in his head. Whereas, other humans may only be able to see or visualize a partial or incomplete picture of something at best, Christopher on the other hand, can see everything in its complete entirety, instantly! And yet, as remarkable as this may seem, it doesn't come without any drawbacks. For unfortunately, this advanced ability makes it very difficult for him to cope and fit in within a rigid, pre-structured environment.

~

Later, during the week, two days after Christopher and Elisabeth's visited the Fitzgerald School; Christopher is now enrolled at a different school. The name of the school is McKinley Grade School, which happens to be an all colored children's school.

At McKinley, Christopher spends most of his days isolated from the other students. He doesn't prefer it this way, but he has no other choice, because none of his classmates want to socialize or play with him. Apparently, this is the case, both inside and outside of the classroom.

Today is Friday, the last day of another school week. It's a bright and sunny day. And Christopher is on the school playground with his class during recess time, when, suddenly, a beautiful ruby-throated hummingbird appears. At the time, Christopher happens to be sitting all alone by himself on a wooden bench watching from a distance while the other children are playing together and having fun.

The fluttering hummingbird now proceeds to fly, undetected by the children, over the playground and towards Christopher. And then, it stops, and it hovers for a moment right above his head. Then, suddenly, something amazing happens. It gently lands and perches itself upon his hand.

As Christopher examines the hummingbird, he is absolutely astonished by its natural beauty and intricate design.

Next, another amazing thing happens. And that is, Christopher slowly lifts his hand up (the one that the hummingbird is perched upon), so that the bird is now level with his eyes — to get a closer look at it. Now, looking eye to eye with it, he takes his free hand and he proceeds to gently stroke its velvety smooth wings with his index finger. And, although the ruby-throated hummingbird in flight has a wing beat rate of up to 53 beats per second, it doesn't move! It just sits there perfectly still upon Christopher's hand, allowing him to closely examine it, and stroke its delicate wings!

A short time later, after Christopher is done thoroughly examining the hummingbird and petting its wings, he smiles at it, and he says: "Goodbye, birdie!" And immediately the hummingbird takes flight, and it proceeds to fly away.

Suddenly, there's a lot of commotion on the playground. As Christopher looks up and in the direction of the noise, he notices that in the distance, two boys are stomping their feet up and down on the ground. Curious as to why they are doing this, he gets up from the bench, and he walks over towards them, in order to get a closer look.

As Christopher approaches the two boys, he observes that they are killing ants, and enjoying every moment of it. Enraged by what he sees, Christopher runs over to them, and he yells: "Stop it! Stop it! You're killing them!" But the boys don't listen to him. They don't stop. So Christopher, using his body as a protective shield, quickly drops down and positions himself like an umbrella over the ants to protect them from harm. In response, one of the bullies named Derrick Bruterman, gets really mad, and he kicks Christopher really hard in his stomach, and he says to him: "What's the matter, yellow freak? Can't you stand seeing stupid little ants gettin stepped on?" Afterwards, he and his friend laugh their foolhardy heads off at Christopher, and then they turn and walk away.

~

The next day, Saturday, Elisabeth takes Christopher on an outing to the Minnesota, Como Zoo. There is much to see there. It has a large variety of different species of animals. There are lions, tigers, bears, zebras, camels, giraffes, monkeys, gorillas, wolves, penguins, peacocks, roosters, chickens, hens, and many other fun creatures to enjoy and see.

The time is 10:50 AM. It's almost time for a live show to begin. "Starkey, the Amazing Sea Lion" is about to perform. The show starts in 10 minutes.

World renowned "Starkey," and his trainer are known for putting on a fun and exciting outdoor water show for their audiences. With great anticipation, Elisabeth and Christopher hurry over to the aquatic building to see the show.

When Elisabeth and Christopher finally arrive at the aquatic building, they make their way to the grandstand, so that they can find seats before the show begins. The place is packed with people, but, luckily, there happens to be two empty seats located near the center of the bleachers. The show is scheduled to start any moment.

After working their way to their seats, Elisabeth can't help but to notice that she and Christopher are getting some strange looks from the people there, which makes her feel very uncomfortable. Noticeably, everyone in the stands has their eyes fixed upon them. As a matter of fact, the people are so preoccupied with Christopher and Elisabeth that they don't even realize that the show has already begun.

Enough is enough! Finally, Elisabeth gets up, and she takes Christopher by the hand, and they quickly exit the bleachers.

Upon exiting the bleachers, Elisabeth notes that the crowd is still gawking at her and Christopher, so she boldly speaks up, and she says to the curious onlookers: "Haven't you people ever been taught that it's rude to stare?" And then, with a sarcastic tone in her voice, she says to them: "Why don't you take a picture? It'll last longer!" Afterwards, she and Christopher promptly leave, and they venture off into another area of the park.

The next place that Christopher and Elisabeth visit at the zoo is the Greenhouse Conservatory. The Conservatory is a large, domed shaped, glass building that is surrounded by windows. The glass windows are an important structural feature of the Greenhouse. They allow valuable sunlight to penetrate through, which is vitally essential, because the building is used to house and display various kinds of trees, plants, and flowers, which naturally require a lot of sunlight in order to germinate, grow, and stay healthy.

Interestingly, this is Christopher's first time in a greenhouse. As he enters the doorway, he immediately observes and feels the warmth of the sun's rays penetrating through the window panes. He also smells the lovely, aromatic fragrance of the many beautiful flowering plants and trees, which spontaneously causes his eyes to light up, and his face to beam with ear-to-ear grins.

As Christopher and Elisabeth progressively move along the Greenhouse visitor's stone pathway, he frequently stops to touch, feel, and smell the flowers and various species of plant life. Truly, this is by far, the highlight of his visit to the zoo! And, after preferably spending much of their day there, Elisabeth and Christopher leave and go home.

14

FUNHOUSE MIRRORS

AND

SCARY TIMES

The year is 1957. Christopher is now twelve years old. The month is July. And it's summer break. This means no school until the next school year. However, what is even better is that today is Saturday, and the traveling "Funfest Carnival," happens to be in town. Elisabeth is driving Christopher there so that they can spend the whole day together, and have some fun.

After Christopher and Elisabeth arrive at and enter the Carnival, Elisabeth asks Christopher: "What do you want to do first, Christopher?"

"I want to go into the 'Funhouse of Thrills!'" Christopher points and says.

"Ok, let's do it!" Elisabeth says. And off they go.

Upon entering the 'Funhouse of Thrills,' Christopher and Elisabeth soon find that it is full of surprises. There is a maze of mirrors, a spinning tunnel, a moving staircase, and many other amusing and fun things.

Christopher and Elisabeth are having a blast as they work their way through the Funhouse.

A short time later, upon finally exiting the Funhouse, Christopher and Elisabeth pass by some Funhouse Mirrors that are on display. As they stop and peer into the first mirror, they are simply amazed. It makes their bodies look extremely thin and very tall! Next, stepping in front of another and different mirror, it makes them appear stumpy and flat. And lastly, when they gaze into the third and final mirror, it makes the upper half of their bodies appear long, stretched out, and skinny; and in the lower half, their legs look short and fat.

This happens to be Christopher's first encounter with funhouse mirrors. When he sees himself in the mirrors, he doesn't know quite what to think at first. Bewildered and a bit confused, he asks: "Mom, why do I look like that?"

Elisabeth proceeds to try to explain this extraordinary phenomenon. She says: "You don't really look like that son. These are just funhouse distortion mirrors that were created or made to reflect an optical illusion. In other words, when we look into the mirror, our eyes are not seeing the real or true image of ourselves, but instead, they are deceived, fooled, or tricked by a distorted image that the mirror creates, so that our minds believe what we see, even though the image is only a fake image, and not a real or true reflection of ourselves." Elisabeth now pauses, and then she asks: "Does that make sense, son?"

"Sort of. I guess the mirrors can make us look stupid or like a monster or something, when we're really not," Christopher says.

"That's right! I think you've got it. Good job son!" Elisabeth says.

After leaving the Funhouse of Thrills, Elisabeth asks Christopher: "Are you hungry, son?"

"Yep, I'm starving," Christopher replies.

"How about we grab a quick bite to eat?" Elisabeth asks.

"Ok," Christopher says. And then he and Elisabeth walk over to a nearby refreshment stand to get a hotdog and fries and something to drink.

As Christopher and Elisabeth approach the concession stand, there happens to be a few people standing in line ahead of them, so they enter the back of the line and patiently wait their turn.

After waiting awhile, Elisabeth and Christopher finally arrive at the head of the food line. It is now their turn to be served. But wait! The vender, who happens to be a Caucasian man, acts as though Elisabeth and Christopher are not there. Instead of acknowledging them, he looks right past them, as though they're invisible. And then, pointing to a different customer (a Caucasian man), who is standing in line directly behind Elisabeth and Christopher, the vender says to him: "Can I help you, Sir?"

"Sure," the Man says, as he begins to step around Elisabeth and Christopher, so that he can be served.

Elisabeth, not believing what she is seeing, is thoroughly agitated by the inconsiderate actions of the customer, as he tries to jump in front of her and Christopher, but especially is she appalled by the rudeness of the vender! Reacting immediately, Elisabeth throws her arm out in front of the customer, to block his approach. Then, she turns, and she looks the vender straight in the eyes, and she says to him with a disturbed, but take charge voice: "Wait a minute! You hold on there! You know darn well that we were here before him (the customer who cut in front of them). You wait on us first!"

The vender, who happens to be a racist bigot, gives Elisabeth a sly, fiendish, and irritated look. And then, he nonchalantly takes her order.

A short time later, after eating lunch, Elisabeth and Christopher go on practically every ride at the Carnival. They ride on the "Old Western Railroad Train," the "Ferris Wheel of Lights," the "Musical Carousel of Dreams," and more. They even try their hand at few of the skill challenging arcade games. Truly, it has been a fun filled day for both Christopher and Elisabeth.

Later, after several hours have passed by, Elisabeth is beginning to feel tired. So she says to Christopher: "I don't know about you, son, but your Momma's exhausted! And my feet are starting to kill me! How about we call it a day, and go home?"

"Ok Mom," Christopher replies.

"Did you have fun, son?" Elisabeth asks.

"Yep, it was a lot of fun, mom!" Christopher smiles and says. Afterwards, they leave, and head for home.

~

When Elisabeth and Christopher arrive home from the Carnival, they stop in to check on Archer Tucker.

Hearing them coming through the backdoor of his house, Archer says: "Hey, Elisabeth and Christopher! How was the Carnival?"

"It was a lot of fun!" Christopher excitedly exclaims.

"What about you, Art? How was your day?" Elisabeth asks.

"Not bad. Not too bad at all!" Archer replies.

"That's good. Well, we thought we'd stop in and check in on you before we head to our place. I just need to drop something off there, and then, afterwards, I'll come right back, and I'll fix you some dinner," Elisabeth says.

"That sounds great, but don't feel like you have to hurry. Maggie and I have been snacking on chips and stuff all day," Archer conveys.

"Now, Art, you know better than that! Haven't I told you not to be eating junk like that? It's not good for you!" Elisabeth scolds.

"Yeah, I know. But I like to do it every now and then," Archer answers.

"You incorrigible old man, what am I going to do with you?" Elisabeth giggles and says.

"Continue putting up with me, like you always do, I guess?" Archer replies with a smile.

"Okay," Elisabeth says with a chuckle. She continues: "I'll be back in a just moment, and then I'll make you a good home cooked meal!"

"That sounds great!" Archer says.

As Elisabeth and Christopher are walking from Archer's house to their home, suddenly, Elisabeth collapses, and she falls down flat with her face to the ground. Christopher, who is walking several feet behind her, sees her fall and, he yells: "Mom!" Then, in a hurry, he runs over to and kneels down to help her. However, upon quick examination, he observes that she is not responding at all.

Christopher now begins to panic and cry, and then, as quick as a flash of lightning, he jumps to his feet, and he runs inside of Archer's house shouting: "Archer! Archer!"

When Archer hears Christopher calling him, he is startled and, he asks: "Christopher, what's the matter?"

"My mom, she fell down and she's not getting up!" Christopher explains.

"Oh my goodness! I'll call the paramedics!" Archer says. And he picks up the telephone and dials the operator.

"May I help you?" the operator says on the other end of the phone line.

"Yes. I happen to be blind. There's been an accident! Someone is badly hurt! Please send the paramedics at once! The address is 423 Summit Hill. Please hurry!" Archer says.

A short time later, when the paramedics arrive, they examine Elisabeth and find that she is breathing, but unconscious. So they put her on a stretcher, and then they place her in the back of the ambulance.

While the paramedics are putting Elisabeth in the ambulance, Christopher is standing there in utter shock! Afterwards, the men close the backdoor of the vehicle, get in, and then they begin to drive off.

As the ambulance proceeds to drive away, Christopher yells out: "Mom! Mom! Come back! Come back!" Then, he starts running as fast as he can after the moving vehicle. He runs all the way to the end of the driveway, and then down to the end of the block. But the vehicle is just too fast! It keeps getting further and further away from him! Now, realizing that he can't catch up to it, Christopher stops running. And he cries out with a mournful and whimpering voice, saying: "Mom!" And then, immediately dropping to the ground upon his knees, he begins to weep profusely.

Poor Christopher! He is traumatized! What is he going to do without his Mother? She is his "Rock of Gibraltar," his "Bright Shining Star." She is the only one that gives his life real hope, strength, and true meaning.

~

When Elisabeth arrives at the Good Samaritan Hospital, she is immediately taken into the Emergency Room (ER), and examined by the ER Doctor. Afterwards, the Doctor phones Archer Tucker and, he says: "Mr. Tucker, I'm returning your phone call. I was told that you called earlier to check on Elisabeth Pascale. Well, she seems to be suffering from an extreme case of exhaustion and dehydration, we are treating her, and currently she seems to be responding fine.

CHARLES SHELTON

However, we will need to run some more tests. Therefore, we're going to admit her and keep her under close observation overnight. And then, she will most likely be released sometime tomorrow."

"That's good. I'm glad to hear that she's doing better. Thanks for calling Doc. I'll be sure to tell her son Christopher the good news when he wakes up in the morning," Archer says.

As it so happens, following Elisabeth's collapse and emergency trip to the Hospital, Christopher is now back at home and in bed. Archer has temporarily moved him into one of the extra bedrooms in his house. However, unbeknown to Archer, poor Christopher is not really sleeping. He simply cannot fall asleep. He is missing his mother all too much!

As Christopher lies there in bed, he begins to panic. And then his mind begins to speed up and then race out of control. First, images of today's events leading up to and after his mother's collapse begin replaying vividly and repeatedly in his mind. And then, without a moment's notice, thousands of past images of his entire life begin to flood forth like a ragging torrent before his eyes. The images are so vast and numerous that it feels like his head is going to explode from the overload of information. In response, Christopher grabs his head with both of his hands. But the pressure only increases and intensifies, until he finally passes out from the severity of the pain.

Later that night, Christopher finds himself out walking through a dense forest of heavily populated trees. As he makes his way through the trees and wild thicket, he begins to hear a very strange sound. It sounds like the voice of a woman crying for help.

As Christopher listens more closely, he discovers that the voice is coming from the direction of the north, and that it seems to be a good distance away. Curious as to whom it could be, he proceeds to walk towards her.

The night is cold and gloomy. Christopher can actually see his breath in front of his face as he breathes the crisp night air. And as he walks, he can hear the rustling, crackling, and snapping sounds of fallen twigs and leaves beneath his feet.

Christopher is both tentative and scared. But he continues to try to make his way towards the mysterious voice.

After traveling for a short distance through the dense forest, he eventually comes to a large clearing that is partly illuminated by a bright moonbeam from above. Looking out and into the clearing, he observes that the ground is covered in tall grass, which is about knee high in length.

Suddenly, a voice cries out again. It is the voice of the woman crying for help. She is saying "Help me! Please help me!"

Immediately, looking up and in the direction of the summonsing voice, Christopher observes that it seems to be coming from a hilltop that is located on the opposite side of the clearing, a distance of about 200 yards away.

Christopher is frightened! A part of him wants to turn back, and yet, a bigger part of him is compelling him to keep moving forward. He stops and pauses for a moment in order to gather himself together. And then, after mustering up courage and strength, he begins to enter the clearing.

When Christopher gets about one fourth of the way into the clearing, suddenly, he is approached by a large, winged creature. But this is no ordinary bird! It has wings like a bat, a face like a jackal, claws like an eagle, and a tail like a scorpion. And, when it flies, it sounds like a mad hornet!

Horrified by what he sees and hears, and realizing that he is in imminent danger, Christopher takes off running, hot-footing it as fast as he can across the clearing. However, because the flying creature is strong and fast, it quickly catches up to him.

Swooping down upon Christopher, the flying creature strikes him on the back of his head with its sharp claws. The blow is so powerful that it knocks him down with his face to the ground!

As soon as Christopher's body hits the ground, he immediately rolls over, and he tries to get up, but within a flash the flying creature is back on the attack! This time it swoops down upon him and it tries to viciously attack his face! Christopher is absolutely terrified! And he begins screaming, and kicking, and wildly swinging his fists at the attacking creature! Then, suddenly, a voice says: "Christopher! Christopher! It's ok! It's alright! You were just having a bad dream!"

When Christopher opens his eyes, he sees that it is Archer Tucker. And, he immediately starts to calm down.

Archer says: "I have good news. I heard from the hospital. The Doctor says that your mother is doing fine, and that she will be coming home tomorrow."

Upon hearing the good news, Christopher breathes a big sigh of relief, and then he smiles and he goes back to sleep. Afterwards, Archer exits the room.

~

The next day, Elisabeth is released and sent home from the Hospital, just as the Doctor had predicted; which is much to the delight of Christopher, who is so happy to be reunited with his beloved mother once again!

As future days, months, and years pass by, Christopher acquires wisdom and knowledge at an electrifying pace. Inherently, he has an insatiable appetite for learning. And he reads every book that he can get his hands on, especially books on science, physics, biology, and horticulture.

15

ONE MAN'S TRASH

ANOTHER MAN'S TREASURE

The year is 1961. Christopher is now sixteen years old. He is about 5 feet 10 inches tall, with a slender build. He looks pretty much the same as he did when he was younger, but now he is just bigger and taller. By nature, he is a wide-eyed, good-hearted person, who wears his heart on his sleeve.

Today, Christopher is mowing Archer Tucker's lawn. He has just finished the job, and after taking a refreshing drink of cool water from the garden hose, he enters Archer's kitchen through the backdoor of his house.

Elisabeth, upon seeing Christopher come in, says to him: "Christopher, I need you to go to the market for me." She then hands him a grocery list and money and, she says: "Here's a list of items that I need for tonight's supper. And here is the money. I want you to be careful and safe, but try to hurry back."

"Okay, I will Mom," Christopher says. Afterwards, he immediately exits the house, gets on his bicycle, and rides off.

~

Christopher has a pretty nifty looking bike. It's a Schwinn Panther. It is a radiant red color, with whitewall tires, chrome fenders, and a white and red two-tone saddle seat. Also, it's conveniently equipped with a large, front, metal carrier basket that is perfect for carrying groceries and other things.

~

Within a short period of time, Christopher finally arrives at the local "Piccadilly Supermarket," and he locks up his bicycle at a bike rack that's located on the side of the building. Next, he enters the store; quickly gathers all of the items on the grocery list; pays for them; and then he proceeds to promptly exit the store.

The groceries are heavy. Christopher is carrying a large, brown paper grocery bag in his arms, with both of his arms firmly wrapped around it. The bag is filled with various items, such as: a roast, canned goods, a head of lettuce, celery, carrots, butter, ice cream, and a loaf of bread, etc.

The moment Christopher steps foot outside the store, he is surprisingly attacked by a large German Sheppard. Oh no! Gasping in fear, he quickly jumps back! And immediately his grocery bag splits open, and some of the cans goods and other items fall to the ground. Luckily, the dog didn't bite him! Thank goodness it was on a leash, and that it was quickly pulled back in the nick of time by its owner! Nevertheless, the dog is still acting crazy, barking and carrying on! To Christopher, it is a very frightful and intimidating experience, to say the least! His poor heart is racing, and his body is trembling, as he stands there with fear etched upon his face!

When the dog's owner, who happens to be Caucasian man, observes Christopher's reaction to his dog's attack, he can't help but to notice the tremendous fear in the young lads face. Nevertheless, in response, he says to Christopher with a cold stare: "Oh, don't worry!

He (his dog) doesn't like Nigger meat!" Afterwards, he and another Caucasian man who is with him, burst out in laughter — a sort of cruel, condescending, and sadistic kind of laughter, that is meant to cause its recipients embarrassment, humiliation, and pain. And then, afterwards the men take their dog and leave.

After the two men and their dog leave the area, Christopher picks up his grocery items that fell on ground, and he loads them and the rest of the groceries into the large, front carrier basket on his bicycle. Then, he gets on his bike, and he rides home.

~

The next day, when Christopher is riding his bicycle home from school, he rides through an alleyway behind the local "Green Thumb Nursery & Landscaping Store." Suddenly, the backdoor of the nursery swings wide open. And out walks a man dressed in casual clothes, with a green apron on. He is carrying something in his hands. Next, he proceeds to throw the object in a nearby trashcan, and then he turns, and he walks back inside of the building, and shuts the door behind him.

Christopher, highly curious as to what the object was that the man threw away, proceeds to ride his bicycle over to the trashcan to investigate. As he approaches the trashcan, he quickly hops off his bike, and he looks inside the can. To his surprise he sees that the discarded object is a small, infant tree, planted in a clay pot.

Bending over and reaching down inside of the trashcan, Christopher proceeds to lift the tree out. And, upon close examination, he notes that the height of the tree is about 10 inches, and that it is a scraggily and sickly looking thing, with a bent branch, and lots of missing leaves.

Immediately, after noting the poor condition of the tree, Christopher takes his shirt off, and he raps it around the base of the tree and the clay pot. Next, he carries the tree over to his bicycle, and he places it in the front carrier basket. Then, he gets on his bike and he proceeds to ride home. But wait! Suddenly, it dawns on him! He can't take the tree home! His mom won't let him keep it! She's tired of him bringing everything he finds home! Thinking quickly, he begins to ride his bike to an old and abandoned Warehouse District in Wright County.

After riding for a while, Christopher eventually comes to a railroad crossing. Crossing the tracks, he turns left at the next street, and then he rides his bike down a long, dirt road.

When Christopher gets to the end of the dirt road, he approaches an old, vacant, dilapidated, abandoned, and boarded up building that is surrounded by a tall, chain-link metal fence, with a broken entry gate.

Entering through the gate, Christopher rides his bicycle up to the building, then he gets off, and he walks up to the front door.

As it so happens, the front door of the building is boarded up with a large piece of thick plywood that covers the entire door. Grabbing one end of the board, Christopher tries to pull it off with his hands, but it is nailed too tight to the doorframe. So he quickly looks around the area to see if he can find something that he can use to jimmy or pry the board away.

Running over to the broken entry gate, he finds a loose iron rod lying on the ground. The iron rod is about four feet long and about a quarter inch in diameter. It appears to be the perfect tool for the job. So he bends over, picks it up, and then he returns to the front door. And, after successfully using the rod to pry the board away from the door, he enters the building. Now inside, he begins working his way through several dark rooms towards the back of the building.

Finally, after Christopher arrives at the back of the building, he comes to set of large double doors marked shipping and receiving.

When Christopher opens one of the double doors, he is instantly blinded by bright light. But then, after a moment or so, his eyes become acclimated to the brightness, and he is able to see clearly again.

As Christopher looks around the large, vacant room, he observes that the bright light is coming from sunlight that is shining through upper windows that are positioned close to a tall ceiling, which is about a 50 feet high. The windows are also conjoined closely together, and they surround the entire room. He also notices that a small section of the roof is damaged, and that it is leaking drops of water into a large metal bucket that is situated directly below. Apparently, the water happens to be runoff from last night's rain. He also observes that the entire floor of the room is covered with thick soil, tall grass, and weeds.

Christopher now turns around, and he quickly exits the building. Returning to his bicycle, he lifts the potted tree that's wrapped in his shirt out of the bike basket, and then he reenters the building; walks back to the large vacant room; and enters it.

Upon entering the backroom, Christopher proceeds to walk over to the far southwest corner, and then he stops, and he places the potted tree on the ground. Afterwards, he begins pulling up handfuls of tall grass and weeds.

After pulling up about a six foot circumference of grass and weeds, Christopher picks up a rock, and he takes it and he walks over to the potted tree, and he lifts it up from off the ground. Next, he removes his shirt from the tree base and clay pot. Then he gently strikes the clay pot with the rock. Immediately, upon impact the clay pot breaks and the tree's roots become free.

Christopher now bends over and he picks up a large, jagged piece of the broken clay pot that fell to the ground, and he uses it to dig a hole in the soil, in the center of the area where he pulled up the grass and weeds.

After the hole is large and deep enough, Christopher takes the tree and he places its root system in the hole, and then he covers it with the loose soil. Next, quickly rising to his feet, he takes his shirt, and then he walks over to the bucket of rainwater, and he fully submerses it below the surface of the water. Afterwards, he takes the soaked, drenched shirt, and he quickly walks back over to the tree.

Christopher, now standing directly above the tree, proceeds to ring out the rainwater from his shirt onto the tree and soil below.

After thoroughly watering the tree, Christopher exits the building; puts his wet shirt in the bicycle basket; gets on his bike; and rides home.

Interestingly, over the next days, months, and upcoming years, Christopher continues to visit and nurse the tree to health; utilizing every means possible.

.

16

YEAR OF THE KILLER VIRUS

The year is 1964. A young man wearing a blue janitor's uniform, carrying a plain, metal, dome shaped lunchbox, enters the employee's entrance of the Good Samaritan's Hospital. He is about 6 feet tall, with a medium build.

After he enters the door, he proceeds to walk up to an employee time punch clock, takes his employee timecard out of its assigned slot on a hanging wall rack, punches in, and then returns it to its proper place. Afterwards, he strolls over to a long roll of gray, metal, wardrobe lockers.

As the young man stands at the wardrobe lockers, keying in the code and opening the combination lock on his personal locker; two dark skinned colored men, also dressed in matching, blue janitor uniforms, enter the room, and they proceed to walk towards him.

As the men approach the young man, one of them begins to verbally abuse and ridicule him, saying: "Hey, what's up old yeller?

You yellow banana!"

The second man also quickly joins in on the belittling criticism, saying to the young man: "Hey, freak! What's happenin? You Uncle Tom!"[7]

When the young man hears the insulting remarks coming from the two men, who by the way happen to be his fellow coworkers, he immediately turns towards them, and he looks directly at his attacking ridiculers. But, he doesn't retaliate. No, he doesn't say a single word in reply to them. Afterwards, the two men, who may perhaps misinterpret the young man's silence as a sign of weakness, begin to laugh their heads off at him. They laugh and laugh, till they finally get their fill, and then they turn and walk away.

Sad to say, this is not an isolated case or incidence, but rather, it is a regular, reoccurring part of these bullies daily routine and treatment of belittling and tormenting the young man.

As soon as the two men leave the area, suddenly, a Caucasian man, who is the hospital cleaning staff supervisor, enters the room. And he yells out to the young man standing at the wardrobe lockers, saying: "Christopher… Maurice… Pascale, hurry up! They need you up in the ICU[8] right away! Someone had an accident!"

"Ok, I'll get right on it, Mr. Ferrymen, Sir!" Christopher says.

Christopher is twenty years old. He has been working here at the Good Samaritan Hospital for the past two years. Outwardly, he looks pretty much the same as he did when he was younger, but now, he's just bigger and taller. However, the distinct feature that stands out the most about him is the color of his skin. He is a rare breed. Because his father Randall Pascale was both African American and Native Indian, and his mother Elisabeth is white, the pigmentation of his skin is a very light brown color, with sort of a yellowish, golden

---

[7] An Uncle Tom is a black person, especially a man, who will do anything to be in good standing with white people, including betraying his own culture or people.
[8] ICU (Intensive Care Unit).

glow. And, unfortunately, for this reason, and also the fact that he is living at a time period in history when the white and black races do not typically interracially mix, he doesn't fit in.

Sadly, no matter what Christopher does, or where he goes, he just can't seem to win. He is viewed and treated by the world as a freak of nature. It is as though he is sitting all alone on a fence in between the two separate races. On the one side, he is shunned by whites, who view him simply as an intellectually inferior Negro, and on the other side, he is rejected by blacks who view him as a traitor or enemy. Although he is intelligent, innocence by nature, and good at heart, human society has stamped a price tag upon him, as being a creature of little or no value. And, for this reason, he is a loner, which is a painful plight or condition that he doesn't prefer, but one that is forced upon him by an ignorant, cold hearted society.

∼

When Christopher arrives up at the hospital ICU with his mop and pail; a nurse that is sitting at the Nurses Station, looks him straight in the face. Then, she points her finger in the direction of the accident that he is there to attend to, and she says to him with a crabby, condescending tone: "Patient room, number 315!" And then, quickly handing him a face mask, she continues, saying: "And be sure to put this on!"

After covering his face with the mask, Christopher proceeds to wheel his mop and bucket over to and into the patient's room. As he enters the door, he discovers that there's vomit all over the floor near the patients bed.

Lying in bed is a small child, a little Caucasian girl. She is in fact, only three years old. Her name is Elsie Rinehart. She has recently been hospitalized for having a rare viral disease.

Standing on the opposite side of the girl's bed, away from the area where the vomit lies, is a Caucasian man and woman. They are Elsie's parents. Their names are Margery and Carl. Both of them are wearing protective masks and rubber gloves.

Christopher now proceeds to clean up the mess on the floor,

methodically dipping the mop head over and over again into the bucket of soapy water, ringing it out, and wiping up the floor. As he works, he occasionally glances up at little Elsie. And, although she is very weak and sick, she manages to keep her eyes curiously fixed upon him.

Within a short period of time, the floor is thoroughly cleansed. So Christopher turns and he promptly exit's the room with his mop and pail. Afterwards, he removes his mask, and he walks over to an elevator that is located at the end of the hallway, just pass the Nurses Station, and he waits for it to come.

As Christopher waits for the elevator to come, one of the Nurses approaches the area, and she opens a locked door marked "Medical Supplies," that is located directly across the hall from where he is standing. Afterwards, she enters the room. But the door remains wide open.

While Christopher waits patiently for the elevator to arrive, he glances across the hallway. And, without the Nurse knowing, he peers inside the medical supply room. Wow, to his amazement, he observes that the room is stocked with medicines of all kinds! Never in his life has he ever seen so many drugs! Suddenly, the nurse quickly exit's the room, and she locks the door behind her. She is carrying a medical instrument tray: with a needle, syringe, cotton balls, rubbing alcohol, bandages, and a bottle of medicine on it.

Finally, the elevator now arrives. So Christopher promptly gets in with his mop and pail, and the door closes.

~

After Christopher returns his mop and pail to the Janitors Station, which is located on the first floor, he stops by his supervisor's office to let him know that the cleanup job in the ICU has been completed. As he opens the door and enters the room, his supervisor, Mr. Ferrymen, happens to be watching a live news report on a small television (TV) set.

"I'm finished cleaning up the mess, Boss!" Christopher yells.

"Hush! Be quite!" Mr. Ferrymen angrily says. And then, he quickly turns and refocuses his strict attention on a breaking and shocking news report.

The TV news reporter says: "A number of people in the surrounding areas of Wright County have recently contracted an unknown deadly virus that authorities have named "The Probias Plague." Some have died, and others are being brought into the hospital for quarantine and treatment. Presently, there is no known cure. But doctors and scientists are feverishly working — both hard and around the clock — to stop the spread of this lethal disease. However, they remain baffled as to its means of germination. All they know is that the virus fatally attacks and destroys human organs such as the liver, lungs, and kidneys. And, shortly thereafter, it terminates its victims. Also, the thing that is unprecedented and unique about this strange virus is that it is a discriminatory one, in that it only attacks and infects females!"

After hearing the news report, Christopher returns to work. And, later, after the completion of his workday, he returns home.

~

The next day, when Christopher arrives at work, his supervisor, Floyd Ferrymen, says to him: "Christopher, I need you to run an errand. I need you to take the 'Hospital Pull Cart,' and go over to 'Sunrise Pharmaceutical Drugs,' to pick up a small shipment of stuff."

"Ok, Mr. Ferrymen," Christopher says.

"And, be careful! Because some of the items are fragile. But try to hurry back!" Mr. Ferrymen adds.

"I will," Christopher replies.

~

Sunrise Pharmaceutical Drugs is located a distance of about five blocks away from the Good Samaritan Hospital. The Hospital Pull Cart is the perfect size and means of transport for picking up small shipments of medical supplies. In essence, the Pull Cart is really just a large wagon, with wooden guard rails, and with the name 'Good

Samaritan Hospital' displayed on both sides.

~

When Christopher arrives at Sunrise Pharmaceutical Drugs with his Pull Cart, he is highly impressed by the sheer size of the company. The building is gigantic!

Walking up to the Security Guard Station, Christopher says to the guard on duty: "I'm here to pick up an order for Good Samaritan Hospital."

"Ok," the guard says. And then, pointing to a visitor's login sheet, he says: "Sign in here."

After Christopher signs the login sheet, the guard hands him a visitor's Identification Badge (ID), and says: "Take this badge, and go to the 'Shipping and Receiving Department.' It's located at the southwest corner of the building." He then points Christopher in the right direction, and sends him on his way with his Pull Cart.

A short time later, after Christopher finds and arrives at the Shipping and Receiving Department, the shipping clerk has him wait while he processes the Good Samaritan Hospital's order.

~

Finally, after the shipping clerk is done pulling Christopher's order of medical supplies, he then proceeds to transfer the items, one by one, from a wooden pallet that's attached to the front end of his forklift, into Christopher's Pull Cart. And after he's finished doing that, he has Christopher sign a document that confirms that the shipment was received. Afterwards, he sends him on his merry way.

Shorty after Christopher leaves Sunrise Pharmaceutical Drugs; when he's on his way back to the Good Samaritan Hospital, he passes by some construction workers that are working on the construction of a new brick building that's being built across the street. Christopher vividly and distinctly recalls that his supervisor, Mr. Ferrymen told him to hurry back. So he's moving at a pretty fast pace — almost running with the Pull Cart. Suddenly, one of the boxes falls out of the cart and onto the sidewalk. In response,

Christopher yells: "Oh no!" Then, he immediately stops and picks up the item, and closely examines it. Fortunately for him, nothing seems to be damaged. So he places the box back into the cart, and he hurries on his way.

When one of the members of the construction crew sees Christopher running with the Hospital Pull Cart, he laughs, and he yells out with a loud voice, concerning him, saying: "Wow! Look at that boy go! That Nigger really wants him a job!" Afterwards, he and the rest of his fellow crew members begin to laugh out loud at Christopher.

The moment Christopher hears what the construction worker says, he quickly turns to look at him, but he doesn't say anything in reply. And, although it hurts him to be spoken of this way and ridiculed, he decides to suck it up and not retaliate. Instead, he just turns back around, and he hurries on his way. And, within hardly no time at all, he arrives back at work with the medical supplies in hand.

Later, after the completion of a long workday, when Christopher gets home, unfortunately, he finds that his mother Elisabeth has fallen ill. She has a high body temperature of 104 degrees. And she is lying in bed. Temporarily, she has been moved into an extra bedroom in Archer Tucker's house. Christopher observes that both Archer and a visiting Doctor, named Henry Murdock, are in the room with her. However, he decides to remain outside.

After the doctor is finished examining Elisabeth, he and Archer step outside of the room, and they close the door behind them. Then, the Doctor says to Archer: "I suspect that Elisabeth has possibly contracted the Probias Plague, but it's too early to tell for sure." He continues: "If her condition hasn't improved by tomorrow morning, I want you to call the hospital and have her admitted to the ICU isolation ward."

"I will, thanks Doctor Murdock," Archer says. Afterwards the Doctor leaves.

The moment Christopher overhears the Doctor's medical

evaluation of his mother Elisabeth; he becomes very sad and upset; and he turns and he runs out of the house and into the backyard; and he begins to cry. But then, suddenly, a thought pops into his head, and a strange look falls upon his face. Afterwards, he quickly gets on his bike, and he rides away.

~

Later that night, Christopher returns home, and he enters Elisabeth's bedroom, in order to check on the status of her condition. Quickly observing that she has grown worse, he says: "Hi Mom."

Elisabeth is so tired and weak that she can barely open her eyes. Nevertheless, recognizing the sound of Christopher's voice, she says to him with a faint voice: "Hi Son. Your Momma's not feeling well."

"I've got something for you, Mom," Christopher says. Then he proceeds to reach into his pants pocket and, he pulls out a small bottle that is filled with some sort of liquid. Next, he gently lifts Elisabeth's head up from off the pillow, and he gives her the liquid to drink.

After Elisabeth drinks the liquid, Christopher lays her head back down upon the pillow, and she falls fast asleep. Afterwards, he exits the room, and then he leaves home again.

~

It is now 3:00 AM. Up in the ICU of the Good Samaritan Hospital, a nurse at the Nurses Station is being relieved of her duty by another oncoming staff member, who is also a nurse.

The oncoming Nurse says: "Hey Francine! How was your night?"

"Hi Jill. It's been pretty crazy! I haven't had much time to relax!" Francine replies.

"What's tonight's work agenda look like?" Jill asks.

As Nurse Francine turns and proceeds to show Nurse Jill a detailed list of duties and provides her with a rundown on things,

Christopher quietly enters the ICU, and he secretly seeks pass the preoccupied Nurses. And then, immediately afterwards, he slips into room 315, where the sick little girl named Elsie Rinehart is stationed.

When Christopher enters Elise's room, he notices that she's out cold. Quietly approaching her bed, he reaches into his pants pocket, and he pulls out a small bottle of liquid, and he unscrews the cap. Next, he gently lifts her head up from off of the pillow.

The moment that Christopher raises Elise's head up, she begins to wake up. So he looks her in the eyes, and he smiles, and says to her in a soft tone: "It's ok honey; I have some medicine for you." He then proceeds to slowly pour the contents of the bottle into her mouth.

As soon as Christopher is finishing pouring the liquid into Elise's mouth, suddenly, Elise's mother walks into the room. Immediately, recognizing that Christopher is not one of the hospital's doctors or nursing staff, she panics and she says to him: "Who are you? What are you doing in here? And what was that that you just gave to my daughter?"

Christopher, sensing that he's in trouble and not knowing what to say, he panics, drops the bottle, and then he turns and quickly bolts out of the room!

Elsie's mother yells: "Help! Somebody stop him! Please, help!"

The loud commotion draws a lot of attention.

When the nurse at the Nurses Station turns to see what's happening, she sees Christopher exiting Elise's room. So she immediately yells out to him, saying: "Hey, you! Stop!" But he doesn't listen. He just proceeds to run as fast as he can towards the nearest exit, which happens to be a staircase; and he enters it, and begins quickly descending down several long flights of stairs.

Christopher's only thoughts are to get to the first floor and exit the building as fast as he can. When he finally reaches the bottom of the stairwell, he quickly opens the door and exists onto the first floor. However, to his surprise, he is met by two waiting policemen, who grab and arrest him. And, after immediately handcuffing him, they lead him out of the hospital, and put him in the backseat of their squad car, and drive away.

A short time later, after arriving downtown at the Wright County Jailhouse, Christopher is thrown into an interrogation room for questioning and examination. There are three plain clothes police officers present in the room with him.

The head policeman, who is the first to speak up, sternly says to Christopher: "What where you doing in the Rinehart's daughter's hospital room, boy?"

Christopher is trembling and scarred! Feeling overwhelmed and intimidated, he lowers his eyes to the floor, and he remains silent.

The head officer now becomes very impatient with Christopher, and he forcefully says to him: "This is the last time that I'm going to ask you, boy! I said, what where you doing there?"

Christopher now looks up at the interrogating officer and, he says to him: "I wasn't doing anything!" In response, the officer raises his arm and he strikes Christopher real hard across his face with the back of his hand. Instantly, Christopher's mouth starts to bleed.

A second policeman now steps forward and, he says to Christopher: "Do you know what happens to colored boys who touch little white girls, boy?" The officer then proceeds to loosen the thick belt from around his fat waist. Then he takes it off, raps it around his fist, and he slugs Christopher right in the face. As a result, the hard blow immediately knocks him out.

Later that night, Christopher finds himself out walking through a dense forest of heavily populated trees. As he makes his way through the trees and wild thicket, he begins to hear a very strange sound. It sounds like the voice of a woman crying for help.

As Christopher listens more closely, he discovers that the voice is coming from the direction of the north, and that it seems to be a good distance away. Curious as to whom it could be, he proceeds to walk towards her.

The night is cold and gloomy. Christopher can actually see his breath in front of his face as he breathes the crisp night air. And as he walks, he can hear the rustling, crackling, and snapping sounds of fallen twigs and leaves beneath his feet.

Christopher is both tentative and scared. But he continues to try to make his way towards the mysterious voice.

After traveling for a short distance through the dense forest, he eventually comes to a large clearing that is partly illuminated by a bright moonbeam from above. Looking out and into the clearing, he observes that the ground is covered in tall grass, which is about knee high in length.

Suddenly, a voice cries out again. It is the voice of the woman crying for help. She is saying "Help me! Please help me!"

Immediately, looking up and in the direction of the summonsing voice, Christopher observes that it seems to be coming from a hilltop that is located on the opposite side of the clearing, a distance of about 200 yards away.

Christopher is frightened! A part of him wants to turn back, and yet, a bigger part of him is compelling him to keep moving forward. He stops and pauses for a moment in order to gather himself together. And then, after mustering up courage and strength, he begins to enter the clearing.

When Christopher gets about one fourth of the way into the clearing, suddenly, he is approached by a large, winged creature. But this is no ordinary bird! It has wings like a bat, a face like a jackal, claws like an eagle, and a tail like a scorpion. And when it flies, it sounds like a mad hornet!

Horrified by what he sees and hears, and realizing that he is in imminent danger, Christopher takes off running, hot-footing it as fast as he can across the clearing. However, because the flying creature is strong and fast, it quickly catches up to him.

Swooping down upon Christopher, the flying creature strikes him on the back of his head with its sharp claws. The blow is so powerful that it knocks him down with his face to the ground!

As soon as Christopher's body hits the ground, he immediately rolls over, and he tries to get up, but within a flash the flying creature is back on the attack! This time it swoops down upon him and it tries to viciously attack his face! Christopher is absolutely terrified! And he begins screaming, and kicking, and wildly swinging his fists at the attacking creature.

Finally, after much effort, Christopher is able to knock the creature off of him. Then, he quickly rises to his feet, and he starts running again across the clearing. But the relentless winged creature is not giving up! It keeps chasing after him and getting closer!

Christopher, not knowing what to do, is thoroughly petrified! Then, suddenly, out of nowhere comes a ferocious, ravaging beast. It has a head like a lion, a body like a leopard, long fangs like a saber tooth, and sharp claws like a bear.

With dynamic power and lighting quick speed, the wild beast runs straight at Christopher. And in an instance, it springs off its hind legs and it leaps high into the air above his head. As it does, it quickly grabs hold of the winged creature in flight with its large mouth, and then it lands back down upon on the ground. Next, without delay, the wild beast quickly utilizes its front feet to pin the flying creature down, and it begins viciously ripping and tearing it apart.

Shocked and horrified by what he sees, Christopher turns and he begins running again, hoofing it as fast as he can across the clearing!

After running the entire, remaining distance of about 175 yards, Christopher finally makes it safely across the clearing to the foot of a hill on the other side. However, this is no ordinary hill. It's about 300 feet high. Also, its surface is covered with large rocks and stones.

Christopher is exhausted! Panting and breathing heavily from running, he proceeds to sit down alongside the hill with his back against a big boulder, so that he can catch his breath and rest up a bit. And then, suddenly, he hears the sound of the woman's voice again. She is saying: "Help me! Please help me!"

Immediately rising to his feet, Christopher quickly discerns that the summonsing voice is coming from an area on top of the hill.

The setting and situation feels all so strange and eerie! Christopher is afraid to follow the voice, but at the same time he can't find it within himself to turn away from someone in need of help. So after mustering up enough courage and strength, he begins the slow climb to the top of the hill. However, he soon finds that climbing the steep and rocky incline is not so easy. The going is extremely tough! But, within a matter of time, he eventually manages to finally make his way to the top.

The moment Christopher arrives at the top of the hill, a light rain begins to fall. Quickly looking around, he scouts the area to see if he can spot the woman in need of help. But it's too dark and hard to see. So he yells out in a loud voice (hoping that she will hear him and respond), saying: "Hello! Is someone there?" But there is no answer. Suddenly, loud sounds of crackling and thunder occur, followed by a heavy downpour of torrential rain, mixed with damaging hail.

Christopher, realizing that he needs to seek cover immediately, quickly looks around for a place of possible shelter. But, because the area is covered in dense darkness, it's just too hard to see! Suddenly, without warning, powerful flashes of lightning occur. And, although this is extremely scary, fortunately, the bright light from the lightning is so bright that it completely lights up the sky above and the ground below, providing Christopher with enough light to see.

Quickly, scanning the horizon with his eyes, Christopher happens to spots a cave nearby. It's located about 50 yards away from him. So without hesitation, he proceeds to run as fast as he can towards it. But the faster he runs, the worse the storm gets!

The rain is now falling like buckets from the sky, along with pelting hailstones! Also, there are loud and ominous cracklings and rolling sounds of powerful thunder! And lightning is flashing and striking nonstop everywhere, producing startling, and explosive, big bang noises!

Finally, Christopher manages to make it safely to the cave. Thank goodness! He is so happy to be out of the falling hail and rain!

The moment Christopher enters the cave, the lightning abruptly stops, and everything quickly turns pitch-black again. Nevertheless, the cave proves to be the perfect shelter to provide needed protection from the storm.

Christopher's clothes are soaking wet, and he is beginning to feel cold. In an attempt to warm himself, he proceeds to lie down on the floor of the cave with his body curled up in a fetal position. Tired and exhausted, his eyes are feeling heavy, and within a matter of an instance, he proceeds to fall fast asleep.

Sometime later, when Christopher awakens from sleep, he notices that the rain and hail have stopped, and that daylight is beginning to appear through an overcast sky that is covered in dense, gray clouds. Stepping outside of the cave and scanning the horizon, he observes that the entire ground is covered in huge slabs of stone. Suddenly, he hears a startling, rattling sound! It appears to be coming from behind him.

As Christopher slowly turns to look behind him, he sees three, intimidating, fierce creatures standing on top of the cave, just above his head.

The creatures look somewhat like large lizards. But they have fiery colored, red eyes. The lower part of their body has four legs. Their upper body has two arms that are equipped with humongous, asymmetrical pinchers that resemble lobster claws, but only much sharper! And their tails are like rattle snakes.

Fearful and shocked by what he sees, Christopher begins to backpedal slowly. Then, he quickly turns, and begins running away as fast as he can!

The instant that Christopher begins to flee from the lizard-like creatures, they immediately jump down from the top of the cave to the ground below, and they begin chasing after him in hot pursuit!

The lizard-like creatures are extremely fast! And, within no time at all, they catch-up to Christopher, and they begin nipping at his legs and heels with their powerful, razor sharp pinchers!

Christopher is in a frantic panic! What's he going to do? He's running as fast as he can, and yet, the creatures are right behind him! What can he do to lose them? Suddenly, as he looks up and into the not too far distance ahead of him, he sees that he is fast approaching a ravine. Thinking quickly, it occurs to him that if he can jump across it, then he can get away safe. But wait! As he gets closer to it, the ravine appears to be just too wide and too deep for him to jump across. Oh no! What's he going to do now?

What a dilemma! Christopher knows that if he stops running the lizard-like creatures will catch him, and use their powerful pinchers to crush and tear him apart! Yet, on the other hand, if he attempts to jump the ravine, and he falls short of the distance, he will fall over 300 feet to his death at the bottom, upon jagged rocks! Or, if by chance, he happens to miss the deadly rocks, he will plunge into the depths of a raging river that flows rapidly through the ravine, and be swept away! Either fate could prove to be deadly!

Now, with only a split second left to react, Christopher decides to go for it. Approaching the edge of the ravine, he takes a deep breath. And then, like an Olympic broad jumper, he pushes off with his left leg, really hard, and he leaps as far as he can go across the ravine.

When Christopher jumps the ravine, the lizard-like creatures follow right behind him. However, they immediately fall over the edge of the cliff! Two of them plummet and fall upon the jagged rocks at the bottom of the ravine, and upon impact their bodies explode and burst apart!

As far as the fate of the third lizard-like creature goes, it just barely misses the rocks! But it falls into the water, and is quickly swept away by the raging river!

Christopher, on the other hand, is still airborne and approaching the opposite side of the ravine. But wait! It doesn't look like he's going to make it either! He has already reached the height of his jump, and now he is starting to descend downwards. Oh no!

As Christopher is falling, he lets out a mournful howl and big scream! And then, suddenly, loud, clanking sounds occur. And a deep voice says: "Quite down in there, boy!"

A policeman is standing at the door of a jail cell, with a billy club in his hand. He had overheard noises coming from Christopher Pascale's cell, and he came to investigate.

Christopher, now awake and acknowledging the officer's presence, says to him: "Sorry, Officer!" Apparently, he was having a bad dream.

The policeman now turns and walks away.

~

The time is 8:00 AM. Archer Tucker is sleeping in the living room of his home. It looks like he had fallen asleep last night while he was sitting in his favorite chair. The fact is, the poor guy was so worried about Elisabeth being ill, that he just couldn't sleep; and after sitting up most of the night, he eventually nodded off.

Archer now begins to awake to the soothing aroma of freshly brewed coffee, and the sizzling sound and pleasing scent of frying bacon.

Assuming that Christopher is up and cooking, Archer gets up, and he proceeds to walk into the kitchen.

158

Upon entering the kitchen, Archer says: "Um! Um! Um! Man, that sure does smell good!"

"Good morning, Art," Elisabeth says.

"Elisabeth! It's you! I didn't expect you to be up! I thought it was Christopher!" Archer says, surprised and amazed. He continues: "How are you feeling?"

"I feel great!" Elisabeth replies.

"That's wonderful to hear!" Archer smiles and says. He continues: "We were so worried about you last night! I thought for sure that you would still be in bed this morning!"

"Thanks for being concerned, but today, I couldn't feel any better!" Elisabeth cheerfully exclaims.

"How are you this morning, Art?" Elisabeth asks.

"Oh, I'm doing fine. But, I'll be even better, once I get some of that good smelling coffee that you made!" Archer says.

"Sure, here let me pour you some. And, how about some bacon, eggs, and biscuits too?" Elisabeth says.

"Sure, that sounds great!" Archer smiles and says. He then asks: "Do you mind if I turn the radio on?"

"No, I don't mind at all, go right ahead," Elisabeth says.

Archer now walks over to and he sits down at the kitchen table, which is located next to a window. And he reaches for the radio that's seated on top of the window ledge, and he turns it on. Immediately, the refreshing sound of soothing, easy listening music begins to fill the air.

~

The time is 8:15 AM. Up in the ICU of the Good Samaritan Hospital, the door to room 315 slowly opens, and in walks a nurse carrying a medical instrument tray with items on it. Startled by what she sees, her jaws drop open! And, involuntarily dropping the tray on the floor, she says: "Oh, my God!" Afterwards, she quickly turns and she proceeds to run out of the room and down to the Nurses Station where a doctor happens to be standing.

Overcome with emotion, the startled nurse says to the doctor: "Doctor, Laurence, come quick!"

Walking fast, the nurse leads the doctor to room 315, which happens to be the room where the little girl named Elsie Rinehart, is stationed.

When the Nurse and Doctor enter Elsie's room, the Doctor is simply amazed by what he sees! Elsie is wide awake, sitting up in bed, singing, and playing with her doll!

Doctor Laurence, with a shocked look on his face, says to the nurse: "It's unbelievable!"

In the meantime, Elsie's mother and father, Margery and Carl Rinehart are in the elevator, enroute to Else's room. They are returning from the hospital's cafeteria that's located on the first floor. Both of them were in Elsie's room earlier this morning, but then they stepped out for a moment, while she was sleeping, in order to clear their heads and to get some coffee.

Now, as it so happens, the startling news about Elise's improved condition has spread like wildfire amongst the hospital staff; and more Doctors and Nurses, who are hearing the good news about her, have come to see her; as a steady flow of them are entering and leaving her room.

~

When Elise's parents, who are now returning from the cafeteria, reach the Nurses Station in the ICU, they notice that there's a lot of commotion and activity going on in their daughter's room. Margery, imagining that the worst has happened, panics, and she says to Carl: "Oh no! What has happened to our Daughter?" Then, she and Carl make a mad dash to her room to find out.

~

The moment Elise's parents enter her room, they simply cannot believe their eyes! Their daughter is up and doing well! Now, overwhelmed with emotion, Margery begins to cry tears of joy! Reaching out her hands, she approaches her daughter, lifts her out of bed, and she proceeds to hug and kiss her over and over again. And, she says to her: "Look at you! You're all better now! Your Momma loves you so much, my beautiful little princess!"

Elsie's father Carl is also overcome with emotion, and he begins to breakdown and cry. At seeing this, his wife Margery walks over to him with Elsie in her arms, and they all unite in a big family hug.

Carl, with tears streaming down his face, now takes Elsie into his arms, and he hugs and kisses her, and says: "Daddy loves you baby girl!"

Elsie's Mother now turns, and she admiringly looks at Doctor Laurence, and she says to him: "Thank you so much Doctor Laurence for saving our daughter from the Probias Plague!"

"To be honest with you, Mrs. Rinehart, we don't know how your daughter recovered from the carcinogenic virus," Doctor Laurence says. He continues: "Up until this morning we had seen no improvement in her medical condition. As a matter of fact, her condition had only grown progressively worse. And we were at our wits end as to what to do for her next."

"Well then, how do you explain her remarkable turnaround?" Mrs. Rinehart asks.

"I don't know what to tell you. The only explanation that I can offer at this time, is that the human body is a remarkable thing; sometimes, it will find a way to heal itself. I guess in Elise's case, this happens to be the exception!" Doctor Laurence says.

Eventually, after the Doctors and Nurses leave Elise's room, Margery, with a puzzled look on her face, says to her husband Carl: "There's something very strange going on here, Carl!"

"What do you mean?" Carl asks.

"It just doesn't seem to add up or make any sense what's so ever!" Margery says.

"What doesn't make sense?" Carl asks.

"It doesn't make sense how Elise could have gotten better on her own, after all, you seen the bad shape that she was in! Even the Doctors had given up all hope!" Margery replies.

"I think that it's what Doctor Laurence said. That the human body is a remarkable thing, and that sometimes it finds a way to heal itself!" Carl says.

"Yeah, but overnight? She had the Probias Plague, Carl! Also, what about the other patients that have it, they haven't gotten any better! I have a feeling that there's something more to it!" Margery says.

Coincidently, as it so happens, news reporter, Brent Richardson, from KDWA SpyCast News has just arrived at the Good Samaritan Hospital, in order to investigate and report on the viral outbreak. As he enters the hospital, he happens to overhear one of the nurses say to a fellow nurse: "Isn't it amazing how the little three year old girl up in the ICU fully recovered from the deadly virus?"

"I know what you mean. It's a miracle! Her parents must be so happy! I hear that she's being discharged from the hospital today!" the 2nd Nurse says.

The Reporter excuses himself and, he says to the two nurses: "Excuse me, but I couldn't help but to overhear your conversation about the little girl. Do you mind if I ask what her name is?

"I believe her name is Elise. Yep, that's right, Elise Rinehart," the 1st Nurse replies.

"What floor is the ICU on?" the Reporter inquires.

"The third floor," the 2nd Nurse says.

"Thank you!" the Reporter says. Then he turns and he heads towards the elevator.

∼

Back up in room 315 of the ICU, the Rinehart's are gathering their daughter's belongings and preparing to take Elsie home. The Doctors have given her a clean bill of health, and she has been officially discharged from the hospital.

While Margery is packing Elsie's bag, she happens to spot a small glass bottle on the floor beneath the bed. Bending down, she picks it up. "It's empty," she says. And then, suddenly, she remembers the colored boy that she saw last night in Elsie's room. She recalls how he was holding the bottle up to Elsie's mouth.

Margery now looks at Carl and, she says: "Carl, wait here and watch Elsie for a moment. I'll be right back." She then walks to the Nurses Station, and she says to the nurse at the desk: "Excuse me nurse. But, there was a colored boy in my daughter Elise's room last night. He gave her something to drink, and then he ran out of the room."

"I just started my shift a little while ago… but, oh yeah, I heard about that!" the Nurse says.

"Do you know what happened to him or where he is?" Margery asks.

"He was arrested and taken to the Police Station," the Nurse recalls.

"Thank you!" Margery says. Then she turns and she hurries back to Elsie's room.

∼

When Margery gets back to Elsie's room, she says to her husband: "Let's go, Carl! Grab Elsie's bag."

Carl, noticing that Margery is in a major hurry to leave, says to her: "What's the big hurry, Margery? Is there something wrong?"

"I don't know, but I think that I might have made a big mistake!" Margery says.

"A mistake. What mistake?" Carl asks.

"Come on, I'll tell you all about it on the way," Margery replies.

"Where are we going?" Carl inquisitively asks.

"To the Police Station," Margery answers.

"To the Police Station? What for," Carl asks.

"You'll see!" Margery says.

~

News reporter, Brent Richardson is still on the first floor of the Hospital. He is standing at the elevator door waiting for the elevator to come. Also, the two Nurses that he had spoken to earlier about Elsie are standing nearby. Suddenly, the elevator door opens and out steps the Rinehart family. Instantly, one of the nurses recognizes Elise. So she quickly approaches and says to her: "It's Elise! Our little miracle girl! Are you leaving us today sweetie? I'm so happy for you!"

When news reporter, Brent Richardson, who had just stepped into the elevator, hears the name Elsie, and the Nurse talking to her, he quickly steps back out before the door closes. And he approaches Elise, and he says to her parents: "Excuse me, Sir and Ma'am, but is this Elsie Rinehart?"

"Yes, why do you ask?" Margery replies.

The reporter introduces himself. And then he proceeds to inquire, first hand information, about Elsie's illness and recovery.

~

Back at Archer Tucker's home, Archer and Elisabeth have just finished eating breakfast.

"Thanks, Elisabeth. That was a wonderful breakfast!" Archer appreciatively says.

"You're welcome, Archer!" Elisabeth replies.

Suddenly, the music abruptly stops playing on the radio, and then, over the radio waves comes the following news report. A male voice says: "We are interrupting this program to bring you the following live news report. Hello, this is Reporter, Brent Richardson, reporting to you from KDWA SpyCast News. We are broadcasting live from the Wright County Jail. Standing here next to me is the Rinehart family. With us are Carl and Margery, and their three year old daughter, Elise. As radio listeners, I think that you'll find their story most interesting!" He continues: "Mrs. Rinehart, what brings you and your family to the County Jail today?"

"We are here to speak to one of the inmates that we believe has had a profound effect on the life of our three year old daughter, Elsie," Margery relates.

"I believe the inmate that you're referring to is a young colored man named, Christopher Pascale?" the News Reporter says.

"That's correct!" Margery replies.

The moment Elisabeth and Archer hear Christopher's name mentioned on the radio, they are shocked!

"It's Christopher!" Elisabeth yells out. Then she and Archer continue to listen attentively to the news report.

News Reporter, Brent Richardson now asks Margery: "Mrs. Rinehart, can you tell us your story?"

"Sure. Up until early this morning, our daughter Elise was extremely ill! She had been diagnosed and hospitalized at the Good Samaritan Hospital for having an extremely rare viral disease, for which there is no known cure. Authorities are calling it the "Probias Plague." Over several days her medical condition had grown progressively worse, and the Doctors at the hospital were not offering any hope that she would ever recover, but then, a very strange, amazing, and wonderful thing happened!" Margery says.

"What was that?" the News Reporter asks.

"Last night, when I was up in the hospital ICU with Elise, at one point, I had stepped out of the room for a moment, in order to take care of a personal matter. But, then, when I returned, I saw a young colored boy leaning over my daughter Elsie's bed. In fact, he was pouring a small bottle of something into her mouth. Of course, at seeing this, I panicked, and I said to him: 'Who are you? What are you doing in here? And, what was that, that you just gave to my daughter?' This of course frightened the boy, and he quickly ran out of the room. But, a short time later, he was caught and arrested by the police. I don't know what the mysterious bottle of liquid was that the boy gave to our daughter? All we know is that now, she is no longer ill! As matter of fact, as of this morning, the Doctors have given Elsie a totally clean bill of health, and she was officially discharged from the hospital about a half hour ago!" Margery says.

As Margery is relating her story, Elisabeth begins to recall that Christopher had also given her a bottle of something to drink last night, when she was lying ill in bed. Then she begins to connect Elise's miraculous recovery to her own.

Elisabeth is worried and afraid for Christopher. She says to Archer: "Oh no! My poor Christopher is in jail! I've got to get down there right away!"

"Yes. I understand! You better go!" Archer says.

Elisabeth quickly gets up, grabs her purse, and she runs out of the house, jumps in her car, and then speedily drives away.

~

By the time Margery Rinehart has finished giving News Reporter, Brent Richardson her story, a sizable, mixed-race crowd of people

166

have formed in front of the County Jailhouse. They are there in order get the scoop on what's going on. Both white and black people have assembled.

~

Eventually, Elisabeth's finally arrives at the County Jailhouse. Upon seeing a large crowd of people standing in front of the building, she quickly pulls her car over to the curb and parks across the street. Then she gets out, and she runs over to the Jailhouse. And, after working her way through the crowd, she finally manages to make her way up to the front door of the building. But, when she tries to enter the Jailhouse, she is immediately stopped by two policemen who are standing guard.

Elisabeth says to the Policemen: "I need to get in there to see my son!"

"We're sorry Ma'am, but nobody is allowed to go in!" one of the officers responds.

"But, I need to get in to see my son!" Elisabeth says.

"I'm sorry, but we have strict orders not to let *anyone* in!" the Policeman says.

"But, he's only a boy!" Elisabeth exclaims.

"I'm sorry, but there's nothing that I can do!" the Policeman replies.

While Elisabeth is speaking to the Police Officer, it happens that Carl Rinehart is standing nearby in the crowd, and he overhears the discussion between Elisabeth and the Policeman.

Carl feels bad for Elisabeth, and, although, not knowing who she is, he approaches and says: "Excuse me, Ma'am. But I couldn't help but overhear your conversation. I'm sorry to hear about your son. It must be hard?"

"Yes, it is!" Elisabeth exclaims.

"What's your son's name?" Carl asks.

"His name is Christopher. Christopher Pascale," Elisabeth says.

"You're kidding me? Well, I'll be!" Carl says, with a surprise look on his face. Then, suddenly, he spots a close friend standing in the crowd. And then, continuing their conversation, Carl says to Elisabeth: "May I ask, what is your name Ma'am?"

"My name is Elisabeth," Elisabeth replies.

"Hi, Elisabeth," Carl says, as he reaches out and shakes her hand. He continues: "I may be able to help you. Wait here for a moment. And I'll be right back."

After Carl leaves Elisabeth's side, he proceeds to walk over to his friend in the crowd, and he whispers something in his ear. Afterwards, the two of them approach Elisabeth.

"Elisabeth, this is my good friend, Francis Higgins. He's going to help you to see your son," Carl says.

"It's a pleasure to meet you, Elisabeth," Mr. Higgins says. He continues: "Carl tells me that your son is locked up in jail, and that they won't let you see him."

"Yes, Mr. Higgins, that's correct!" Elisabeth confirms.

"Well, let's see what we can do about that! Please come with me," Mr. Higgins says. Then the two of them, along with Carl, proceed to approach the front door of the jailhouse.

When Elisabeth, Mr. Higgins, and Carl reach the front door of the jailhouse, they are met and stopped by the two police officers standing guard.

Mr. Higgins says to the policemen: "I demand to see the Chief of Police, Richard Bioff!"

"And whom might you be?" one of the Police Officers asks in a rude tone.

"I'm Alderman, Francis Higgins!" Mr. Higgins says.

"Yes, Mr. Higgins! I'll get him right away, Sir!" the Policeman now respectfully says. Then, he turns and he quickly enters the building, and within a matter of moment or so he returns, along with Chief Bioff.

The moment Chief Bioff steps outside of the jailhouse, he sees Alderman, Francis Higgins standing there, and his face lights up with a big smile, and in a delighted tone he says to him: "Why, if it isn't my good old friend Alderman, Higgins! What brings you down here today?"

"Hello, Chief Bioff. This is my friend, Elisabeth," Mr. Higgins says, as he fully directs his attention to Elisabeth. He continues: "Her son happens to be one of your inmates, and she would like to see him."

"Sure! I think we can arrange that!" the Chief smiles and says. And, turning to Elisabeth, he says: "Hi, Elisabeth. What's your son's name?"

"His name is Christopher Pascale," Elisabeth says.

The Chief is stunned! And with a puzzled look on his face, he says to Elisabeth: "You mean that colored boy that was brought in last night?"

"Yes, that's him! That's my Christopher!" Elisabeth confirms.

"Well, I don't know if we can let you see him?" the Chief says.

"But you just said that I could see him!" Elisabeth says, both shocked and confused.

"Yeah, but…" responds the Chief.

Alderman Higgins, immediately recognizing that Chief Bioff is about to go back on his word; steps forward, and in a friendly fashion, he gently takes the Chief by his arm, and he says to him: "Chief, come here for a moment." He then proceeds to lead him over to a semi-private area. And he turns and faces him, and says: "Now, Chief, you owe me one. I need you to let this woman see her son!"

"Yeah, but I didn't know that the colored boy was her son! Since when do we start giving coloreds special privileges and treatment? After all, he's being held on some very serious charges — that being aggravated assault, and attempted murder of a little white girl," Chief Bioff remarks.

"Now, chief, from what I was told, that's not true. Also, the girl's own parents are here to drop all charges!" Alderman Higgins says. He continues: "So what do you say; can Mrs. Pascale please see her son?"

After pausing to think about it for a moment, the Chief says: "Alright, I'll grant you this favor this time!"

"Thanks, Chief! I appreciate it!" Mr. Higgins says.

As they turn and proceed to walk back over towards Elisabeth, the Chief says to Mr. Higgins: "Francis, why do you always bring me things like this?"

"Because our wives happen to be sisters," Mr. Higgins smiles and says.

~

When Chief, Bioff, and Alderman, Higgins approach Elisabeth, they are joined by Margery, Elsie, and Carl Rinehart.

The Chief says to Elisabeth: "Follow me, Elisabeth." Afterwards, all of them: Elisabeth, Margery, Elise, Carl, Alderman Higgins, and Chief Bioff approach and enter the jailhouse together.

When KDWA SpyCast News reporter Brent Richardson sees Elisabeth, along with Chief Bioff and the others entering the

Jailhouse together, he attempts to follow them through the door, but he is quickly restrained and pushed back by the two policemen standing guard.

~

A jail cell door opens. And a policeman yells out: "Christopher Pascale!"

"Yes," Christopher answers.

"Your mother is here. You are free to go!" the Policeman says.

Upon hearing the exciting news, Christopher immediately hops out of bed and he quickly exits the cell; after which, he is then led by two escorting police officers through a series of secured doors, and then into the lobby of the criminal booking area.

The moment Christopher and the policemen enter the booking area, Christopher immediately spots his mother Elisabeth, and she sees him too. In response, they spontaneously run to each other, and warmly embrace.

Christopher excitedly says: "Mom, you're well!"

"Yes, I am son. It's a miracle!" Elisabeth replies.

Elisabeth, now recognizes that Christopher has a split lip, and stains of dried up drops of blood on his shirt. So she says to him with a concerned voice: "Christopher, you're hurt! You've been bleeding! What happened?"

"Don't worry Mom, I'm fine!" Christopher says, as he quickly shrugs it off.

While Christopher and Elisabeth are talking to one another, the Rinehart family approaches them. Their daughter Elsie is in the arms of her father Carl.

When Christopher sees Elsie, he is very happy to see her. With joyful eyes, and an endearing smile, he says to her in a soft and cheerful tone of voice: "Hey little one! I'm glad to see that you're well!"

"Hi," Elise replies, as she flashes a big smile back.

Elisabeth, now, respectfully acknowledging the Rinehart's authority and willingness to have her son Christopher released from jail, says to them: "Mr. and Mrs. Rinehart, I want to thank you so much for dropping all charges on my son Christopher."

"No problem, it's the least that we could do! After all, your son saved our daughter Elsie's life!" Carl says.

Margery Rinehart now turns and she addresses Christopher, and she says to him: "Christopher, can I ask you a question?"

"Sure," Christopher says.

"When you were up in our daughter Elsie's hospital room last night, what was in the bottle that you gave to her?" Margery asks.

"It was Dexatromvonseratomin," Christopher replies.

Bewildered and amazed by what he said, a dead silence falls upon everyone in the room.

Christopher continues: "But, for short, I call it 'Emerald Green.' It's a natural medicine!"

"Where did you get it from?" Margery asks.

"From a tree," Christopher replies.

"From a tree," Margery says.

"Yes, a tree. It's a very special tree!" Christopher remarks.

"What makes it so special?" Margery asks.

"It's special because it's the only one of a kind. I planted, nurtured, and raised it myself!" Christopher explains.

"Where is this tree?" Carl asks.

"It's in a secret place," Christopher says.

"I knew that it was you that made our daughter well. Thank you so much!" Margery says.

"You're welcome!" Christopher replies.

"Christopher, is it also because of your "Emerald Green," that I too am not sick anymore?" Elisabeth asks.

"Yes, Mom. I administered a dose of it to you last night when you were sick in bed," Christopher says.

"I remember!" Elisabeth says. Then she begins to cry tears of joy. And she hugs her son, and kisses him on his cheek.

A police officer now approaches the Rinehart's and Pascale's, and he says to them: "I'm sorry folks, but I'm going to have to ask you to break it up, and move along!"

"Ok officer, we're leaving right now," Carl says. He then turns to Elisabeth, and asks: "Elisabeth, do you and Christopher need a ride home?"

"No, my car is parked right across the street. But thanks anyways!" Elisabeth says.

Next, the police officer proceeds to escort all of them out the building.

~

As the Pascale's and Rinehart's exit the Police Station, SpyCast News reporter, Brent Richardson, and a large crowd of curious people are still patiently waiting outside. Suddenly, a woman in the crowd points her finger at Christopher, and she yells out: "There he is! There's Christopher!" And like a herd of stampeding cattle, the excited crowd begins rushing towards him.

When Elisabeth sees the crowd rushing in upon them, she realizes that she needs to get Christopher to safety immediately! Quickly, glancing across the street, she looks over to the location where her car is parked. But wait! Her car is missing! In response, she says out loud: "Oh no! My car is gone! It must have gotten towed!"

"Don't worry, we'll take you home! Follow us, quickly!" Carl says.

Without delay, and with news reporter, Brent Richardson and the crowd starting to press in upon them, Elisabeth and Christopher manage to slip away, and they quickly follow the Rinehart's to their car.

After running a little ways, the Rinehart's and Pascale's finally make it safely to Carl's car. Then, they immediately pile in; Carl starts the engine; and they drive away.

Elisabeth, now feeling a sigh of relief, but still shocked and bewildered by the crowd's response, says: "My goodness! What was that all about?"

"The people must have heard about Christopher, and how he healed Elise of the Probias Plague. And now they want to see him!" Margery says.

"Wow, that was crazy! I'm glad that you and Carl were there to give us a ride home!" Elisabeth exclaims.

In the meantime, back at the County Jailhouse, Chief, Richard Bioff picks up the receiver of his rotary desk phone, and he dials out. And, after several rings, a man answers on the other end.

Chief Bioff says: "Mr. Harrington, this is Chief of Police, Richard Bioff. How are you?"

The Chief pauses to listen to a Mr. Harrington's response, and then he continues, saying, in regards to his family: "Good! How are the wife and son?"

Again, the Chief pauses to hear a response. Then he continues, saying: "Good! Say, the reason I called is that I just came into contact with something very intriguing and very lucrative, that I think you would be highly interested in. It's guaranteed to make the two of us a whole lot of money!"

The Chief again pauses to hear a response, and then he says: "I'd rather not talk about it over the phone. But instead, how about we meet tonight at eight o'clock down at Lucky Luchino's Restaurant, and I'll tell you all about it then?"

Once again, the Chief pauses for a response, and then he says: "Oh, and by the way, make sure that you bring all of the guys along with you too!"

Finally, after pausing to hear one final response, the Chief ends the call, by saying: "Ok, see you tonight!"

~

Carl Rinehart's car now pulls up in front of Archer Tucker's house and stops. And then, Christopher and Elisabeth get out and wave goodbye.

"Thanks for the ride home!" Elisabeth says, as the car slowly drives away. Afterwards, she and Christopher proceed to walk up to the house and enter in.

17

THE GATHERING

It is 7:50 PM. And a man and woman walk into Lucky Luchino's Restaurant, and request a table for two. The Restaurant Host says: "I'm sorry, Sir. But as you can see, we have a packed house tonight. Presently there's about a 30 minute wait for a table. However, if you'd like, you may take a seat at our cocktail bar, and we'll call you as soon as one becomes available."

"Ok, that will be fine," the Man says. Afterwards, he and his lady friend walk over to and seat themselves at the cocktail bar.

The front door of the restaurant opens again. And, in walks two men dressed in formal attire. As they proceed towards the Host Station, the Host says: "Good evening, Mr. Leachman!"

"Is the boss in?" Mr. Leachman asks.

"Yes. He is, Sir. He's in the backroom with the others!" the Host relates.

"Ok, good!" Mr. Leachman says. And then he and the other man with him head straight for the backroom.

~

After Mr. Leachman and his friend arrive at and enter the backroom of the Restaurant, Mr. Leachman immediately walks straight up to Michael Harrington, who is seated in a chair at the head of a long conference table. Interestingly, Michael looks pretty much the same as he did 20 years ago, but now he's just older, and a little more filled out.

When Michael sees Mr. Leachman approaching him, he smiles and he stands up, and he says: "Well, if it isn't my good old friend Mayor, Jarvis Leachman! I'm glad that you could make it!"

"I wouldn't have missed it for the whole world!" Mayor Leachman says. Afterwards, both men give each other a cordial hug and a hardly hand shake. But then, suddenly, the Mayor notices Michael's wristwatch. And, being highly impressed, he says: "Wow! That's a really nice watch that you're wearing Michael!"

"Thank you," Michael replies.

"Where did you get it?" Jarvis asks, out of curiosity.

"I won it in a poker game," Michael says, after pausing for a moment. But, in truth he knows that the watch really belonged to Randall Pascale, the young colored man that he killed some 20 years or so ago; a murder that he happened to get away with, Scott Free, because the local law authorities failed to properly investigate the crime. And, who, also at the time, according to their own secretive words, said: "We don't deem it necessary to investigate this crime any further, seeing that it happened to an insignificant, colored boy."

Michael Harrington now addresses everyone present, and he says: "Let's be seated!"

~

After everyone is seated at the conference table, Michael says to the group: "I, the owner of this fine restaurant establishment, and foremost, the original founder and CEO (Chief Executive Officer) of 'Sunrise Pharmaceutical Drugs Corporation,' the number one Pharmaceutical Company in the nation, in which all of you have invested stock, first of all would like to thank our dear friend, the Chief of Police, Richard Bioff, for calling together this important meeting."

The Chief smiles, nods his head, and lifts his drinking glass in acknowledgement and appreciation of Michael's sincere words.

Michael continues, saying: "And now that all of us are here, we can get started. I suppose that all of you have heard the exciting news about a recent medical cure that was discovered, which can cure the fatal virus, the "Probias Plague." And, who knows what else it might cure? The human race has never seen anything like it! It's a medical breakthrough of epoch proportions! I know that it sounds wonderful. And it is! However, there's one huge problem associated with it. The problem is, this medical wonder was not found or brought forth by us. But rather, it was discovered by some Negro boy."

Michael continues: "Gentlemen, I don't know what your take is on this, but we absolutely cannot allow a medical breakthrough of this magnitude to be credited to someone else, let alone this boy! Can you just imagine what this could do to our reputation and image? Also, think about all the money that we stand to lose out on! Because people will no longer solely depend on Sunrise Pharmaceutical Drugs for their medicinal cures anymore. It could completely ruin us! But not only that, it could also start to change the way white citizens of Frogtown start to view the colored people of Shytown. Rather than looking upon them as a weaker race, with inferior intellectual capabilities, they might start to view them as equals, which according to my opinion would be a huge mistake that could wind up costing us dearly!"

Michael continues: "Need I remind you that the notion that the black race is inferior; was a lie that was masterly and artfully contrived in the past by the founding forefathers of this great country. In a nutshell, what they conceived and perpetrated amounted to slander or character assassination. The result of which, destroyed the African slaves' image, their true character. In return, they were given a new identity, a made up image, which was that of a dumb, brute beast; a lie which has stayed the course of time throughout many generations, and which has worked out beautifully to the personal advantage and financial prosperity of the white race down to this very day!"

As Michael is speaking to the gathered group; sitting there with him in attendance, are some of the top leaders of the community; highly affluent men of enormous wealth, and prestigious, influential power.

One man at the meeting; a big business tycoon named, Earnest Rockwell, speaks up and he says: "We simply cannot allow things to change! I personally have too much to lose!"

"Me too," another man says.

"What can we do to stop this thing from happening?" a third man asks.

"We have to act on this thing fast, before the situation gets out of hand!" Michael says. He continues: "But, we also need to be extremely shrewd and highly innovative! Like our forefathers, we must devise a plan that will ultimately work for our benefit as leaders, as well as for the white populous in general."

Archbishop, St. Oliver Earl Glance, who happens to be in attendance at the meeting, speaks up and he asks: "What do you have in mind, Michael?"

"The human mind can easily be deceived. Think about a skilled magician, and how he uses sleight of hand techniques, distractions, smoking mirrors, and deception to create artfully contrived false images or illusions to fool the eyes and deceive the minds of his audience," Michael says.

Michael, now smiles, and then he leans forward, and he says: "Well then, this is what we're going to do…"

18

KEEPER OF THE TREE

After having spent the night in jail, Christopher is so happy to finally be back home. Later that night, while is sleeping, he begins to dream a dream. He is fleeing from three intimidating, fierce creatures. The creatures look somewhat like large lizards. But they have fiery colored, red eyes. The lower part of their body has four legs. Their upper body has two arms that are equipped with humongous, asymmetrical pinchers that resemble lobster claws, but only much sharper! And their tails are like rattle snakes.

Fearful and shocked by what he sees, Christopher begins to backpedal slowly. Then, he quickly turns, and begins running away as fast as he can!

The instant that Christopher begins to flee from the lizard-like creatures, they immediately jump down from the top of the cave to the ground below, and they begin chasing after him in hot pursuit!

The lizard-like creatures are extremely fast! And, within no time at all, they catch-up to Christopher, and they begin nipping at his legs and heels with their powerful, razor sharp pinchers!

Christopher is in a frantic panic! What's he going to do? He's running as fast as he can, and yet the creatures are right behind him! What can he do to lose them? Suddenly, as he looks up and into the not too far distance ahead of him, he sees that he is fast approaching a ravine. Thinking quickly, it occurs to him that if he can jump across it, then he can get away safe. But wait! As he gets closer to it, the ravine appears to be just too wide and too deep for him to jump across. Oh no! What's he going to do now?

What a dilemma! Christopher knows that if he stops running the lizard-like creatures will catch him, and use their powerful pinchers to crush and tear him apart! Yet, on the other hand, if he attempts to jump the ravine, and he falls short of the distance, he will fall over 300 feet to his death at the bottom, upon jagged rocks! Or, if by chance, he happens to miss the deadly rocks, he will plunge into the depths of a raging river that flows rapidly through the ravine, and be swept away! Either fate could prove to be deadly!

Now, with only a split second left to react, Christopher decides to go for it. Approaching the edge of the ravine, he takes a deep breath. And then, like an Olympic broad jumper, he pushes off with his left leg, really hard, and he leaps as far as he can go across the ravine.

When Christopher jumps the ravine, the lizard-like creatures follow right behind him. However, they immediately fall over the edge of the cliff! Two of them plummet and fall upon the jagged rocks at the bottom of the ravine, and upon impact their bodies explode and burst apart!

As far as the fate of the third lizard-like creature goes, it just barely misses the rocks! But it falls into the water, and is quickly swept away by the raging river!

Christopher, on the other hand, is still airborne and approaching the opposite side of the ravine. But wait! It doesn't look like he's going to make it either! He has already reached the height of his jump, and now he is starting to descend downwards. Oh no!

As Christopher is falling, he lets out a mournful howl and big scream! And then, with a burst of renewed energy, he begins kicking his legs—like he's riding a bicycle. Luckily, the movement of his legs increases his forward momentum and gives him just the right amount of added height and distance that he needs to clear the ravine.

Interesting to note, is that when Christopher clears the ravine, his body lands only just a few inches past the edge of the cliff. Anything less, and he would have fallen to his death. Wow! What a close call!

Christopher is so thrilled to be safe and alive! As he lays there with his back against the ground, he breathes a big sigh of relief, and he takes in several deep breaths of fresh air. But then, suddenly, he hears a woman's voice. She is saying: "Help me! Please help!"

Christopher, now quickly rises to his feet, and he looks around the area. But he doesn't see anyone. Neither does he hear the voice anymore, which could help him to locate her. So he cries out with a loud voice, saying: "Hello! Is anyone there?" But there is no answer!

Christopher is exhausted! So he sits down on the ground to rest up a bit. But, just as soon as he starts to relax, the sound of the woman's voice occurs again. She is saying: "Help me! Please help!"

Once again, Christopher hops to his feet. But this time he tries to quickly pinpoint from what direction the voice is coming. As he listens closely, he observes that the voice appears to be coming from behind an elevated ridge that lies to the north, about 50 feet away from him. So without wasting any time at all, he proceeds to run there to take a look.

When Christopher reaches the top of the ridge, he climbs over the embankment, and he looks around, but strangely he finds that no one is there. The only thing standing in front of him is an old and decrepit tree, with a few dead leaves on it. And what a strange sight it is! The tree is bound with four heavy, iron chains that stretch upwards from the four corners of the earth, clear up to the very top of its upper limbs and branches.

Christopher, with a highly puzzled look on his face, and disappointment in his voice, mutters to himself in a low undertone, saying: "There's no one here, just an old tree! But, I could have sworn that I heard the sound of a voice coming from here?" Then, he turns around, and he begins to leave. Suddenly, he hears a voice behind him say: "Help me!"

Quickly turning back around, Christopher yells: "Hello! Is anyone there?" But again, he neither hears nor sees anyone, anywhere!

A moment of dead silence ensues.

Christopher is absolutely stymied! Where could the person be? He is starting to lose hope. Again, he calls out with a loud voice, saying: "Hello! Is anyone there? Where are you? Answer me!" But still, there's no answer.

Out of sheer frustration, Christopher now verbally utters to himself, saying: "Oh, forget it! What's the use?" Then, suddenly, he hears the voice again, saying: "Help me!"

At hearing the voice, Christopher says to himself "Wait a second. Am I hearing what I thought I heard? I know that I'm not losing my mind." He then takes a couple of steps backwards, and he proceeds to raise his head upwards at the old tree. And then, addressing the tree, he says to it: "Hello! Was that you?"

"Free me!" the Tree says.

Stunned, startled, and amazed, Christopher quickly takes a giant step backwards! Not believing what his ears just heard. That an object, such as a tree, could actually be communicating with him, he again asks the tree: "Was that you that was calling me?"

"Yes, it was me? Free me!" the Tree says.

"Well, I'll be! It was you!" Christopher's says, as his jaws drops open in sheer wonder and amazement.

Christopher now points to the thick iron chains that hang down from the tree, and he says to the Tree: "Who did this to you?"

"An enemy," the Tree replies.

"An, enemy. What enemy," Christopher asks.

"The enemy of the tree!" the Tree says.

"But, why would anyone want to harm you?" Christopher asks.

"The enemy is bent on destroying the world! I am a valuable source of life. I help to sustain all life forms on earth. Without me, everything will soon die! That is why you must help me, before it's too late!" the Tree says.

"What do you want me to do?" Christopher asks.

"Remove the chains, and free me!" the Tree says.

"But how am I to do that?" Christopher asks.

"You'll find a way. It's been prophesied that one day 'The Keeper of the Tree' will come and set me free. And you, Christopher, are he!" the Tree says.

~

Sadly, the truth is, planet earth has lost its natural healing powers. The reason being is because of man's careless and senseless polluting of the earth and its surrounding environment. The effect has wreaked havoc upon many things, but most importantly upon the trees in particular. The result is that the trees are now sick. They no longer contain the vital elements or properties that are needed to help cleanse the earth of enemy pollutants, and diseases.

Interestingly, trees not only produce life giving oxygen, but also they are the earth's natural cleansing, filtering, and regenerative system. The curing power that they possess is contained within their leaves.

Normally, the properties of the trees leaves contain special purifying agents that work to keep the earth's air and environment clean. The sun works to release these healthy properties into the surrounding atmosphere and environment, which in turn produces the perfect chemical balance that is needed to keep the earth and its inhabitants healthy. These miraculous agents also help to purify the rain, oceans, lakes, rivers, and soils. However, now that the trees lack the regenerative and curative powers that they once possessed, they are no longer able to cleanse planet earth, and keep it in perfect ecological balance, which makes it more susceptible for problems and diseases to arise.

Unfortunately, the earth's wellbeing isn't the only thing being threaten. In addition, mankind itself has personally become recipients of the trees misfortune. Because the trees are sick, and are failing to produce and release their natural purifying agents into the earth's biosphere, the chemical makeup of humans is slowly being altered. As a direct result, humans are now lacking certain necessary agents or properties in their bodies that are needed to keep them healthy. This makes them highly susceptible to sickness, disease, and premature aging and death. You see, just like the air, oceans, lakes, rivers, and soils, mankind's health and prosperity is also dependent upon the natural curative properties of the trees leaves.

As dismal and complicated as the problem may seem, manmade pollution is the root cause of the trees illness and weakened state. Due to his mismanagement, carelessness, and greed, mankind has damaged this natural cleansing, filtering, and regenerative system, which has resulted in serious problems to the ecosystems, and all of earth's life forms, including humans. A problem that has now reached alarming status, and which will ultimately lead to the extinction of all life forms, including the human race. As it presently stands, Wright County is the first to feel its horrific affects. But wait! There is still hope that the problem can be fixed! However, man is quickly running out of time! If something isn't done soon the damage will become irreversible!

~

Christopher, doubting that he is the foretold 'Keeper of the Tree,' but yet willing to help, says to the old, talking Tree: "I don't know if I am the foretold 'Keeper of the Tree,' but I'll see what I can do." He then proceeds to walk over to one of the four iron chains that are individually pinned to the ground with a large, steel stake, and he grabs hold of the stake with his bare hands. And then, struggling and straining with all of his might, he pulls upward on it. However, the stake does not move. Christopher can't even budge it, not even one inch! It's just too deeply imbedded in the ground.

Thinking that he might have better success with one of the other stakes, he proceeds to run over to it, and he tries to dislodge it from the ground. However, he quickly finds that it too is solidly fixed and immoveable!

Now, feeling completely helpless and defeated, Christopher says to the Tree: "I can't do it! They're impossible to pull up and remove!"

"You can do it! There's got to be another way!" the Tree says.

After carefully surveying and accessing the situation for awhile, Christopher observes that the four iron chains, that stretch upwards from the ground to the crown of the tree that they are individually connected to a large, iron ring that's located at the top and center of the tree. He also observes that the large ring seems to be fastened together with some type of locking device. He reasons that if he can reach and unlock the center ring, that perhaps this might release the four chains, and set the tree free. However, this will not be an easy task. It will require him to climb all the way to the top of the tree; a feat that he does not wish to attempt. But, unfortunately, he realizes that there seems to be no other way.

Christopher is terrified by the very thought of the climb. He says to the Tree: "Ok, Tree. I think the only possible way to free you, is for me to climb up to the very top of you, and unlock the center ring that holds the four iron chains together. However, that's not the biggest obstacle that stands in my way. The biggest problem is that I suffer from acrophobia. In other words, I am deathly fearful of heights! There's absolutely no way that I can climb all the way up there!"

"Yes you can! You can do it! I believe in you!" the Tree says.

Christopher pauses to think about it for a moment, and then after taking several deep breaths of fresh air, he proceeds to walk over to the tree, and he begins his slow upward climb.

As Christopher inches his way up the tree, he is so focused on the climb that he doesn't realize that danger is lurking in the not so far distance, for something is closely watching him. It is a large, carnivorous reptile or snake, with a head like a dragon. This enormous, frightening looking, monstrous Dragon Snake Beast is equipped with huge fangs! And its body is about 30 feet long! Totally aware of Christopher's presence, it begins to slowly slither its body along the ground, moving towards him and the tree.

After Christopher reaches the second set of lower tree limbs, he stops climbing for a moment, in order to calm his nerves and gather himself together. And then, after regaining his composure, he continues his upward climb.

The further up the tree that Christopher climbs, the more difficult it becomes for him.

Finally, after a considerable amount of concentrated effort, Christopher eventually reaches the halfway point of his climb. But then, he makes the biggest mistake of his life. He looks down. Oh no! Upon seeing the height and distance that he is up and away from the ground, only intensifies his fears! Immediately, his heart begins to beat faster and faster, and his body begins to quiver, shake, and grow weak. Poor Christopher is scarred out of his wits, as he clings on tight to the tree, with his arms wrapped firmly around it! Not wanting to proceed any further, he just sits there frozen, straddling a tree limb with his legs, and holding on to the tree trunk for dear life!

As Christopher sits there motionless in the tree, three hungry vultures appear in the sky overhead. And they begin to continuously circle the air above the tree, watching, and just waiting for him to fall.

When the Tree sees that Christopher has stopped climbing, and that the enemy Dragon Snake is close by, it begins to earnestly implore him, saying: "Keep going, Christopher! Come on, you can do it! Please, hurry! We're running out of time!"

After listening to the urgent prodding's of the Tree, Christopher takes a deep breath, and after mustering up courage, he continues his upward climb.

Eventually, although the going is extremely tough, Christopher finally completes his climb to the top of the tree. But wait! Just as soon as he reaches the top, the Dragon Snake arrives at the base of the tree.

Completely unaware that a monstrous Dragon Snake Beast is there, and that impending danger is near, Christopher reaches out his hand and he grabs hold of one of the iron chains that is nearest to him. And then, audibly speaking out loud to himself, he says: "Now, what I do?"

"You must remove the lock that holds the center ring and chains together!" the Tree says.

However, this is easier said than done. It's not going to be an easy task, because in order to get to and remove the lock, Christopher must stand up on top of the highest tree limb.

Realizing what he must do, Christopher gingerly proceeds to slowly raise his body up by holding on to both the tree trunk and an upper tree branch for security and stability. And, after much concentrated effort, he manages to finally stand up on top of the tree limb. But then, suddenly, he loses his footings and grip, and he slips and begins to fall. Oh no! But wait! As Christopher is falling, he somehow manages to quickly reach out and grab hold of the tree limb that he was standing on. Wow, what a miraculous save! However, he's still not out of the woods yet. Now, hanging from the tree with both of his feet dangling, he must try to pull himself back up and onto the limb.

When the Vultures, who are still circling the sky above, observe that Christopher is in trouble, they become increasingly excited in anticipation for him to fall.

Christopher is struggling, doing all that he can, not only to hold on to the tree limb, so that he doesn't fall, but also to climb back up upon it.

Finally, after struggling and straining with all of his might, he manages to pull himself back up and onto the tree limb.

Christopher, realizing that he just escaped a major catastrophe, breathes a big sigh of relief! However, little does he realize that his troubles are far from being over! For the Dragon Snake, who is at the base of the tree, is beginning to work its way up towards him!

When the Tree sees that the Dragon Snake is moving upwards towards Christopher, it cries out to him, saying: "Christopher, watch out! Watch out! For the enemy is here!"

When Christopher hears the Tree's foreboding alarm, he immediately looks downward and he sees the Dragon Snake coming towards him. Shocked and frightened by what he sees! He panics, and he says: "What in the world is that! Oh no! What am I going to do?"

Poor Christopher is trapped like a rat, with nowhere to go! But then, suddenly, he spots a nearby tree branch that resembles a sword. So he climbs out and over to it, and he breaks it off, so that he can use it as a weapon, in an attempt to fight and hold off the monstrous Dragon Snake Beast.

The Dragon Snake, who has slowly drawn closer, now approaches the tree limb that Christopher is perched upon, and then it proceeds to slowly slither its way out towards him.

As the Dragon Snake gets close to Christopher, it begins to coil its upper body, and then in a flash, it lunges forward and strikes at him!

Christopher, welding the tree branch in his hand like a sword, instantly thrusts it forward at the Dragon Snake's head! In response, the Dragon Snake quickly moves backwards! But then, without hesitation, it immediately strikes a second time!

Once again, Christopher thrusts his stick out forcefully at the Dragon Snake. This time the sharp pointed end of the stick happens to hit him in one of its eyes, and it pokes it out!

The Dragon Snake is furious! With a loud hissing noise, it lunges forward and it strikes at Christopher a third time! This time Christopher manages to swat him real hard on top of his head with his stick, and it quickly retreats. But the Dragon Snake is tenacious. Still not giving up the fight, it lunges forward and it strikes a fourth time! In response, Christopher immediately swings his stick at it, but this time the Dragon Snake grabs it with its mouth, plucks it from his hand, and the stick falls to the ground.

Christopher is now totally unarmed; recognizing this, the Dragon Snake strikes at him a fifth time! In response, Christopher manages to dodge out of its way, but then he loses his balance, slips off the tree limb, and he begins falling to the ground!

As Christopher falls, like a lifeless ragdoll from the top of the tree, his body strikes against several tree limbs and branches on his downward flight, which is extremely painful. However, inadvertently, this helps to somewhat reduce and slow down the speed of his fall. Nevertheless, when his falling body finally approaches the bottom of the tree, he still hits the lowest tree limb really hard, and then he falls to the ground.

Fortunately for Christopher, the tree limbs and branches did help to significantly soften the final impact of his fall. However, the force is still great enough that it knocks him unconscious.

Sometime later, when Christopher regains consciousness, he finds that the Dragon Snake is hovering directly over him, and staring him right in the eyes. Christopher is terrified! He doesn't know what to do! So he just remains motionless, in a frozen-like state.

Suddenly, the Dragon Snake begins to strike, but Christopher manages to quickly move out of its way! And then, swiftly rising to his feet, he begins to run!

The Dragon Snake is catlike quick. And within an instance, it chases Christopher down, and it trips him up. Once again, Christopher's body goes crashing to the ground!

With Christopher now lying helplessly with his back against the ground, the Dragon Snake quickly approaches him. Then, raising its ugly head one last time for a final and fatal strike, it hisses at him, and then, opening its large mouth wide, with its huge fangs exposed, it lunges forward to deliver the deathblow! In frightful response, Christopher closes his eyes, grimaces, and screams! Suddenly, a voice calls out: "Christopher! Christopher! Are you alright?"

It's Christopher's mother, Elisabeth. She overheard him, and she has come to wake him up from his bad dream.

When Christopher hears his mother's voice, he begins to awake from sleep. Still feeling groggy, he asks: "Is that you, mom?"

"Yes. It's me, son. You were just having a bad dream, but it's okay, I'm here now," Elisabeth says.

"It all seemed so real!" Christopher says, as he breathes a big sigh of relief.

"I know, but it's alright now, everything's okay, just go back to sleep," Elisabeth says.

Elisabeth's calm demeanor and soothing voice greatly comforts her son, and he quickly falls back asleep. Afterwards, she exits the room.

~

Early the next morning, while Christopher, Elisabeth, and Archer are eating breakfast at the dining room table, suddenly, they hear the sound of loud noises coming from outside in front of Archer's house. Curious as to what's causing all the commotion, Elisabeth proceeds to get up from the table, and she walks into the living room and over to a large, front, bay window to investigate.

When Elisabeth pulls back the window curtain, to her surprise, she sees that the front lawn is covered with a large crowd of people. Both white and black people are there, young and old.

Elisabeth, now donning a puzzled look on her face, whispers to herself in a low undertone, saying: "What in the world is going on? Why are all of these people here?" Then, she quickly closes the curtain, and steps away from the window.

Christopher now enters the living room, and he says to Elisabeth: "Hey, mom, what's all the noise about?"

"There's a crowd of people outside!" Elisabeth says.

"What do they want?" Christopher asks.

"I don't know, but I'm going to find out!" Elisabeth says, as she proceeds to walk over to the front door, and opens it up.

When the front door opens, Elisabeth is anxiously greeted by several news reporters, including KDWA SpyCast News Reporter, Brent Richardson.

One reporter, who aggressively approaches Elisabeth, asks: "Are you, Elisabeth Pascale?"

"Yes, I'm Elisabeth," Elisabeth replies.

"Does Christopher Pascale live here?" a second reporter asks.

"Yes," Elisabeth says.

"Is Christopher your son?" a third reporter asks.

"Yes. What's this all about?" Elisabeth inquires.

The 1st Reporter asks: "Did your son Christopher give some sort of medicinal cure to a young girl named, Elsie Rinehart, who was hospitalized for having the incurable virus, the "Probias Plague," and now she is well?"

"I don't know what you're talking about?" Elisabeth responds, as she feigns ignorance.

Suddenly, Christopher steps in front of the doorway. Upon seeing him, a person in the crowd yells out, saying: "There he is! There's Christopher!"

The entire crowd now becomes anxiously excited, and they began to entreat him, saying: "Heal us! Please heal us?"

Elisabeth, shocked and taken aback by what the crowd is saying, steps in front of Christopher. Then, protectively shielding him with her body, she begins pushing him back inside of the house. Afterwards, she also steps inside, and quickly closes the door behind them.

Archer Tucker now enters the living room, and he asks: "What's going on, Elisabeth?"

"There's a crowd of people outside!" Elisabeth says.

"A crowd. What do they want?" Archer asks.

"It's a long story. Let's sit down, and I'll explain," Elisabeth says.

After Christopher, Elisabeth, and Archer are seated, Elisabeth tells Archer: "There was a little girl up in the hospital where Christopher works that was extremely ill, apparently she was dying from the Probias Plague. Christopher came to learn of it, and he gave her some sort of curative medicine that he made, which he named 'Emerald Green,' and she got completely well. And now people are beginning to think that he can cure them of their illnesses too!"

"What do you think Elisabeth? Do you think it's possible that what Christopher gave the girl, did in fact cure her?" Archer asks.

"I don't know? All we know is that she no longer has the Probias virus! And what gets even stranger, is that Christopher also gave me some of his Emerald Green to drink when I was deadly sick, and now, I too am well!" Elisabeth says.

"You're kidding me!" Archer says.

"I kid you not. I'm telling you the truth," Elisabeth replies.

"That's incredible!" Archer says.

"Christopher, where did you get this 'Emerald Green' from?" Archer asks.

"I got it from a tree," Christopher says.

"From a tree," Archer says.

"Yep," Christopher says.

"Where is this tree?" Archer asks.

"It's in a secret place," Christopher says.

"Wow, Elisabeth, what are you going to do about this?" Archer asks.

"I don't know. But, if indeed, Christopher's Emerald Green does in fact contain some sort of remedial cure, then I believe that we have a moral sense of obligation or duty to use it to help others. But, of course, that is not mine nor anyone else's decision to make, it's totally up to Christopher, being that it's his Emerald Green," Elisabeth says.

After hearing what his mother Elisabeth says, Christopher without hesitation, says: "I want to help!"

Elisabeth smiles, and she embraces her son, and says: "I love you, Christopher!" Afterwards, Christopher sneaks out the backdoor of the house; gets on his bicycle; and he proceeds to ride it to his secret place, which is located a distance of about two miles away.

After riding for a while, Christopher eventually comes to a railroad crossing. Crossing the tracks, he turns left at the next street, and then he rides his bike down a long, dirt road.

When Christopher gets to the end of the dirt road, he approaches an old, vacant, dilapidated, abandoned, and boarded up building that is surrounded by a tall, chain-link, metal fence, with a broken entry gate.

Entering through the gate, Christopher rides his bicycle up to the building; then he gets off his bike; and he walks up to the boarded up front door. Next, he picks up an iron rod that's lying on the ground next to the door, and he uses it to pry the board away. Afterwards, he walks inside, and begins moving towards the back of the building.

Finally, after working his way through several dark rooms, Christopher comes to a set of large double doors marked shipping and receiving.

When Christopher opens one of the doors, he is instantly blinded by bright light. But then, after a moment or so, his eyes become acclimated to the brightness, and he is able to see clearly again.

The bright light is coming from sunlight that is shining through upper windows that are positioned close to the ceiling, which is about 50 feet high. The windows are also conjoined closely together, and they surround the entire room. Interestingly, positioned beneath the windows, are large, hanging mirrors that are strategically placed, so that light from the sun can bounce off of them and shine and radiate upon the entire room.

Christopher now steps inside the large room, and he shuts the door behind him.

As Christopher looks around the room he sees the most beautiful sight! The entire room is covered with an assortment of lovely flowers, growing shrubs, and plants of various kinds. And in the middle of the garden there's a unique hand crafted Japanese style, arched, wooden bridge that is positioned over a small, lily pad pond containing several large and colorful goldfish. The view of the garden is absolutely, strikingly breathtaking!

The temperature and atmosphere of the room is also perfect. And the lovely aromatic fragrance of the blooming shrubs and scented flowers smells so delightfully refreshingly, that it immediately brings an elated smile to Christopher's face! But, that's not all. Interestingly, in addition to the things already mentioned, the room and garden has many more unique features. As Christopher looks upward, he sees suspended and stretched horizontally across the entire 50 foot high ceiling, from the east side to the west side of the room, is a series of about a dozen garden hoses, with multiple tiny holes punched in them. The hanging garden hoses are supported by wires and clamps. And they hang about 2 feet from the ceiling, in a series of evenly spaced, straight rolls, like rolls of theatre seating that start at the front of a theatre, and then progressively backup to the rear of the room.

Each individual garden hose is capped at one end, which, in this setup happens to be the east end. And the other end of the hose is connected or fed into a single long water pipe that runs horizontally along the west side of the ceiling from the northwest corner to the southwest corner of the room.

The single long water pipe, which the 12 garden hoses are connected to is also capped at one end, which, in this setup is the northwest end. And attached to the other end of the water pipe, at the southwest corner, is another long garden hose that is fed through and out a partly opened window. From there, the hose stretches outside and then downward alongside the building, and then into a large, sealed water basin that sits upon the ground below.

Located on the ground, next to the large, sealed water basin, is a large compost bin that is filled with compost. Also, there are two solar generated water pumps marked #1 and #2 positioned there. And next to the water pumps is a roll of six, individual, large, open, metal barrels for catching rainwater. They are conveniently covered with filter screens to keep unwanted things out, such as leaves, debris, etc. In addition, each of the six open barrels has its own separate hose attached to it. And the hoses are individually and collectively fed into or connected to a single, straight water pipe that is capped at one end. The other end of the water pipe is connected to one end of the solar generated water pump marked #2. The opposite end of water pump #2 is attached to the large, sealed water basin by means of a separate hose.

When the water level in the large, sealed water basin falls below a marked low level, water pump #2 automatically turns on and it drains stored rainwater from the six metal barrels.

As the rainwater travels from the six metal barrels through water pump #2, and then into the large, sealed water basin, it first passes through a series of water filters that are specially designed to remove acid rain sediments and any other harmful impurities.

When the water level in the large, sealed water basin reaches a marked full level, water pump #2 automatically shuts off.

Inside of the building, the floor is covered in thick rich soil. And strategically placed and buried beneath the surface of the soil are multiple moister sensors, which are used to monitor the soil's moister level and regulate proper irrigation.

When the soil becomes too dry, the moister sensors trigger water pump #1 to turn on. The pump then draws rainwater from the large, sealed water basin, by means of an attached hose, and then up and through another hose that's attached to the opposite end of water pump #1 — This hose extends from the ground, all the way up to and inside the building, through the open window.

Once its inside the building, the rainwater then flows through the single long water pipe that runs horizontally alongside the west side of the ceiling from the southwest corner to the northwest corner of the room, and then through the 12 suspended garden hoses that hang from the ceiling, where it is released and dispersed to fall like soft, gentle rain upon the plants, shrubs, and flowers below.

Truly, this is an elaborate and complicated irrigational system for keeping the plants and flowers watered regularly. But even more impressive and amazing than all of this, is a very special tree that is planted in the northwest corner of the room. Its magnificent appearance is one of absolute splendor, from the base of its sturdy trunk, to the top of its luxurious crown.

The height of the tree reaches clear up to the top of the 50 foot high ceiling. Its foliage has a rich and luxuriant, deep green hue that shines like waxed fruit in the supermarket. And there are light green shoots of new growth at the tips of its limbs and branches, indicating signs of healthy growth and vigor.

The tree is planted in soil that is rich in healthy minerals and proper nutrients. And, like the plants, shrubs, and flowers, it too is watered frequently.

~

After Christopher is done admiring his beautiful indoor garden, he bends over and he picks up an old, empty, metal coffee can that has a garden trowel in it. Afterwards, he proceeds to make his way from the wooden entryway doors of the large room towards the tree.

As Christopher walks, he moves along a winding path that is paved with beautiful decorative stone, and then up and over the arched wooden bridge; and then across more paved stone.

When Christopher reaches the end of the pathway, he proceeds to walk up to the tree's drip-line. Then, he kneels down, with both knees situated upon the ground, and he begins digging into the soil with the garden trowel.

After reaching a depth in the soil where the feeder roots reside, Christopher stops digging. Then, he reaches into his pants pocket and pulls out an army pocket knife. Next, he proceeds to lop off several of the feeder roots and he places them inside the coffee can.

Afterwards, he puts the knife back into his pants pocket.

Next, Christopher unbuttons a pocket on his twill shirt, and he pulls out a small plastic bag that contains a mysterious, thick, green ointment. Opening the bag, he reaches in and he takes some of the ointment, and he spreads and rubs it on the tree, in the area where he lopped off the feeder roots.

As soon as the mysterious ointment touches the tree, it begins to emit dazzling rays of spectacular light — like sparkling, gleaming, beautiful gemstones. And then, something amazing happens. During the exact moment that the ointment is applied, the areas of the tree that were lopped off, immediately begin to mend and heal within an instance of time!

After observing this astounding phenomenon, Christopher closes the plastic bag, and he puts it back in his shirt pocket. Next, he covers the hole that he dug with loose soil, and then he stands upon his feet with the coffee can in his left hand. Next, he walks underneath the tree's crown canopy. And, reaching out his right hand, he begins picking some of the leaves off a few of the lower hanging branches. These too, he places in the coffee can. Afterwards, he takes the can, and he proceeds to walk around the tree to a door in the room that's located several feet from the tree, directly behind it.

Entering through the door, Christopher, steps inside a small room resembling a chemistry lab. Although small in size, the room has a window. And directly beneath the window seal is a long table that has various objects on it; items that you would normally find in a chemistry lab. Things such as glass beakers, test tubes, flasks, funnels, thermometers, tubing, flask stands, tongs, and a Bunsen burner, etc.

After entering the lab, Christopher walks over to the table, and he sets the coffee can down upon it. Next, he grabs a large, round-bottomed distillation boiling flask with sidearm, which contains rainwater from the large, sealed water basin that's located outside of the building. And he pours the entire contents of the coffee can into it. Afterwards, he inserts a rubber stopper containing a thermometer into the top opening of the flask. Then he secures the boiling flask to a flask stand, which has a Bunsen burner situated directly beneath it.

Next, Christopher connects the boiling flask's arm to a condenser tube, which is separately being held in place by its own stand. Then he connects the opposite end of the condenser tube to a piece of bent glass tubing. Lastly, he places the opposite end of the bent glass tubing into a large collection flask.

Finally, after Christopher completes his setup, he uses a flint spark lighter to light the Bunsen burner, and he makes an adjustment to the flame. Afterwards, he returns to the tree, and he lies down beneath it, and falls fast asleep.

Sometime later, when Christopher awakens from sleep, he gets up and he returns to his lavatory. Approaching the flasks, Christopher observes that the liquid in the distillation boiling flask has run pretty much empty, and that the collection flask is now full of liquid, which is "Emerald Green." So he turns off the Bunsen burner. Then he removes the collection flask from off its stand, and he pours as much of its contents as he can, via a funnel, into an unbreakable glass jug that is marked with his initials, CMP. The remainder of the contents he leaves in the flask.

After inserting a cork into the unbreakable jug's opening, Christopher places the jug into a sturdy canvas, carrying bag. Then, he takes an eyedropper off of his lavatory shelf, and he puts it in his shirt pocket, and buttons down the pocket flap. Next, he proceeds to take the bag containing the jug of Emerald Green outside, and he puts it in the front carrier basket of his bicycle. And then, he returns to the front door of the building, and he replaces the board. Afterwards, he returns to his bike, gets on it, and rides home.

Interestingly, the moment that Christopher leaves the area; a man, who was in hiding, walks from around the building where Christopher was. It is Michael Harrington! Both slyly and sneakingly, he had followed Christopher to his secret place, and was spying on him. And after confirming that Christopher is gone, he pries the board away from the front door, and he enters the building.

~

After traveling on his bicycle for a while, Christopher finally arrives at the backdoor of Archer's house. Stopping quickly, he gets off his bike; puts the kickstand down; takes the canvas bag containing the Emerald Green out of the bicycle carrier basket; and then he enters the house.

As Christopher enters the backdoor, he yells: "Mom, I'm home!"

Elisabeth is sitting in the living room, and the moment she hears Christopher's voice, she gets up and she walks towards him. Upon seeing him, she says: "Hi, son. You're back!" And, quickly spotting the canvas bag, she asks: "Is that the Emerald Green?"

"Yep," Christopher says, with a nod of his head. Afterwards, he and Elisabeth walk over to and open up the front door of the house, and they step outside.

Amazingly, the large crowd of people is still there; congregated upon Archer's lawn.

As Christopher steps outside the house, a person in the crowd yells out: "It's Christopher!"

Elisabeth shouts to the crowd, saying: "Everybody, form a line!"

Quickly forming a line, the people begin to approach Christopher, one by one. As they do, he has them open their mouths, and he uses his eyedropper to give each of them a drop of his Emerald Green.[9]

Finally, after Christopher administers the last dose of Emerald Green to the last person in line, he dismisses the crowd, and they slowly begin to leave. Suddenly, several squad cars arrive at Archer's home, and a number of policemen quickly hop out. And they aggressively approach Christopher.

---

[9] Because Emerald Green is so potently strong, one drop is all that a person needs.

The lead officer in charge says to Christopher: "Are you, Christopher Pascale?"

"Yes," Christopher says.

"You're under arrest for theft!" the Policeman says. And then, taking Christopher by the hand, he handcuffs him, and he begins reading him his Miranda Rights.

When Elisabeth sees what's happening, she is taken aback! Quickly, stepping forward, she asks the Policeman: "What's going on? What's this all about? What are you doing to my son?"

"He's under arrest for theft!" the lead Officer remarks.

"For theft," Elisabeth says."

"Yes, for theft!" the Officer replies.

"You're making a big mistake! My son didn't steal anything!" Elisabeth says.

"Lady, you can take it up with the Judge! But for now, he's going to jail!" the Policeman says. Afterwards, he and the other police with him take Christopher into custody; confiscate his jug of Emerald Green; and they expeditiously proceed to escort him to a squad car.

When the crowd of people observes that Christopher is being arrested and taken to jail, they become agitated and angry, and several of them begin to shout out sharp remarks at the police, saying things such as: "You sick cowards! Where are you taking him?" and, "Leave him alone, you pigs!"

When the police hear what the crowd is yelling, they remain silent, as they continue to quickly escort Christopher to their vehicle. And, after putting him in the backseat, they get in, and drive away.

Immediately, after Christopher is gone, the crowd disperses, and they leave and go to their separate homes.

19

ON TRIAL

Two days have passed sense Christopher's arrest. And Elisabeth and Archer find themselves sitting in a courtroom down at the Wright County Courthouse. They are nervously and patiently awaiting the start of Christopher's hearing. The day prior to this, at his arraignment, he pled not guilty to the charge of first-degree theft.

The courtroom is packed with people. It is standing room only. Suddenly, the Court Bailiff yells out: "This court is now in session! All rise for the honorable Judge, Harry C. Matheson!"

Immediately, everyone respectfully rise from their seats, and they remain standing while the judge enters the courtroom and is seated. Afterwards, they sit back down.

The court bailiff now says out loud: "This is the case of Sunrise Pharmaceutical Drugs verses Christopher Maurice Pascale."

Christopher is sitting at a table, next to his Defense Attorney, Mr.

Garvey Atwater.

To start things off, Sunrise Pharmaceutical Drugs high profile Prosecuting Attorney, Mr. Eugene Ratcliff, who is sitting at a table adjacent from Christopher, rises to his feet. Addressing Judge Matheson, he says: "Your Honor, I would like to call Mr. Bruce Wylie to the stand."

Bruce Wylie promptly approaches the witness stand, is sworn in, and is then seated.

After Mr. Wyle is seated, Attorney Ratcliff approaches him, carrying a small bottle of liquid, and then he sets it down on top of a table nearby. Next, he looks at Mr. Wylie, and he says to him: "Mr. Wylie, can you tell the court what you do for a living?"

"Yes. I am the Head Supervisor at Sunrise Pharmaceutical Drugs," Mr. Wylie replies.

"Good! So you must know your company's inventory and products very well!" Attorney Ratcliff says.

"That's correct," Mr. Wylie answers.

Attorney Ratcliff now turns, and he retrieves the bottle of liquid, which he had momentarily set on the table, and then, he hands it to Mr. Wylie, and he says: "Mr. Wylie, can you identify this for the court?"

"Yes, I can. It's a bottle of our CX252," Mr. Wylie confidently says.

"When you say *our,* who are you referring to?" Attorney Ratcliff asks.

"The *company* that I work for, 'Sunrise Pharmaceutical Drugs,'" Mr. Wylie replies.

"Thank you! No further questions," Attorney Ratcliff says. And then, he turns, and he returns to his seat.

After Attorney Ratcliff returns to his seat, Judge Matheson addresses Christopher's representing Attorney, Garvey Atwater, and he asks: "Does the defense have any questions for the witness?"

"No, Your Honor," Attorney Atwater says.

"You may step down, Mr. Wylie," Judge Matheson says, as he turns and looks at him.

After Mr. Wylie returns to his seat in the audience, Prosecuting Attorney, Eugene Ratcliff once again speaks up, and he says: "Next, I would like to call to the stand, Mr. Jack Truculent."

Jack Truculent promptly approaches the witness stand, is sworn in, and is then seated.

After Mr. Truculent is seated, Attorney Ratcliff once again approaches the witness stand, but this time he is carrying Christopher's canvas bag with the jug of Emerald Green in it. And, after temporarily setting it down on the table nearby, he turns, and he looks at Mr. Truculent, and he says to him: "Mr. Truculent, can you tell the court what you do for a living?"

"I'm a senior Chemist and Physicist," Mr. Truculent says.

"How long have you been doing this type of work?" Attorney Ratcliff asks.

"For over 20 years!" Mr. Truculent replies.

"Wow! That's pretty impressive! So you're an expert! You must really know your stuff!" Attorney Ratcliff smiles and says.

"Yes, I do," Mr. Truculent proudly says with a big grin.

Attorney Ratcliff now turns, and he picks up the canvas bag. And he pulls out the jug of Emerald Green. Afterwards, he addresses the court; shows them the jug; and says to them: "This is 'Item #1,' which was confiscated from the accused. Yesterday, samples of this; and I quote 'Emerald Green,' were taken along with (pausing, he quickly turns and grabs the bottle of CX252 off the table, and he also holds it up for the court to see), this sample of CX252. Both were sent to Mr. Truculent's lab for thorough examination!"

Attorney Ratcliff now turns and he looks at Mr. Truculent, and he says to him: "Mr. Truculent, when you analyzed samples of both 'Emerald Green' and 'CX252' at your lab, what was the result of your analysis?"

"I found that the chemical composition of both Emerald Green and CX252 are chemically indistinguishable," Mr. Truculent says.

"For the court, in layman's terms, what do you mean when you say that they are *chemically indistinguishable*,'" Attorney Ratcliff asks.

"It means that they are absolutely identical!" Mr. Truculent replies.

"Thank you! No further questions," Attorney Ratcliff says. And then, he turns, and he returns to his seat.

Defense Attorney, Garvey Atwater now approaches the witness stand. Then turning and addressing the court, he proceeds to asks them a rhetorical question, saying: "What does the term *identical* mean?" And then, reaching into his pants pocket, he pulls out his wallet, opens it up, takes out a photograph, and he hands it to the witness, Gary Truculent. Next, he says to him: "Mr. Truculent, can you describe to the court what you are holding?"

"It's a photograph of you!" Mr. Truculent says.

"Thank you!" Attorney Atwater says. Then, after quickly retrieving the photograph from Mr. Truculent, he turns, and he readdresses the court, along with Mr. Truculent, and he says (as he holds up and displays the photograph for all to see): "Actually, this is *not* a photograph of me. But, instead, it is a photograph of my, and I quote *'identical'* twin brother!" He continues: "My name is *Garvey* Atwater! This is my brother *Harvey* Atwater!"

Prosecuting Attorney, Ratcliff, immediately speaks up, and he says to the Judge, "Objection, Your Honor! What does this have to do with the case?"

"Overruled. I want to see where he's going with this," Judge Matheson curiously says.

Defense Attorney, Garvey Atwater goes on to explain, saying: "The term, and I quote *'identical'* is relative, not absolute. For instance, my brother and I are said to be, quote *'identical'* twins. Yet, interestingly, in some ways we are not. Take for example our fingerprints. Our fingerprints are *not* identical. As a matter of fact, they don't even match! My brother Harvey's fingerprints identify, not me, but *him alone* as *'Harvey'* Atwater! And the same is true regarding my fingerprints, they identify, not him, but *only me* as *'Garvey'* Atwater!" He continues: "In the Judicial System, fingerprints in criminal cases are used to identify individuals, to verify their distinct, identity! They can even provide strong proof of evidence that can be used to place a person at the scene of a crime! And they can also be used to convict them in a court of law!" He continues: "The differences between me and my brother Harvey's fingerprints are just as different as Judge Matheson's fingerprints are from Mr. Truculent's." He continues: "Does that mean that my brother Harvey and I, and other so called *'identical'* twins, are not, in fact, truly *identical?* In reality, perhaps not. Why? Because the term, and I quote *'identical'* is relative, not absolute!"

Attorney Atwater now turns, and he looks at Mr. Truculent, and he says to him: "So, Mr. Truculent, now that we have gotten that out of the way; based on what I just said, would you still conclude that Emerald Green and CX252 are absolutely *'identical?'*"

"Well, since you put it that way, I guess, maybe not," Mr. Truculent says, with a nervous stutter in his voice, and a baffled look on his face.

"Thank you. No further questions," Attorney Atwater says. Then he turns, and he returns to his seat.

Prosecuting Attorney, Ratcliff, now realizing that Attorney Atwater has just finished cleverly sowing doubts in the court's mind, as to whether CX252 and Emerald Green are in fact one and the same, now stands up at his chair, and he readdresses Mr. Truculent, saying to him: "Mr. Truculent, let me rephrase my question that I asked you earlier; when I asked you to reveal the results of your analysis of Emerald Green and CX252. What I meant to say was; when you analyzed the samples of both Emerald Green and CX252 at your lab, did you find that they *matched?*" Attorney Ratcliff asks.

"Yes, they *matched!*" Mr. Truculent says.

"Thank you. No further questions," Attorney Ratcliff says, as he flaunts a cocky grin.

After the prosecuting attorney gets through speaking, Defense Attorney, Garvey Atwater gets up, and he re-approaches the witness stand, and he says to Mr. Truculent: "Mr. Truculent, if Emerald Green and CX252 did by chance happen to *'match,'* what are the possibilities that they both came from or where derived from the same source? For instance, who's to say that Sunrise Pharmaceutical Drugs didn't steal the original source, 'Emerald Green,' and then tried to pass it off as their own, relabeling it as 'CX252?'"

"Objection, Your Honor! I object! That's preposterous! Absolutely, absurd! Who's on trial here anyways?" Attorney Ratcliff yells to the Judge.

Suddenly, a loud uproar breaks out in the courtroom! In response, Judge Matheson strikes his gavel several times, and he yells out: "Order... order in the courtroom!" Immediately, the courtroom settles down and becomes quiet.

After order is restored in his courtroom, Judge Matheson says: "Objection, sustained!" Then, he turns, and he looks at Attorney, Garvey Atwater, and he sternly cautions him, saying: "Mr. Atwater, one more outburst like that, and I'll have you in contempt of court!" Next, he turns and he addresses the Court Stenographer, and he says to her: "That last statement will be stricken from the records." In response, the Court Stenographer nods her head in agreement.

Judge Matheson is fuming! He now glares at both attorneys (Ratcliff and Atwater), and he says to them: "It's getting a little out of hand here! I need a break! Let's take a 20 minute recess! This court will reconvene at 11:00 AM!"

~

Later, when the court reconvenes, Michael Harrington slips into the courtroom, and he quietly takes a seat in the back row.

Once again, to start things off, Prosecuting Attorney, Eugene Ratcliff rises to his feet, and he says to Judge Matheson: "Your Honor, I would like to call to the stand, Christopher Maurice Pascale!"

Christopher approaches and takes the witness stand. Next, the court bailiff approaches him. And he has him place his hand on a Bible, and he says: "Do you, Christopher Maurice Pascale, swear to tell the whole truth and nothing but the truth, so help you God?"

"I do," Christopher says. And then he sits down.

After, Christopher is sworn in, Attorney Ratcliff approaches the witness stand, and he says to Christopher: "Mr. Pascale, have you ever been to Sunrise Pharmaceutical Drugs?"

"Yes. I was there once," Christopher says.

"When was that?" Attorney Ratcliff asks.

"Not that long ago," Christopher replies.

"What did you go there for?" Attorney Ratcliff asks.

"My Boss sent me there to pick up some packages," Christopher explains.

"Where do you work?" Attorney Ratcliff asks.

"I don't work there anymore. But at the time, I was working at the Good Samaritan Hospital," Christopher says.

"So, what was in the packages?" Attorney Ratcliff asks.

"I don't know?" Christopher responds.

In response, Attorney Ratcliff turns, and he walks over to the prosecutor's table, and he grabs a document, and then he returns to talk to Christopher.

After Attorney Ratcliff re-approaches the witness stand, he hands Christopher the document, and he says to him: "Mr. Pascale, I want you to take a good look at this document, and then tell the court what it is."

"It's an invoice," Christopher replies, after quickly examining it.

"That's correct! And from what company does it say that the invoice is from?" Attorney Ratcliff asks.

"Sunrise Pharmaceutical Drugs," Christopher says.

"That's correct! And whose name is signed at the bottom of the page?" Attorney Ratcliff asks.

Christopher, once again, quickly scans the document with his eyes. Then, he pauses for a moment, and he says: "It's my name, Christopher Pascale."

"That is also correct! And if you look at the items listed on the invoice, you will find that item #6 is for a case of something. What item does it list?" Attorney Ratcliff asks.

Christopher pauses for a moment; and then he says: "A case of CX252," Christopher says.

"That's correct! And when you picked up the case of CX252, along with the other items listed, on the day that you visited Sunrise Pharmaceutical Drugs, did you inappropriately take and keep some CX252 for yourself?" Attorney Ratcliff asks.

"Objection, Your Honor! Just because my client picked up and delivered some medical supplies, doesn't make him a thief!" Defense Attorney, Garvey Atwater shouts out to the Judge.

"Sustained," Judge Matheson says.

Attorney Ratcliff, now quickly switches or changes his thought process. And he says to Christopher: "Mr. Pascale, can you tell the court where you got the jug of Emerald Green from?"

"I got it from a tree," Christopher says.

Attorney Ratcliff, not fully comprehending what Christopher means, says: "You got it from a what?"

"From a tree," Christopher replies.

"Do you mean that the jug of liquid was lying by a tree, and that you came along and picked it up?" Attorney Ratcliff asks.

"No, Sir. I mean, I manufactured it from a tree," Christopher says.

"Oh. So you made it? And how did you do that?" Attorney Ratcliff asks.

"I extracted natural samples from the tree, and then used them to liquefy Dexatromvonseratomin," Christopher replies.

Attorney Ratcliff is stunned by Christopher's intelligent response, and he says: "Wow! That's pretty impressive! Can you tell the court what that means?"

"Sure. It means to produce Emerald Green," Christopher says.

Thoroughly astonished and amused by Christopher's clever response, the courtroom instantly erupts into laugher! In response, Judge Matheson strikes his gavel several times, and he yells out: "Order… order in the courtroom!"

As Judge Matheson tries to restore order, Attorney Ratcliff turns and he inconspicuously glances over at Michael Harrington, who is seated in the back row of seats. In response, Michael looks back at him, and he nods his head, as though he is giving Attorney Ratcliff his approval to proceed with something.

~

After order is restored in the courtroom, Attorney Ratcliff turns and he faces Christopher. And he continues his discussion by readdressing the subject of the tree. He says to Christopher: "Mr. Pascale, so if you used the properties from a tree to make Emerald Green, then where is this tree located?"

"It's in my secret place," Christopher replies.

"Do you mean in your imagination?" Attorney Ratcliff asks.

"No. It's a real place, and a real tree. I raised it from infancy," Christopher relates.

"From infancy," Attorney Ratcliff says.

"Yes, Sir," Christopher replies.

"How long did it take for you to grow this tree?" Attorney Ratcliff asks.

"A long time," Christopher says.

"Do you have any photographs of this tree that you can share with the court?" Attorney Ratcliff asks.

"No," Christopher answers.

"Well, then how can you prove that it really exists?" Attorney

Ratcliff asks.

"I don't know?" Christopher says.

"Can you tell us where it's located?" Attorney Ratcliff asks.

Christopher is reluctant to answer the question, because the tree is his, and out of fear he doesn't want to disclose the whereabouts of its secret place. Finally, after pausing for a moment, he answers, saying: "No, I can't do that."

"So, the tree really doesn't exist!" Attorney Ratcliff says.

"I didn't say that. I said, I can't tell you where it is," Christopher replies.

"Why not," Attorney Ratcliff asks.

"Because it's mine," Christopher answers.

"Obviously, you don't want to tell us, because you know that it really doesn't exist! Isn't that right?" Attorney Ratcliff says.

"It does too exist!" Christopher says in an irritated tone.

"Then, prove it!" Attorney Ratcliff emphatically says.

"I object, Your Honor! He's badgering my client!" Defense Attorney, Garvey Atwater yells to the Judge.

"Sustained," Judge Matheson says.

Attorney Ratcliff turns towards the Judge, and he says to him in sugarcoated speech: "Your Honor, I just want Mr. Pascale to produce evidence that the tree exists, that's all!"

Attorney Ratcliff now turns back towards Christopher. Readdressing the question, but this time conveying it in a gentler way, he says to him: "Christopher, will you tell us where the tree is?"

"I can't," Christopher replies.

Defense Attorney, Garvey Atwater again intervenes in behalf of his client, and he says to the Judge: "Your Honor, can I have a few moments to talk to my client?"

"You may. Let's take a 30 minute recess," Judge Matheson says. Then striking his gavel on a sound block, he says out loud: "This court will reconvene at 12:30 PM!"

"Thank you, Your Honor," Attorney Atwater says to the Judge.

~

During recess, Christopher is taken from the witness stand into a private room, so that his lawyer, Garvey Atwater, can consult with him in private. Christopher's mother Elisabeth is also invited to be there.

Attorney Atwater looks at Christopher, and he says to him: "Christopher, I really want to help you. But the only way that I can do this, is that you've got to tell them where the tree is. It's the only way that you can prove your innocence."

"But, I can't! It's mine! I'm afraid that if I tell them, they will come and take it away from me!" Christopher says.

"I understand your fears son. But it's our only defense!" Attorney Atwater replies.

Elisabeth now speaks up, and she says to Christopher: "Christopher, I believe you son. You have never lied to me before. And God knows that you certainly are not a thief!" She continues: "Now, I know that you have a very important and tough decision to make here. It's probably the hardest thing that you've ever been asked to do? And you know that, whatever decision you make, that I will be there to support you either way. But, I'm going to ask you to take into consideration that if you are convicted, that they can put you away for a long time. As a mother, I know it's selfish on my part, but I don't think that I could bear seeing you locked up. I love you too much!"

Christopher begins to cry, and he hugs his mom, and he says: "I love you too, mom!"

Attorney Atwater looks at Christopher, and he says to him: "Christopher, if I could somehow arrange with the court, to let you personally go along with them and show them where the tree is, would you be willing to do that?"

Christopher thinks about it for a moment. And then, he says: "Well... I guess I could do that."

"Ok, I'll see what I can do. I can't promise you anything, but I'll try," Attorney Atwater says.

~

After the 30 minutes of recess is over, the court reconvenes. And Christopher is back on the witness stand. So Prosecuting Attorney, Eugene Ratcliff now approaches him, and he says: "Well, Mr. Pascale, what is your decision? Will you tell us where the tree is?"

In response, Christopher looks over at his Attorney, Garvey Atwater for support. And then, he turns his attention back to the Prosecuting Attorney, and he says to him: "I'm not sure?"

When Attorney Ratcliff hears Christopher's response and finds that it's not what he expected him to say, he gets upset; loses his composure; and he says to him in an angry tone: "What do you mean that you're not sure! You had plenty of time to think about it!"

Quickly intervening in Christopher's behalf, his attorney, Harvey Atwater says to the Judge: "Excuse me, Your Honor! Can we (that is both attorneys) approach the bench?"

"Yes, you may," Judge Matheson says.

Both attorneys now walk up to the bench. And Attorney Atwater says to the Judge: "Your Honor, for personal reasons my client is reluctant to divulge the location of his tree. However, if he were allowed to go along with, and personally show the court where it is, he would be willing to do that."

"Wait a minute! Hold on a second!" Judge Matheson says. He continues: "Now, let me get this straight. Are you saying that you want me to release a prisoner, so that he can lead you to the tree?"

"Sort of... I guess, Your Honor. However, he will still be in police custody," Attorney Atwater reasons.

"Are you nuts!" Judge Matheson remarks. He continues: "Not only is this a very unusual and highly irregular request, but also the kid's a prisoner! What if he were to escape?"

"I assure you that, that won't happen! He will be escorted by armed guards!" Attorney Atwater answers.

Judge Matheson looks at Attorney Ratcliff, and he says to him: "Mr. Ratcliff, what do you think about this?"

"I don't have a problem with it Judge," Attorney Ratcliff says.

Judge Matheson pauses; and he thinks about it for a moment. And then, he looks at Attorney Atwater, and he says to him: "I tell you what, Mr. Atwater; I'm going to go out on a limb here and give you my permission. However, I'm holding you *personally responsible* if anything goes wrong!"

"Thank you, Your Honor! I promise you, nothing will happen!" Attorney Atwater says.

"It better not, for your sake!" Judge Matheson sternly replies. Afterwards, he formally addresses the court, and says: "This court is adjourned! And it will reconvene tomorrow morning at 9:00 AM!"

~

A short time later, after court is adjourned, Christopher is taken, and then transported by armed policemen to the secret location of his tree. Also, Judge Matheson, both Attorneys (Eugene Ratcliff and Garvey Atwater), along with Christopher's mother, Elisabeth, and a few other key people that where present in the courtroom are also invited to go along.

~

When Christopher, the Police, the Judge, the Attorneys, and the group of invitees all arrive at the location of Christopher's tree, they exit their vehicles, and then they walk up to an old, dilapidated, vacant, and boarded up building that is surrounded by a tall, chain-link, metal fence, with a broken entry gate. And, after successfully removing the board from the front door of the building, the group promptly steps inside.

Interestingly, after everyone is inside of the building, Christopher is allowed to lead the way to his tree.

Working their way through several dark rooms towards the back of the building, Christopher and the group finally arrive at a set of large, double doors, marked shipping and receiving. However, before they enter the room, Christopher turns and he says to everyone: "Can I get everyone's attention please?" And then he pauses for a moment.

After getting the groups full and undivided attention, Christopher continues, saying: "My tree, is behind these closed doors. As you walk towards it, be sure to use the winding, stone pathway, and wooden walk bridge. And please, stay out of my plants and flower beds! Thank you." Afterwards, he turns, and he opens one of the large doors.

The moment Christopher opens the door, he and everyone with him are instantly blinded by bright light! The light is coming from sunlight that is shining through upper windows (surrounding the entire room), which are positioned close to a 50 foot high ceiling.

After a moment or so passes, the eyes of Christopher and everyone with him become acclimated to the brightness, and they are able to see clearly again.

As Christopher and the people enter and look around the large room, they see that the entire room is vacant, completely empty!

Christopher is shocked! Thinking within himself, he says: *"What in the world happened to my beautiful indoor garden? But most importantly, where is my tree?"*

After the people see that the room is completely vacant, they begin to clamor and speak negative things amongst themselves.

Prosecuting Attorney, Eugene Ratcliff, now steps forward, and he says to everyone: "Well folks, as you can see, there definitely is no tree here!"

In response, Christopher looks at his mom (who is exhibiting signs of sadness and disappointment on her face), and shaking his head back and forth in disbelief over what has happened, he says to her: "But Mom, I was telling the truth! There was a tree! Somebody, took it!"

"Okay everybody, let's break it up!" the head Policeman in charge yells to the group. In response, everyone turns, and they start to head back outside.

After everyone is outside of the building, the police then proceed to escort Christopher back to their squad car, and they get in, and leave.

Elisabeth and the group of people, realizing that nothing more can be done, also leave, and they go their homes.

∼

The next day, down at the County Courthouse, before court reconvenes, Defense Attorney, Garvey Atwater is having a private meeting with his client Christopher, and his mother Elisabeth.

Attorney Atwater looks at Christopher, and he says to him: "Christopher, they (that is the court) want to strike a deal. They said that if you admit that you lied, and that you mistakenly took 'CX252,' and passed it off as your own, as 'Emerald Green,' that they are willing to drop all charges. Otherwise, if you don't, they say that they have no recourse but to push for maximum sentencing. And, if convicted, it will be a long time before you are illegible for parole."

"I can't do that! I'm not a liar!" Christopher says.

218

When Elisabeth hears Attorney Atwater say maximum sentencing, she becomes frightened. Then, her emotions take over, and she says to Christopher: "But Christopher you must; otherwise, they're going to put you away for a long time!" She continues: "Think how it will hurt us! You are my only child — my only son! I won't be able to bear it if you are locked up and away from me! To be free is more important than anything else!"

"Is it really, Mom?" Christopher asks, as he looks her in the eyes. He continues: "Is it more important than keeping one's integrity — the identity of knowing who you truly are?"

"I don't know, son. I guess that's a decision that you'll have to make," Elisabeth says.

A short time later, after Christopher's and his Attorney's meeting is over, the court reconvenes. And Christopher is put back on the witness stand.

Prosecuting Attorney, Eugene Ratcliff now approaches Christopher, and then, he turns to the court, and he says: "The evidence is clear! There was never a tree that produced a miracle drug! It was a fairytale story that was concocted or made up (pausing, he quickly turns, looks, and points his finger at Christopher), by a young lad that was seeking special attention and personal gain!" Next, turning back towards the audience, Attorney Ratcliff continues, saying: "The charge is very serious! One that is worthy of full indemnification! However, my client, Sunrise Pharmaceutical Drugs, out of the goodness of their heart, is willing to drop all charges, that is, if the accused is willing to admit that he lied, and that he mistakenly took 'CX252,' and passed it off as his own concoction, which he labeled 'Emerald Green.'"

A lot of chattering and noise breaks out in the courtroom! In response, Judge Matheson strikes his gavel several times, and he yells out: "Order in the courtroom!" Immediately, the courtroom settles down and becomes quiet. Then, the Judge turns his attention to Christopher, and he says to him: "Christopher Maurice Pascale, do you confess to the charges?"

Christopher, with a heavy heart, and a very sad look on his face, turns, and he looks at his mother Elisabeth. And after thinking about it for a moment, he says: "Yes."

Once again, a loud uproar breaks out in the courtroom! In response, Judge Matheson again strikes his gavel several times, and he yells out: "Order in the courtroom! I said, order in the courtroom!"

After the people quiet down, Judge Matheson says: "This case is suspended, and the defendant is free to go!"

As Christopher and Elisabeth exit the front door of the courthouse, they are immediately swarmed upon by news reporters and a large waiting crowd. One of the reporters quickly shoves a microphone in Christopher's face, and he says: "Christopher, what would you like to say to the people in your behalf?" In response, Christopher keeps silent. However, his mother Elisabeth speaks for him, and she simply says to the reporter: "No comment!"

Suddenly, as quick as the flip of a light switch, the crowd turns on Christopher, and like an agitated, restless, and raging sea, several of them begin yelling out mean and cruel things at him, saying things such as: "You lying fool!" and, "We should have known better!" and, "Go home liar!" and, "You yellow freak! Go back to where you belong!"

In response to the crowd's reaction, Christopher and Elisabeth keep silent. And they hurry to their parked car, quickly get in, and they drive home.

～

During the next few days and upcoming weeks, Sunrise Pharmaceutical Drugs is highly esteemed and praised by the local news media, television networks, and radio stations for their recent court victory, and, especially, for the development of their new miracle drug 'CX252' that has completely halted the Probias Plague, and which, is also successfully being used to cure various other diseases as well. On the other hand, things aren't going so well for Christopher. Since his trial, he has been painted and treated by the public as being the worse person on the face of the earth! And, because of this, for the next several weeks he doesn't go anywhere. He just stays at home in complete isolation, locked up in his room.

Poor Christopher! His mother Elisabeth has never seen him like this before, so despondent and down in the dumps. He's even beginning to think that it would have been better, if he had never been born!

Finally, after some time has passed, Elisabeth eventually convinces Christopher that he needs to get out and about. Today, she invites him to ride along with her, as she runs some local errands. Initially, he balks at the idea at first, but then he agrees to go with her.

It is a nice and sunny day. The first place that Elisabeth travels to is the Post Office; the second is the Grocery Store; and then, lastly, she makes a stop at the Drycleaners.

At each stop, Elisabeth invites Christopher to accompany her. But he refuses, and says: "I'll just wait here in the car, Mom."

While Elisabeth is on her last stop, which is at the Clean & Press Drycleaners, the sunny weather abruptly starts to change, as heavy clouds begin to quickly roll in.

The Drycleaners happens to be located in a small, strip mall-like area.

Christopher, who has elected to stay in the car, happens to notice that a small convenience store, which is located next to the Drycleaners, is having a big sidewalk sale. So, out of curiosity, he gets out of the car, and he walks over to one of the display racks. And he begins rummaging through some of the items for sale.

As Christopher stands in front of the convenience store, browsing through merchandise, three Caucasian men happen to be nearby, loitering next to their parked car.

Suddenly, loud sounds of rolling and rumbling thunderstorms occur in the sky overhead. In response, one of the Caucasian men looks at Christopher, and he proceeds to yell out, concerning him, saying: "I didn't think I'd ever see a Nigger still hanging around during a thunderstorm!" Afterwards, the man and his friends begin to laugh out loud at Christopher.

Christopher, in rapid response to the nasty remark and the rude behavior of the men, promptly turns, and he looks at them. But he doesn't say a word.

Immediately, identifying Christopher, one of the men says out loud to his friends: "Hey, isn't that, Christopher Pascale, the lying and thieving boy that's been in the news?"

"Hey, you're right, it is him!" they confirm and say.

When Christopher realizes that he has been recognized, he is embarrassed. So he quickly turns, and he proceeds to walk hurriedly back to his mother's car.

As Christopher scurries to the car, the three men begin shouting horrible things at him, saying: "You better get out of here, you lying, thieving Nigger!" and, "Don't you come around here no more, boy!" and, "You good for nothing, rotten Nigger!"

A short time later, after Christopher returns to the car, Elisabeth exits the Drycleaners. Then, she quickly hops in the vehicle; starts the engine; drives off; and heads for home.

~

Over the next several months, things are looking pretty good in Wright County. All traces of the Probias Plague are gone. And its citizens in general seem to be in pretty good health.

One day, when Christopher and Elisabeth are shopping at a local department store, suddenly, one of the other customer's (someone that they don't know), collapses, and he falls to the floor. Apparently, he is having seizures. Luckily, one of the store employees immediately spots him, and she quickly calls for emergency medical assistance.

Within no time, proper medical personal is instantly there on the spot to help the man. And, afterwards, he is taken to the hospital.

Later that evening, after Christopher and Elisabeth have returned home from shopping, and they have finished eating dinner; they turn on the television set, so that they can watch their favorite TV show, which is the "Ed Sullivan Show." Suddenly, the program is interrupted by a breaking news report.

The TV News Reporter says: "Several people in the surrounding areas of Wright County have recently contracted an unknown virus, which authorities have named 'Skelexianervosis' or 'the Crippling Virus.' Early symptoms of the virus include headaches, nausea, and fever, followed by uncontrollable seizures. Unfortunately, those who are being brought into the Good Samaritan Hospital for isolation and treatment, end up, within days, becoming permanently paralyzed from the waist down. Doctors and scientists are working both hard and around the clock to stop the spread of this horrendous disease. However, they remain baffled as to its origin. All they know is that the damaging virus attacks and destroys the nervous system, and then, shortly thereafter, it cripples its victims."

Now, turning and directing his attention to a visiting guest, the News Reporter continues, saying: "Present with us is Michael J. Harrington, the founder and CEO of Sunrise Pharmaceutical Drugs."

"Mr. Harrington, can you tell us what affect your miracle drug 'CX252' is having on this current virus?" the Reporter asks.

"Well, unfortunately, so far, CX252 remains totally impotent as a cure for 'Skelexianervosis.' However, we hope to…" Michael Harrington goes on to explain.

While Mr. Harrington is being interviewed by the News Reporter, the camera angle happens to capture his wristwatch, which immediately catches Elisabeth's eye. When she sees it, she is completely shocked and stunned! And she cries out: "Oh no! It can't be!"

"Are you ok, Mom? What's the matter?" Christopher worriedly asks.

Elisabeth points at the TV, and she says: "Do you see that wristwatch that the man to the left of the TV screen is wearing?"

"Yep, I see it," Christopher replies.

"That's your father, Randall's watch!" Elisabeth says.

"What do you mean... that's my father watch?" Christopher asks.

Elisabeth explains, saying: "Your father's wristwatch was one of a kind. It was the only one ever made in the entire world. I bought it for him as a gift just before he died. And, that man on the news, whose name is Michael Harrington, is wearing it!" She continues: "I knew Michael in the past, and now, I seriously suspect that he had something to do with Randall's death!"

After Christopher is done listening to his mother's story, he turns, and he continues to watch the remainder of the news report. And, during the entire time, he doesn't take his eyes off of Michael Harrington.

Later, as it turns out, Christopher decides to spy on Michael Harrington. So, for several days, he waits outside, at both his home and his job, and he secretly follows him wherever he goes.

Today, is Tuesday. It is early morning. And Michael Harrington is about to leave home for work. Suddenly, the front door to his house opens, and out walks Michael, his wife Felicia, and their son Jake, who is about ten years old. Michael kisses Felicia, and he hugs Jake. And then, he says goodbye, and he hurries to his car.

"Don't be late for dinner tonight, Dear!" Felicia yells to Michael.

"I won't, Honey!" Michael hollers back, as he gets into his car, and slowly drives away.

As soon as Michael drives off, Felicia and Jake reenter the house, and they close the door behind them.

Unbeknown to the Harrington's, in the not too far distance, Christopher Pascale happens to be secretly watching them. He is on his bicycle.

~

After Michael leaves home, he drives his car to Sunrise Pharmaceutical Drugs Corporation, which is located a relatively short distance away from his home. Once there, he parks his vehicle in the CEO's reserved parking slot of the employee parking lot, and then he enters the building.

Immediately, after Michael enters the building, Christopher pulls into the Sunrise Pharmaceutical's parking lot on his bicycle. And, after placing his bike in the employee bicycle rack, he reaches into his front carrier basket; takes out a beautiful bouquet of freshly cut flowers; and then, he promptly walks up to and enters the building.

Interestingly, if somebody didn't clue you in or tell you, you probably wouldn't be able to recognize Christopher, for he is in disguise. He is sporting a fake mustache and wig. And he is dressed like a floral delivery man, wearing both a cap and full uniform.

The moment Christopher enters the lobby of the building, he walks straight up to the company's visitor's appointment desk.

"Can I help you?" the Secretary asks Christopher.

Christopher flashes the bouquet of flowers with a card attached, in the secretary's face, and he says: "Yes. I have a delivery for Mr. Michael Harrington."

"Okay. That will be Room 106," the Secretary says. And, quickly pointing her finger in that direction, she continues, saying: "To get there, what you want to do, is walk straight ahead until you get to the hallway, and then, take a right turn, and you'll find Room 106 on your left."

"Thank you," Christopher says. Afterwards, he proceeds to walk there.

Within no time, Christopher arrives at Room 106. Suddenly, the door swings wide open, and a man exits. Christopher, however, doesn't enter in. Quickly scanning the entire, large room with his eyes, he spots Michael Harrington, who is sitting with a group of people inside an enclosed glass conference room that is situated in the far, left corner of the room.

The door to Room 106 now closes.

Strangely, instead of entering the room, Christopher turns, and he walks away. Afterwards, he steps inside the men's bathroom, which is located directly across the hallway.

When Christopher enters the bathroom, he places the bouquet of flowers down on top of a dome shaped trashcan, and then he washes his hands in the sink; dry's them with a paper towel; tosses the towel in the trashcan; and then he exists the bathroom without the flowers.

After leaving the bathroom Christopher promptly exits the building, mounts his bicycle, and he proceeds to ride it around to the back of the building, to the location of the conference room, where Michael Harrington is sitting with the group of people.

Approaching the conference room, Christopher hops off his bike, and then he quietly walks over to and stands directly beneath the window. Luckily, the window happens to be open, and he is in the perfect spot to overhear every word.

Michael Harrington, addressing the group of people in the room, says: "This latest virus, 'Skelexianervosis,' also known as the 'Crippling Virus,' which has recently cropped up in Wright County, leaves us completely baffled and terrified. For it renders its victims totally crippled! Unfortunately, our CX252 remains impotently useless as a cure. And, because of this, need I tell you, that Sunrise Pharmaceutical Drugs is in big trouble? Because of the previous success that our miracle drug CX252 had in stopping the deadly

Probias Plague, and also in curing various other diseases as well, the public is also expecting it to cure this latest virus too! The question is, why is CX252 not working?"

Sunrise Pharmaceutical Drugs top chemist and physicist, Felix Duprey (who happens to be a scientific genius), speaks up, and he says to Michael: "Boss, our medical science and drug research teams, which consists of the top people in their fields in the world, are working hard on it. But, it's a bit more complicated than we thought. Ever since we ran out of the kid's original supply of 'Emerald Green,' we haven't been able to duplicate it. We did exactly what you instructed us to do when we transferred his tree to its new location. We set up everything in the exact and identical places as they were set up in the old building. Interestingly, the tree is still producing medicine, but for some reason, it still remains ineffective as a cure to remedy 'Skelexianervosis.' Even smaller diseases and things that it initially cured, it presently has no favorable effect on them."

Upon hearing Felix Dupery's bad report, Michael Harrington becomes furious! And he says to him in a forceful and demanding tone: "You useless fool! I want you to get back to work on it! And, this time, I want it to work! I don't care what it takes! If a young Negro boy can make it work, why can't you? Get out of here! And don't come back to me until you have effective results!"

After Michael Harrington dismisses his research and development team, Christopher gets back on his bike and he slips away totally undetected. And during the next several days, he continues to stakeout both Michael Harrington's home and Sunrise Pharmaceutical Drugs, to try to find a clue as to where his tree is located.

One day, when Christopher is watching Michael Harrington's residence, an ambulance pulls up, and paramedics get out, and they rush up to and into his house carrying a stretcher.

A short time later, when the paramedics are exiting the house, they are carrying the Harrington's son, Jake, out on the stretcher. Highly concerned, both Michael and his wife Felicia are walking closely alongside of him and the stretcher.

Moving quickly, the paramedics rush Jake over to the ambulance, and they place him inside. His Mother Felicia also gets in the back of the vehicle with him, so that she can ride along. Afterwards, the paramedics close the back doors, hop in the vehicle, and they drive away with the siren on.

When Michael, who has a worried and frantic look on his face, sees that the ambulance has taken off, he runs and he gets into his car, and he follows it to the hospital.

Christopher, who is still watching on in secret, knows where the ambulance is going, so he takes a shortcut with his bike to meet them there.

Eventually, the ambulance arrives at the Good Samaritan Hospital, and the paramedics quickly rush Jake out of the vehicle and into the Emergency Room (ER).

Michael Harrington and his wife Felicia are with their son, but they are not allowed to go inside the ER operating room.

Later, after some time has elapsed, the ER doctor exits the emergency/operating room, and he approaches the Harrington's, who are patiently sitting in the visitors waiting room.

The ER doctor says: "Mr. and Mrs. Harrington. I have both good news and bad news. The *good* news is that we were able to get the seizures under control. However, the *bad* news is, your son Jake has contracted 'Skelexianervosis' — the 'Crippling Virus.'"

When Felicia hears the doctor's bad report on their son's prognosis, she immediately breaks down and starts to cry. And she turns to her husband Michael, and says: "Oh no! Michael, what are we going to do?"

Michael, with a highly despondent and scarred look on his face, shakes his head back and forth in utter confusion, and he says to his wife in a very sad tone: "I don't know, Felicia."

Interestingly, while the Harrington's are consulting with the ER doctor; Christopher happens to be there. He is standing in the not too far distance, secretly hiding and listening to their conversation. Suddenly, a nurse, who happens to be walking by, approaches Christopher, and says to him: "Have you been waiting a long time?"

"No. Not too long," Christopher says.

"Who's here at the hospital?" the Nurse asks.

"An acquaintance," Christopher answers.

"Would you like me to inquire about him or her for you?" the Nurse asks.

"No, that's ok. I'll just wait," Christopher says.

"Ok," the Nurse says. And then she turns and leaves.

Oh no! Christopher's cover is blown! It so happens that while the nurse is talking to him, Michael Harrington overhears their conversation, and he looks up and spots Christopher standing in the distance.

Christopher, now realizing that Michael Harrington sees him, panics, and he begins to leave. But Michael calls out to him, saying: "Hey kid… wait! Please don't go! Don't be afraid! No one's going to hurt you! I just want to talk to you for a moment!" And, slowly approaching Christopher, he continues, saying: "Christopher, my son Jake is very, very, sick!"

"I see that, but what am I suppose to do?" Christopher asks.

"I need you to heal him," Michael says.

"How am I supposed to do that?" Christopher asks.

"Your medicine will cure him," Michael says.

"What medicine?" Christopher asks.

"Your, 'Emerald Green,'" Michael replies.

"My, Emerald Green? I thought you and your company said it was a fraud! And that I had stolen CX252 and passed it off as Emerald Green!" Christopher says.

"I know, we lied! Emerald Green is the real miracle cure, not CX252," Michael says. He continues: "You weren't aware of it, but, one day, I followed you to your secret hideaway, and I stole the Emerald Green that was left in the glass container in your Lab. And then, I took it, and passed it off as Sunrise Pharmaceutical's "*new miracle drug*," which I named CX252."

"That was a rotten thing to do!" Christopher says.

"I know! I totally agree! And, I am very sorry! I hope you can forgive me?" Michael says.

"I don't know?" Christopher replies. "Besides that, where's my tree?"

"I can take you to it! That is, if you agree to make some Emerald Green to cure my son," Michael says.

"I want you to clear my name, and put my tree, and everything else back where they belong!" Christopher demands.

"Ok. I promise! I will do everything you say! Trust me! All I want is for you to first help my son," Michael says. He continues: "Please, Christopher! He's our only child! He's all we've got!"

Christopher thinks about it for a moment, and then, he says: "Alright. I'll do it."

"Thank you! Thank you, so much! Come on, I'll take you to your tree now!" Michael says. Afterwards, him and Christopher exit the hospital together, hop in his car, and they drive to the new location of Christopher's tree.

Eventually, when Christopher and Michael arrive at the new location of the tree, Christopher can barely believe his eyes! Everything inside of the building is setup exactly as it was back at its old location. The room is even the same size. It has the same window and mirror setup. His garden hoses are suspended from the ceiling. His beautiful plant and flower garden look the same. His tree is located in the right corner of the room. Also, his paved decorative stone pathway, and his wooden bridge, along with the lily pad pond containing the colorful goldfish are there. Everything is precisely the same. Even his old, rusty coffee can with the garden trowel is there!

Wasting no time at all, Christopher reaches down, and he picks up the coffee can, and he proceeds to make his way towards the tree, walking along the winding path that's paved with beautiful decorative stone, and then over the arched, wooden bridge, and then across more paved stone.

After Christopher reaches the end of the pathway, he proceeds to walk up to the tree's drip-line. Then, he kneels down, with both knees situated upon the ground, and he begins digging into the soil with the garden trowel.

After reaching a depth in the soil where the feeder roots reside, Christopher stops digging. Then, he reaches into his pants pocket and pulls out an army pocket knife. Next, he proceeds to lop off several of the feeder roots, and he places them inside the coffee can. Afterwards, he puts the knife back into his pants pocket.

Next, Christopher unbuttons a pocket on his twill shirt, and he pulls out a small plastic bag that contains a mysterious, thick, green ointment. Opening the bag, he reaches in and he takes some of the ointment, and he spreads and rubs it on the tree, in the area where he lopped off the feeder roots.

As soon as the mysterious ointment touches the tree, it begins to emit dazzling rays of spectacular light — like sparkling, gleaming, beautiful gemstones. And then, something amazing happens. During the exact moment that the ointment is applied, the areas of the tree that were lopped off, immediately begin to mend and heal within an instance of time!

After observing this astounding phenomenon, Christopher closes the plastic bag, and he puts it back in his shirt pocket. Next, he covers the hole that he dug with loose soil, and then he stands upon his feet with the coffee can in his left hand. Next, he walks underneath the tree's crown canopy. And, reaching out his right hand, he begins picking some of the leaves off a few of the lower hanging branches. These too, he places in the can. Afterwards, he takes the can, and he proceeds to walk around the tree to a door in the room that's located several feet from the tree—directly behind it.

Entering through the door, Christopher, steps inside a small room resembling a chemistry lab. Although small in size, the room has a window. And directly beneath the window seal is a long table that has various objects on it — items that you would normally find in a chemistry lab. Things such as: glass beakers, test tubes, flasks, funnels, thermometers, tubing, flask stands, tongs, and a Bunsen burner, etc.

After entering the lab, Christopher walks over to the table and he sets the coffee can down upon it. Next, he grabs a large, round-bottomed distillation boiling flask with sidearm, which contains rainwater from the large, sealed water basin that's located outside of the building. And he pours the entire contents of the coffee can into it. Afterwards, he inserts a rubber stopper containing a thermometer into the top opening of the flask. Then he secures the boiling flask to a flask stand, which has a Bunsen burner situated directly beneath it.

Next, Christopher connects the boiling flask's arm to a condenser tube, which is separately being held in place by its own stand. Then he connects the opposite end of the condenser tube to a piece of bent glass tubing. Lastly, he places the opposite end of the bent glass tubing into a large collection flask.

Finally, after Christopher completes his setup, he uses a flint spark lighter to light the Bunsen burner, and he makes an adjustment to the flame. Afterwards, he returns to the tree, and he lies down beneath it, and falls fast asleep.

Sometime later, when Christopher awakens from sleep, he gets up, and he returns to his lavatory. Approaching the flasks Christopher observes that the liquid in the distillation boiling flask has run pretty much empty, and that the collection flask is now full of liquid, which is "Emerald Green." So he turns off the Bunsen burner. Then he removes the collection flask from off its stand, and he pours as much of its contents as he can, via a funnel, into an unbreakable glass jug that is marked with his initials, CMP. The remainder of the contents he leaves in the flask.

After inserting a cork into the unbreakable jug's opening, Christopher places the jug into a sturdy canvas, carrying bag. Then, he takes an eyedropper off of his lavatory shelf, and he puts it in his shirt pocket and buttons down the pocket flap. Next, he takes the canvas carrying bag containing the Emerald Green, and he approaches Michael Harrington, who is waiting patiently in the garden.

When Michael sees Christopher carrying the canvas bag, he inquires concerning it, saying: "Do you have it? Is that the 'Emerald Green?'"

"Yep, I've got it!" Christopher says, as he points to the bag with his free hand.

"Great! Are you sure it will work?" Michael asks.

"I'm positive!" Christopher says.

"How can you be sure?" Michael asks.

"I can tell by the taste. I placed some on the tip of my tongue, and it's good," Christopher says.

"Excellent! Let's go," Michael says.

As Christopher and Michael begin to exit the garden, Michael, who is walking directly behind Christopher, says to him: "Ok. That's far enough kid. Give me the bag."

"That's ok. I've got it," Christopher replies.

In response, Michael becomes very angry, and with a loud and demanding voice, he says: "I said! Give me the bag, boy!"

Christopher, now realizing Michael's bad intentions, says: "But, you promised to clear my name, and give me back my tree!"

"What? Do you think that I'm stupid? That would completely ruin me!" Michael says. He continues: "Besides, you ain't nothin but a lowdown Nigger!"

"What did you do to my father, Randall Pascale?" Christopher asks.

"I got rid of him, just like I'm going to do to you!" Michael says.

Suddenly, Michael transforms into a large, carnivorous reptile, with a head like a dragon! This enormous, frightening looking, monstrous, Dragon Snake Beast is equipped with huge fangs! And its body is about 30 feet long!

Completely shocked out of his wits, Christopher immediately begins to flee!

The Dragon Snake is fast, and it quickly chases Christopher down as he tries to escape. Trapping him, it begins to toy with him, like a cat playing a cat and mouse game. It's as though it gets enjoyment out of seeing its prey squirm in fear.

After toying with Christopher for a while, the Dragon Snake suddenly begins to strike, but Christopher manages to quickly dodge out of its way! And then he begins to run! But, because the Dragon

Snake is lightning quick, within an instance it chases Christopher down, and it trips him up. As a result, Christopher's body goes crashing to the ground!

With Christopher now lying helplessly with his back to the ground, the Dragon Snake quickly approaches him. Then, raising its ugly head one last time for a final and fatal strike, it hisses at him, and opening its large mouth wide, with its huge fangs exposed, it lunges forward at him to deliver the deathblow! In frightful response, Christopher closes his eyes, grimaces, and screams! Suddenly, a gunshot is fired, and a bullet hits the Dragon Snake in the back of the head. But wait! The bullet doesn't stop him!

After being struck by the bullet, the Dragon Snake immediately turns in the direction of the fired shot. And it angrily peers at the person holding the gun, who shot him. It's a policeman, who is accompanied by several other policemen.

The Dragon Snake is furious! Leaving Christopher, it quickly moves towards the police, and it proceeds to attack them.

The Dragon Snake opens its mouth wide, and it grabs the lead policemen that fired the shot. And it lifts him up like a feather. Then, it forcefully throws him clear across the room. The policeman's body goes flying like a bird through the air, and then it slams hard into the side of the wooden bridge! Afterwards, he falls lifelessly into the lily pad pond below.

Next, the Dragon Snake quickly turns, and it begins attacking the other policemen too, but they immediately pull out their weapons and open up fire on him. Luckily, their combined firepower proves to be too much for the monstrous beast. And after being hit multiple times with bullets, it falls down flat to the ground, dead!

Interestingly, immediately after the Dragon Snake is successfully put down, something amazing happens. It transforms back into Michael Harrington. He is dead, lying on the ground, with a weapon in his hand. It looks like that dirty, lowdown, rotten snake, got exactly what he deserved!

Christopher is so happy to be alive! As he looks up and in the distance, he sees that Sunrise Pharmaceutical Drugs top chemist and physicist, Felix Dupree is there. As it turns out, he is the one who brought the police. He led them to Michael Harrington, after he had thoroughly related to them his devious and fraudulent dealings, and convinced them of Christopher's complete innocence.

As the Police and Felix approach Christopher, Felix says to him: "Are you okay son?"

"He killed my Father!" Christopher says in a sad voice, as he points to Michael Harrington. Then, he bends over, and he picks up the canvas carrying bag from off the ground. And, opening it up, he reaches inside, and he pulls out a cassette tape recorder; rewinds it; and plays back the recording from the beginning. The recording says:

Michael: "Do you have it? Is that the 'Emerald Green?'"

Christopher: "Yep, I've got it!"

Michael: "Great! Are you sure it will work?"

Christopher: "I'm positive!"

Michael: "How can you be sure?"

Christopher: "I can tell by the taste. I placed some on the tip of my tongue, and it's good."

Michael: "Excellent! Let's go."

Michael: "Ok. That far enough kid. Give me the bag."

Christopher: "That's ok. I've got it.

Michael: "I said! Give me the bag, boy!"

Christopher: "But, you promised to clear my name, and give me back my tree!"

Michael: "What? Do you think that I'm stupid? That would completely ruin me! Besides, you ain't nothin but a lowdown Nigger!

Christopher: "What did you do to my father, Randall Pascale?"

Michael: "I got rid of him, just like I'm going to do to you!"

After listening to the recording, a policeman walks over to Christopher, and he sympathetically puts his arm around him, and he says to him: "Come on son, we'll give you a ride home."

~

As the days, weeks, and months pass by, Christopher is generous with his Emerald Green. Without charge, he freely gives it to everyone in need of it. And all of the people of Wright County benefit greatly from it. 'Skelexianervosis,' the 'Crippling Plague' has completely vanished, and the people in general are much healthier.

Interestingly, in compensation for any and all impunity damages that were done to Christopher, Sunrise Pharmaceutical Drugs Corporation (since the death of its founder and former CEO, Michael Harrington, who is now under the sole ownership and control of his surviving wife, Felicia) generously awards Christopher, free of charge, the new building that his tree is housed within. He becomes the new owner, the sole proprietor, to do with it whatever he pleases. But wait! That's not all! In addition to this, over the next two years Christopher is also granted the privilege and funds by the Wright County Government, to experiment with and medically treat all of its trees that had become sick due to man's reckless polluting of the environment, from which humans had suffered such a harmful and damaging effect, causing them to become more susceptible to sickness and disease.

Amazingly, within a relatively short period of time, Christopher is able to reverse the damage that man has caused to the trees. The trees are now vibrant and healthy once again, producing and dispensing the necessary healing agents and properties that are required to cleanse the environment and aid in keeping humans healthy. Also, equally important and astounding is the fact that people's attitudes and actions towards one another have significantly changed for the better. Gone are the hatreds and prejudices that once stained the land. Instead, all of the people are finally living and working together in love and unity. They have even stopped polluting the environment! What a drastic change and turn of events, all of this has made for both the good and betterment of mankind and planet earth.

20

A NEW DAY

Today is a very special day. In symbol of the highly productive, important, positive, and significant progress and changes that have recently taken place in Wright County, something truly amazing and historic is happening. The Bayridge Dividing Wall — the long and tall, brick, barricade-like structure that separates Frogtown from Shytown is being completely torn down!

The demolition crew consists of a large group of people, composed of both black and white citizens, young and old. They are equipped with bulldozers and dump trucks, and armed with pickaxes, sledge hammers, shovels, push brooms, and various other equipment. All are happily and eagerly working together in love, harmony, unity, and peace, to forever remove the ugly eyesore, the divisive element, which has separated the two communities for decades.

Today, is also special, in that, it is the day that Christopher Maurice Pascale is being honored and awarded for his extremely helpful and most generous contributions to medicine, health, environmental protection, and peace.

"Dear ladies, gentlemen, and youths," the town Mayor smiles and says, as he stands on a raised podium in front of a large, gathered crowd outside. He continues: "For all that he has unselfishly and wonderfully done towards the advancement of medicine, health, environmental protection, and peace; I am both happy and immensely honored to officially declare this day *'Christopher Maurice Pascale Day!'*"

The entire audience erupts into loud cheering and applause!

As Christopher steps up to the podium to receive an award, and deliver a short acceptance speech, his mother Elisabeth, and Archer Tucker proudly sit in the front row of a large crowd of people. Both white and black citizens are there, along with Felicia Harrington, and her son Jake. The incredible thing is that Jake is not sick or crippled. But, instead, he is in perfect health. The reason why, is because on the night that his father, Michael Harrington was killed by the police, Christopher later returned to the Good Samaritan Hospital, where Jake was hospitalized, and he gave him a dose of his Emerald Green, which completely cured him.

After, Christopher is finished delivering his speech, the audience appreciatively applauds and cheers and gives him a warm and long, standing ovation.

Later, following the conclusion of this most momentous and important ceremony and occasion, when Christopher, Elisabeth, and Archer are traveling back home in their car, Elisabeth says to Christopher: "I'm very proud of you son. You're a lot like your father, Randall. And he would be proud of you too!"

Christopher turns and he looks at his mom, and he smiles and says: "Thanks, Mom!" Continuing, he says: "Can I ask you a question?"

"Sure," Elisabeth replies.

"Why couldn't the top chemists, physicists, and scientists of the world duplicate Emerald Green?"

Elisabeth reflects on it for a moment, and then, she says: "Well, you know, I think it's because Emerald Green's cure, is not so much in the tree's natural medicine, as it is in your heart. I think it was your unbiased, unselfish, and outstanding love for people that was the main ingredient. That is what helped cure the people. 'Emerald Green,' is your love, son. That's the real cure!"

Later that night, while Christopher is home sleeping, he dreams a dream. He is trapped and lying with his back flat against the ground. And positioned over him is a carnivorous reptile, an enormous, monstrous, dragon-like snake! The beast has huge fangs, and it's about 30 feet long! Ready for the kill, the Dragon Snake hisses at Christopher, and then, opening its large mouth wide, with its huge fangs exposed, it lunges at him to deliver the deathblow! In frightful response, Christopher closes his eyes, grimaces, and screams! And then, suddenly, out of nowhere, comes a large lizard-like creature with humongous, asymmetrical, powerful pinchers that resemble lobster claws, but only much sharper (this creature happens to be one of the three lizard-like creatures that had previously attacked and chased Christopher — the only surviving one; thought to have died, when it had fallen into the deep river ravine, and was swept away in the torrent), and now, coming quickly to Christopher's aid, and moving ever so fast, it viciously attacks the Dragon Snake! Utilizing its humongous and powerful, razor sharp pinchers, it grabs the Dragon Snake by the neck, and it chops off his head! And, immediately, its body falls to the ground, dead!

After the Dragon Snake is killed, the lizard-like creature, for some unexplained reason, turns and runs away.

Christopher is both shocked and happy to be alive! Picking himself up from off the ground, and without delay, he proceeds to return to the old, decrepit, talking tree, so that he can once again attempt to free it from bondage.

The moment Christopher leaves the area, the three hungry

vultures that have been patiently circling the sky above, instantly descend upon the Dragon Snake, and they begin ripping and tearing it's body apart, and greedily devouring its remains.

In the meantime, Christopher successfully makes his way back to the tree. And after much strenuous effort, he manages to finally climb to the top, where the iron ring that supports the four heavy chains is positioned.

Apparently, the iron ring is the mainstay that holds and supports the massive chains that keep the tree captive. Christopher realizes that if he can somehow reach and unlock it, that this might be the very thing that sets it free.

Gingerly standing up on top of the highest tree limb, and holding on firmly to a tree branch for support, Christopher does something that's highly unimaginative for him. He completely lets go of the branch, and he reaches out for the iron ring with both hands. Wow, what a scary moment!

Christopher is deadly afraid of heights, and because of this his legs are shaking like a leaf on a tree (no pun intended). Luckily, on his first try he is able to grasp hold of the ring. And then, after stabilizing himself, he manages to successfully unlock it. Suddenly, a big explosion occurs! The force from the blast is so strong that it knocks Christopher clear off of his feet, catapulting his body up and away from the tree, to a height of about 200 feet upwards, and a distance of about 100 feet away!

This, however, is no ordinary explosion! In reality, Christopher should have sustained some type of injury from the dynamic blast. And his body, after being projected upward and outward, should have begun to fall and descend rapidly, and then ultimately wind up hitting the ground below really hard. But instead, for some incredible, unexplainable reason, when his body begins its downward flight, it somehow miraculously floats down softly — like a feather floating in a gentle breeze. It's as though he's being cradled and protected by an invisible, giant, helping hand!

When Christopher's falling body eventually reaches the ground, it gently touches down, completely safe from harm. What a miracle!

The moment Christopher is safely situated on the ground, the four heavy iron chains that hold the tree captive, immediately fall to the earth. Then, a massive earthquake occurs! The ground beneath the tree begins to quake, rumble, and shake. And then the tree begins to miraculously stretch and grow to an enormous height! It grows and grows until its very top reaches almost clear up to heaven. Then, suddenly, the cloud covered sky directly above the tree opens up. And a bright beam of light, like a floodlight, breaks through, and it shines directly down upon it, lighting it up for all to see. What an incredibly strong and resplendently beautiful structure the tree has truly become! Afterwards, all of earth's creatures, one and all, come there to reside. And to the tree's branches, all of the birds of heaven stream and fly. All come and take refuge beneath its protective cover, feed from it, and seek its shade. Because the health, prosperity, and happiness they receive from it, will never ever from them fade!

NOTE TO READER

This book is fiction. Any reference to historical events, real people or places are used fictitiously. Other names, characters, places, and events are products of the author's imagination, and any resemblance to actual events or places or persons, living or dead, is entirely coincidental.

www.ingramcontent.com/pod-product-compliance
Lightning Source LLC
Chambersburg PA
CBHW070050260626
47160CB00004B/1161